THE LOST WARRIOR

CREATED BY
ERIN HUNTER

WRITTEN BY
DAN JOLLEY

ART BY
JAMES L. BARRY

HAMBURG // LONDON // LOS ANGELES // TOKYO

The Lost Warrior Vol. 1
Created by Erin Hunter
Written by Dan Jolley
Art by James L. Barry

Lettering - Mike Estacio and Lucas Rivera
Cover Design - Anne Marie Horne
Digital Toning Assistant - Lincy Chan

Editor - Lillian Diaz-Przybyl
Digital Imaging Manager - Chris Buford
Pre-Production Supervisor - Erika Terriquez
Art Director - Anne Marie Horne
Production Manager - Elisabeth Brizzi
VP of Production - Ron Klamert
Editor-in-Chief - Rob Tokar
Publisher - Mike Kiley
President and C.O.O. - John Parker
C.E.O. and Chief Creative Officer - Stuart Levy

A TOKYOPOP® Manga

TOKYOPOP Inc.
5900 Wilshire Blvd. Suite 2000
Los Angeles, CA 90036

E-mail: info@TOKYOPOP.com
Come visit us online at www.TOKYOPOP.com

First published in the United States by HarperCollins *Publishers* 2007
First published in Great Britain by HarperCollins *Children's Books* 2008
HarperCollins *Children's Books* is a division of HarperCollins*Publishers* Ltd
77–85 Fulham Palace Road, Hammersmith, London W6 8JB

The HarperCollins *Children's Books* website address is www.harpercollinschildrensbooks.co.uk

1

Text copyright © Working Partners Ltd 2007
Illustrations © TokyoPop Inc. and HarperCollins Publishers 2007
The author and illustrator assert the moral right to be identified as the author and illustrator of this work

ISBN-13 978-0-00-726967-9
ISBN-10 0-00-726967-6

Printed and bound in England by
Clays Ltd, St Ives plc

WARRIORS

THE LOST WARRIOR

Dear readers,

Welcome to Warriors manga! Brace yourselves — it's the moment you've been waiting for. GRAYSTRIPE IS BACK!

I can't tell you how great it is to see a character I've known on paper for such a long time brought to life in pictures. Graystripe looks every inch the hero! It's true, some bad things happen to him, but I'm quite sure that he secretly loves every moment of the lightning-paced action. Manga brings out the best in Graystripe. He gets to talk tough, and rather than thinking too hard about anything, he can throw a single brooding look to the camera and leap into action. The drawings are so powerful and so direct. Alongside the punchy dialogue, they speak volumes. I LOVE them, and I am so proud of the all-new action Graystripe. Manga Graystripe doesn't mess around; he has one thrilling adventure after another. Well done, Graystripe! Well done, manga!

Sincerely,
Erin Hunter

HARPER COLLINS

ERIN HUNTER

CONTENTS

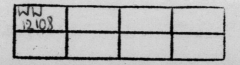

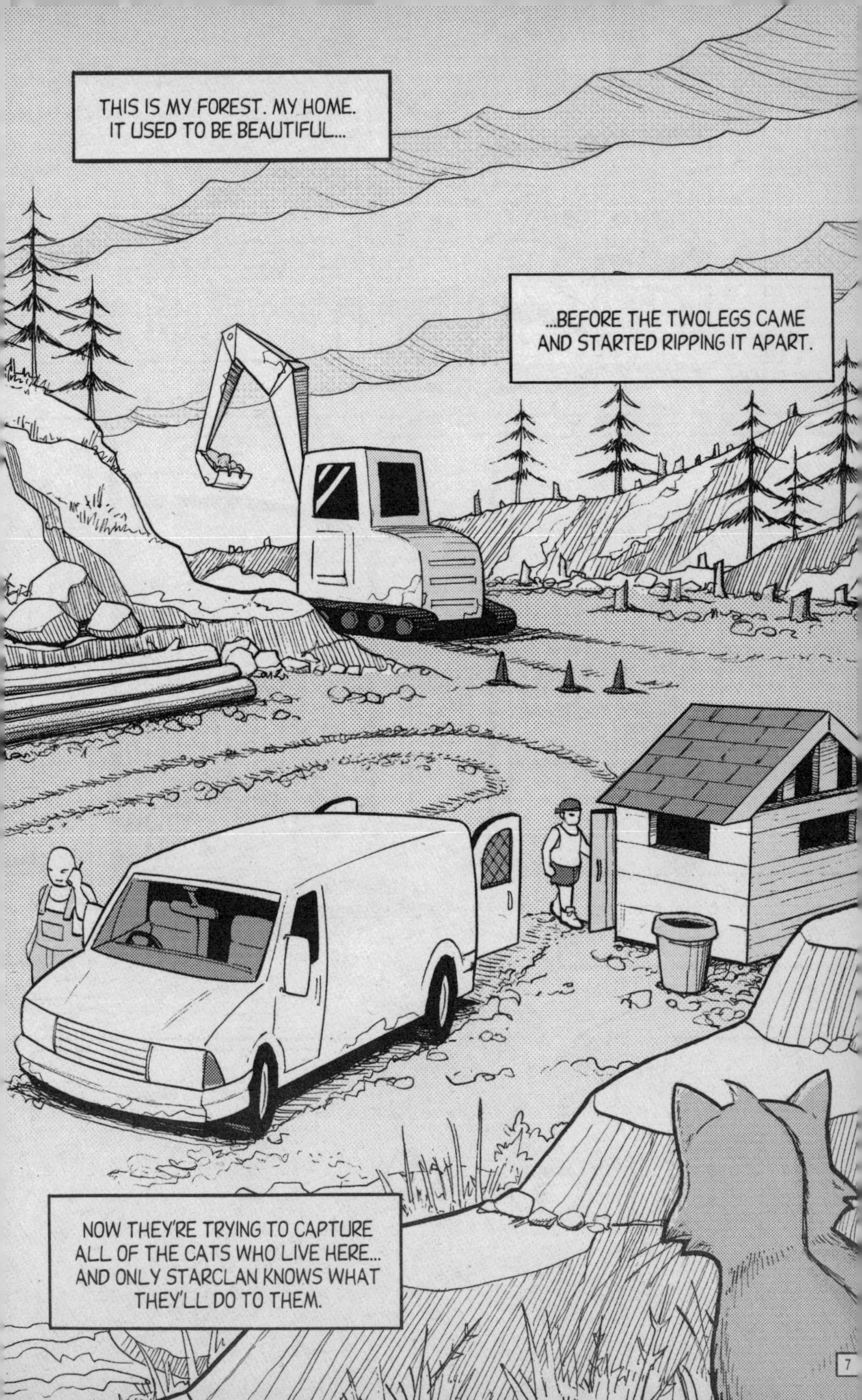
THIS IS MY FOREST. MY HOME. IT USED TO BE BEAUTIFUL...
...BEFORE THE TWOLEGS CAME AND STARTED RIPPING IT APART.
NOW THEY'RE TRYING TO CAPTURE ALL OF THE CATS WHO LIVE HERE... AND ONLY STARCLAN KNOWS WHAT THEY'LL DO TO THEM.

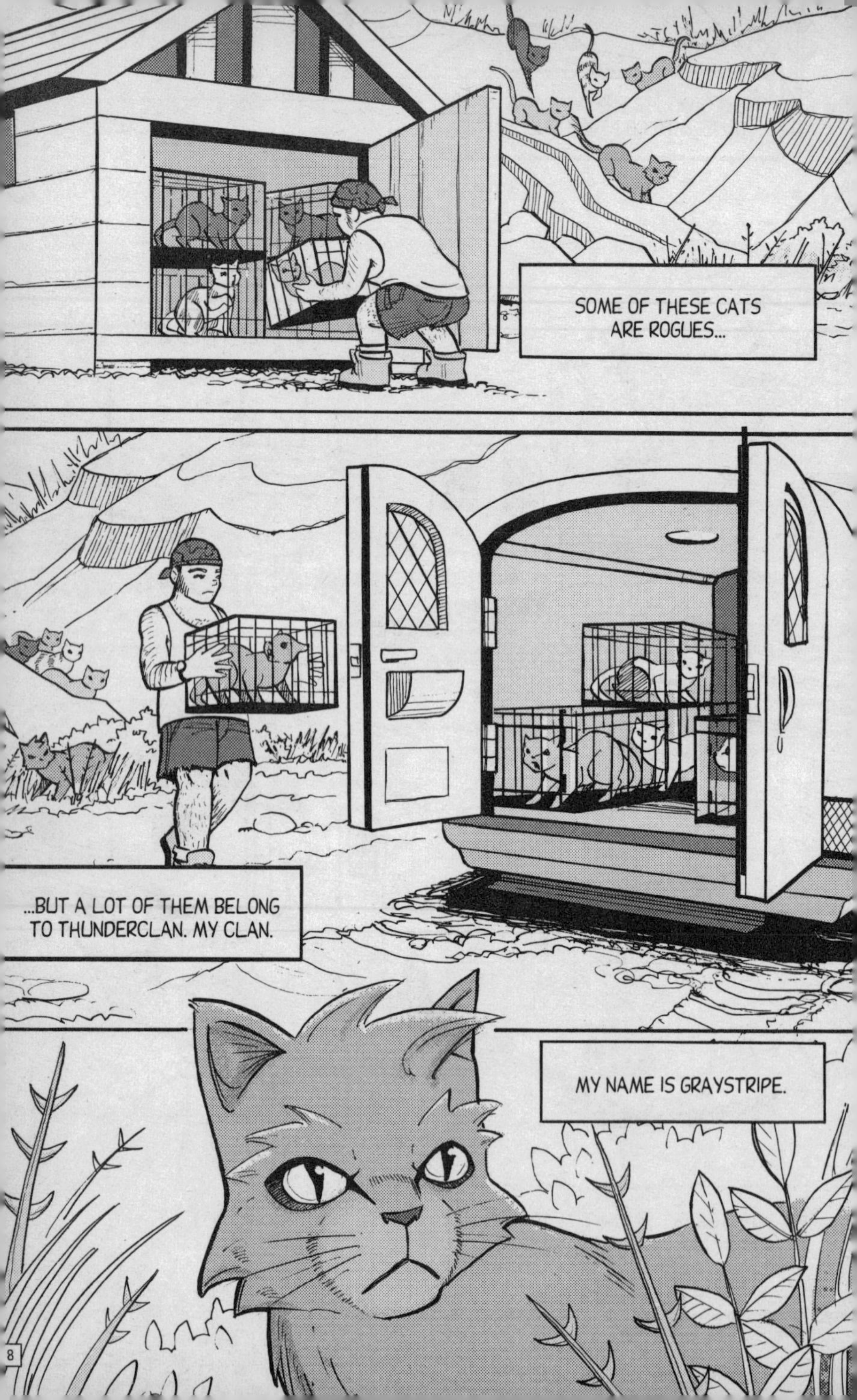
SOME OF THESE CATS ARE ROGUES...
...BUT A LOT OF THEM BELONG TO THUNDERCLAN. MY CLAN.
MY NAME IS GRAYSTRIPE.

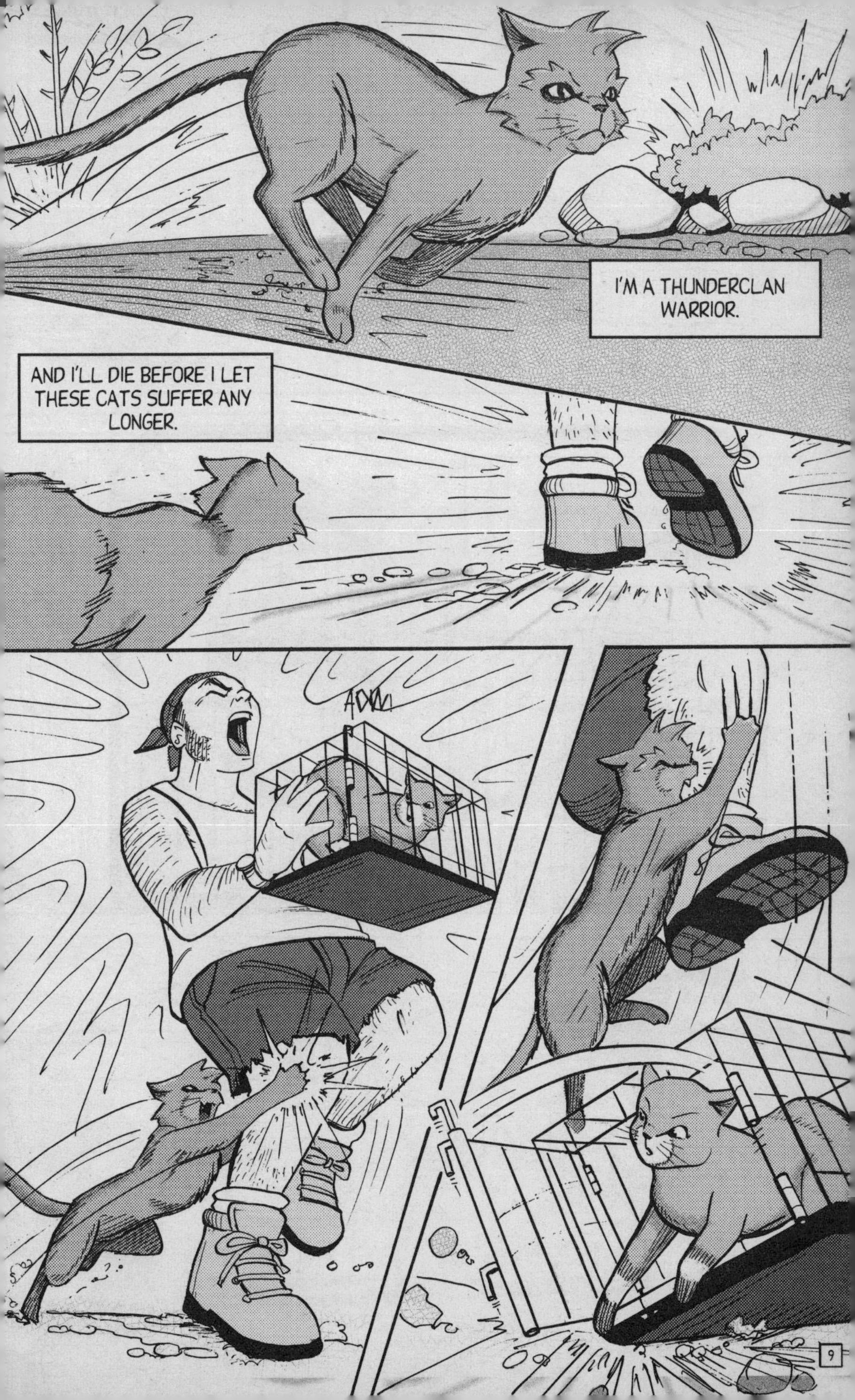
I'M A THUNDERCLAN WARRIOR.
AND I'LL DIE BEFORE I LET THESE CATS SUFFER ANY LONGER.
AOW!

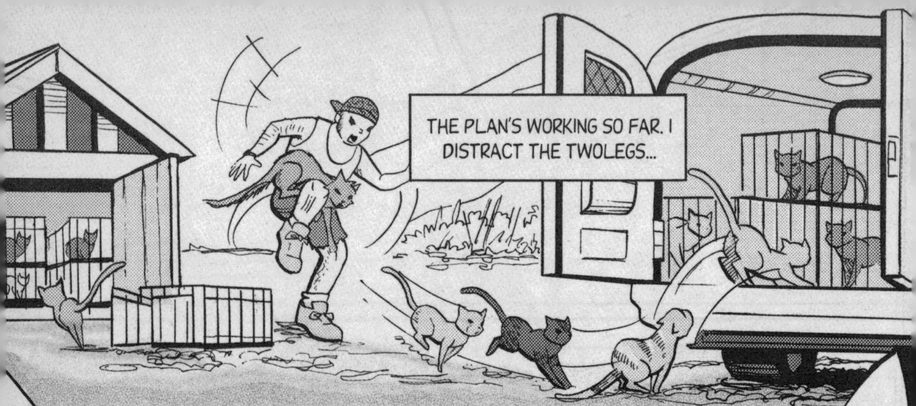
THE PLAN'S WORKING SO FAR. I DISTRACT THE TWOLEGS...
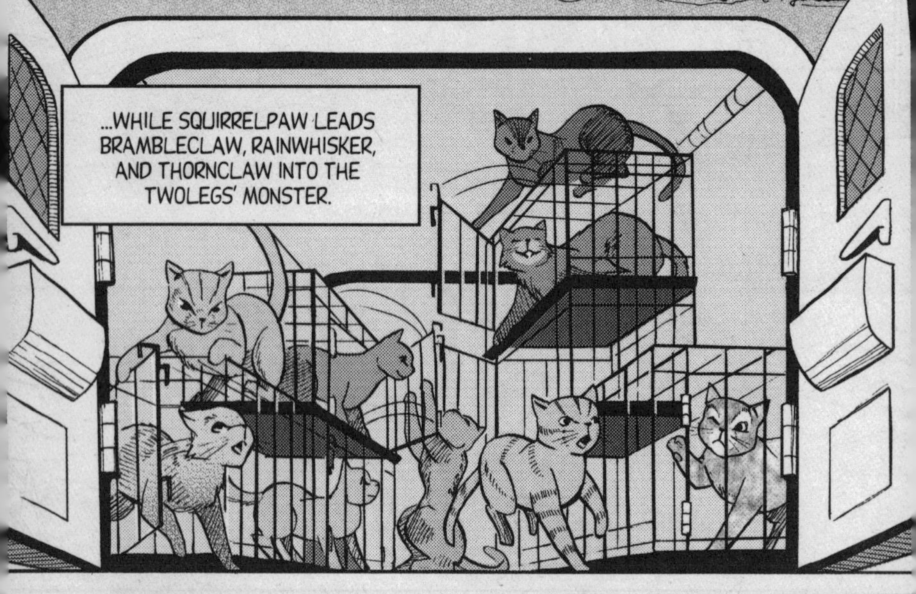
...WHILE SQUIRRELPAW LEADS BRAMBLECLAW, RAINWHISKER, AND THORNCLAW INTO THE TWOLEGS' MONSTER.
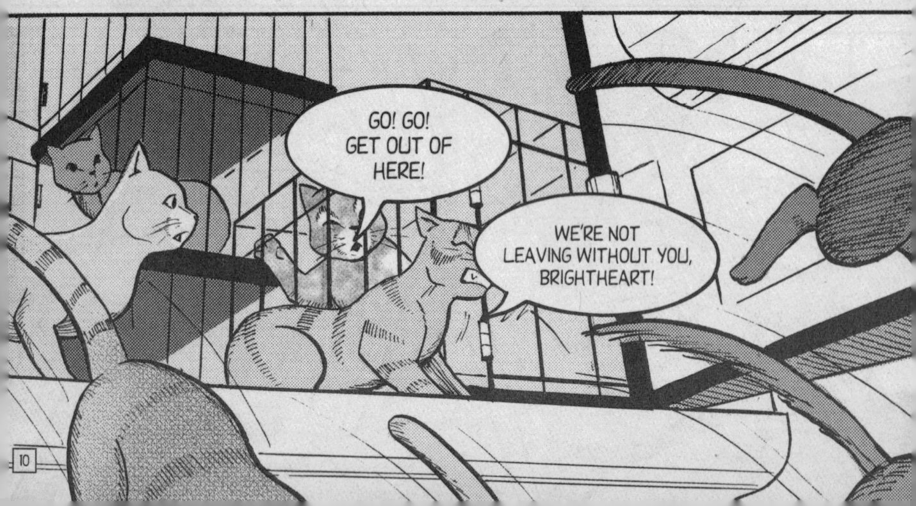
GO! GO! GET OUT OF HERE!
WE'RE NOT LEAVING WITHOUT YOU, BRIGHTHEART!

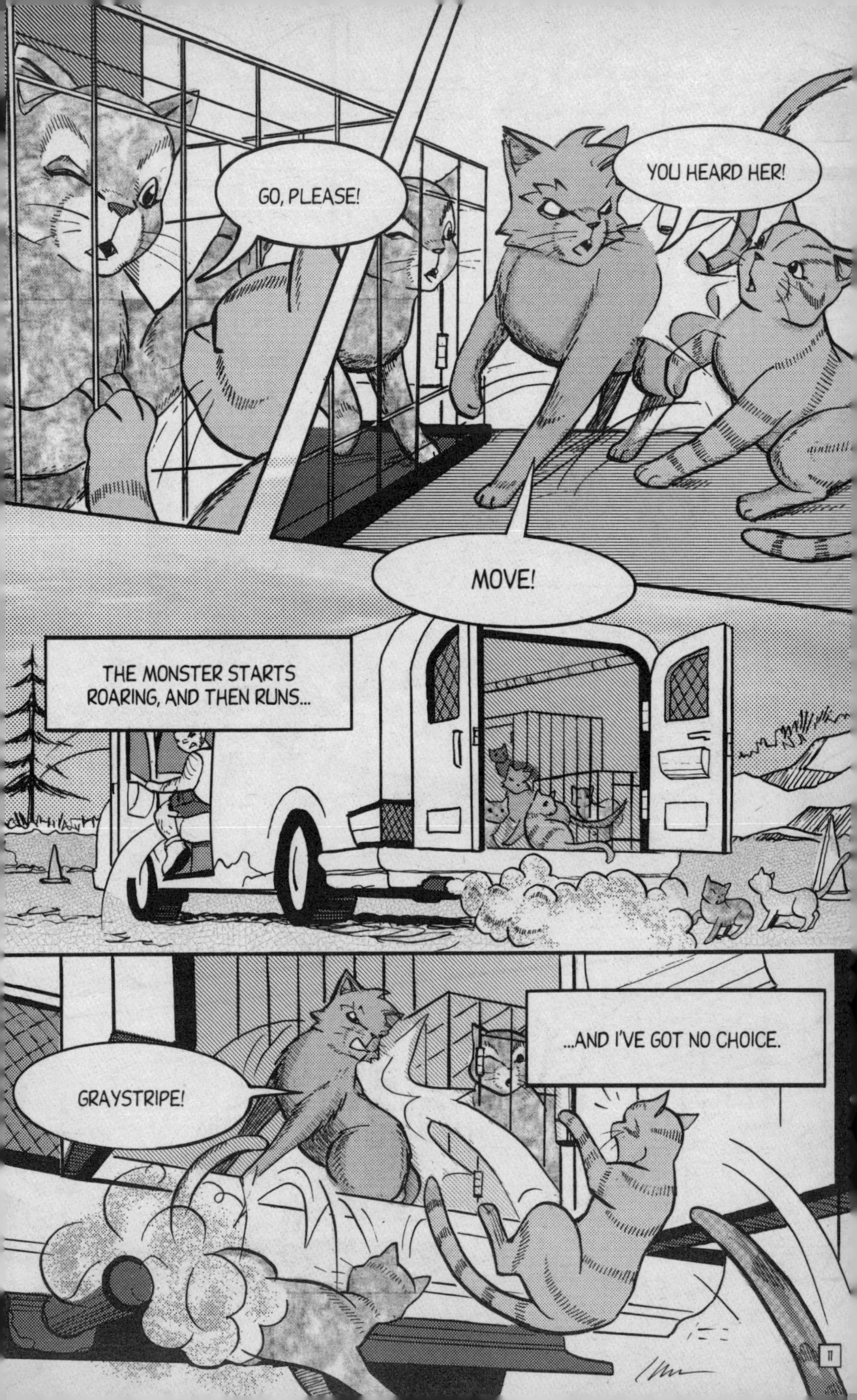
GO, PLEASE!
YOU HEARD HER!
MOVE!
THE MONSTER STARTS ROARING, AND THEN RUNS...
...AND I'VE GOT NO CHOICE.
GRAYSTRIPE!

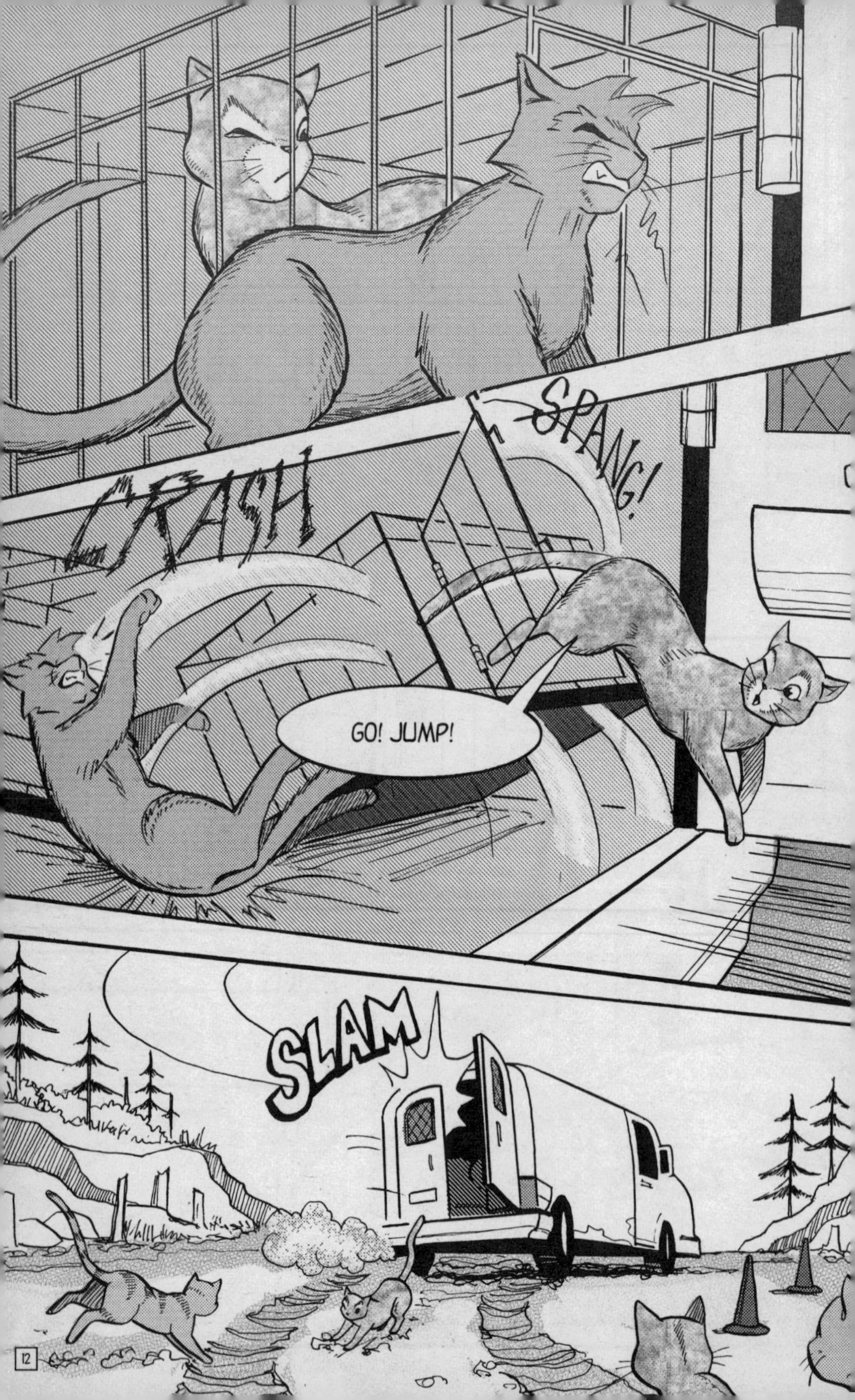
SPANG!
CRASH
GO! JUMP!
SLAM

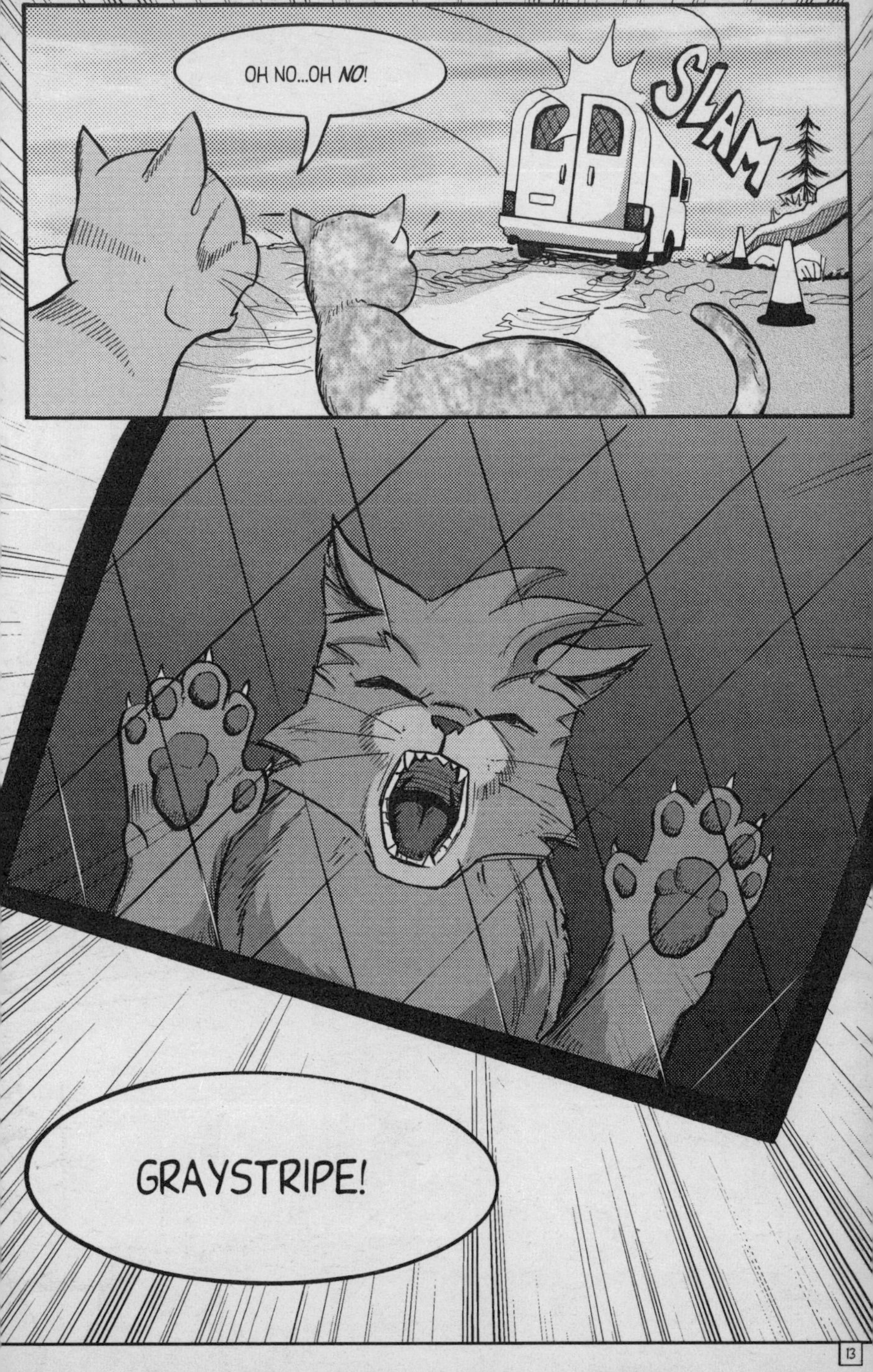

OH NO...OH NO!
SLAM
GRAYSTRIPE!

CHAPTER 1

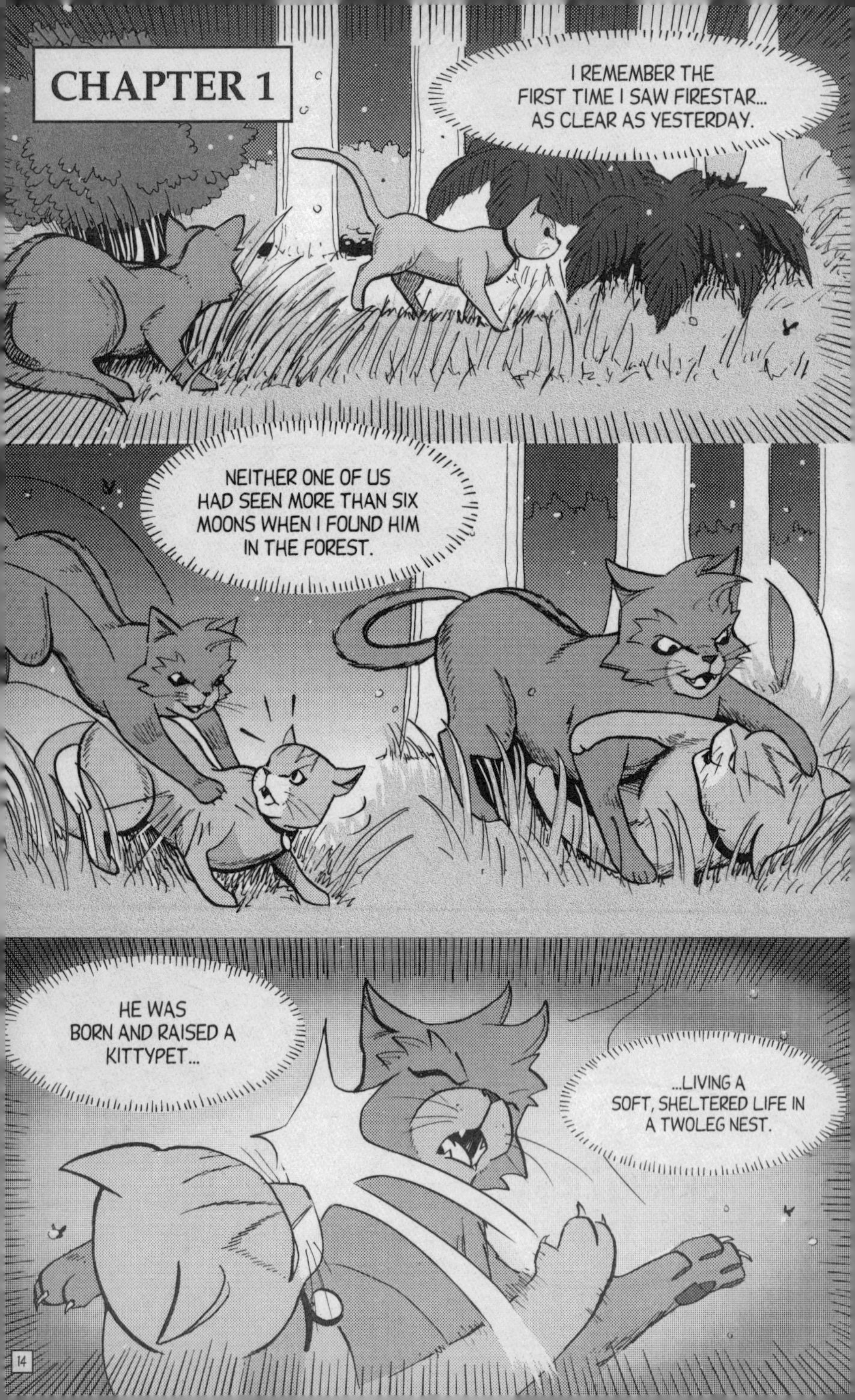
I REMEMBER THE FIRST TIME I SAW FIRESTAR... AS CLEAR AS YESTERDAY.
NEITHER ONE OF US HAD SEEN MORE THAN SIX MOONS WHEN I FOUND HIM IN THE FOREST.
HE WAS BORN AND RAISED A KITTYPET...
...LIVING A SOFT, SHELTERED LIFE IN A TWOLEG NEST.

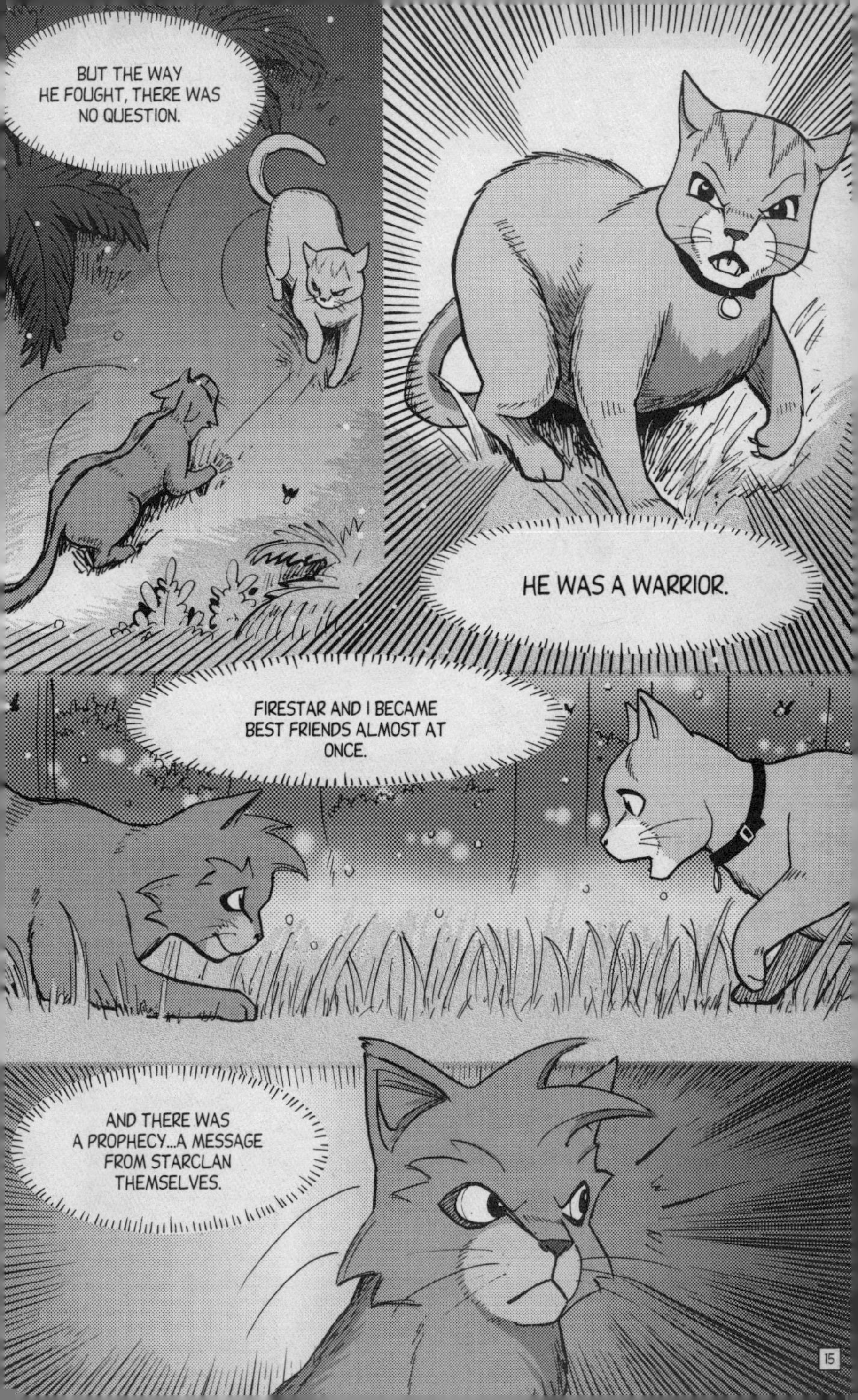
BUT THE WAY HE FOUGHT, THERE WAS NO QUESTION.
HE WAS A WARRIOR.
FIRESTAR AND I BECAME BEST FRIENDS ALMOST AT ONCE.
AND THERE WAS A PROPHECY...A MESSAGE FROM STARCLAN THEMSELVES.

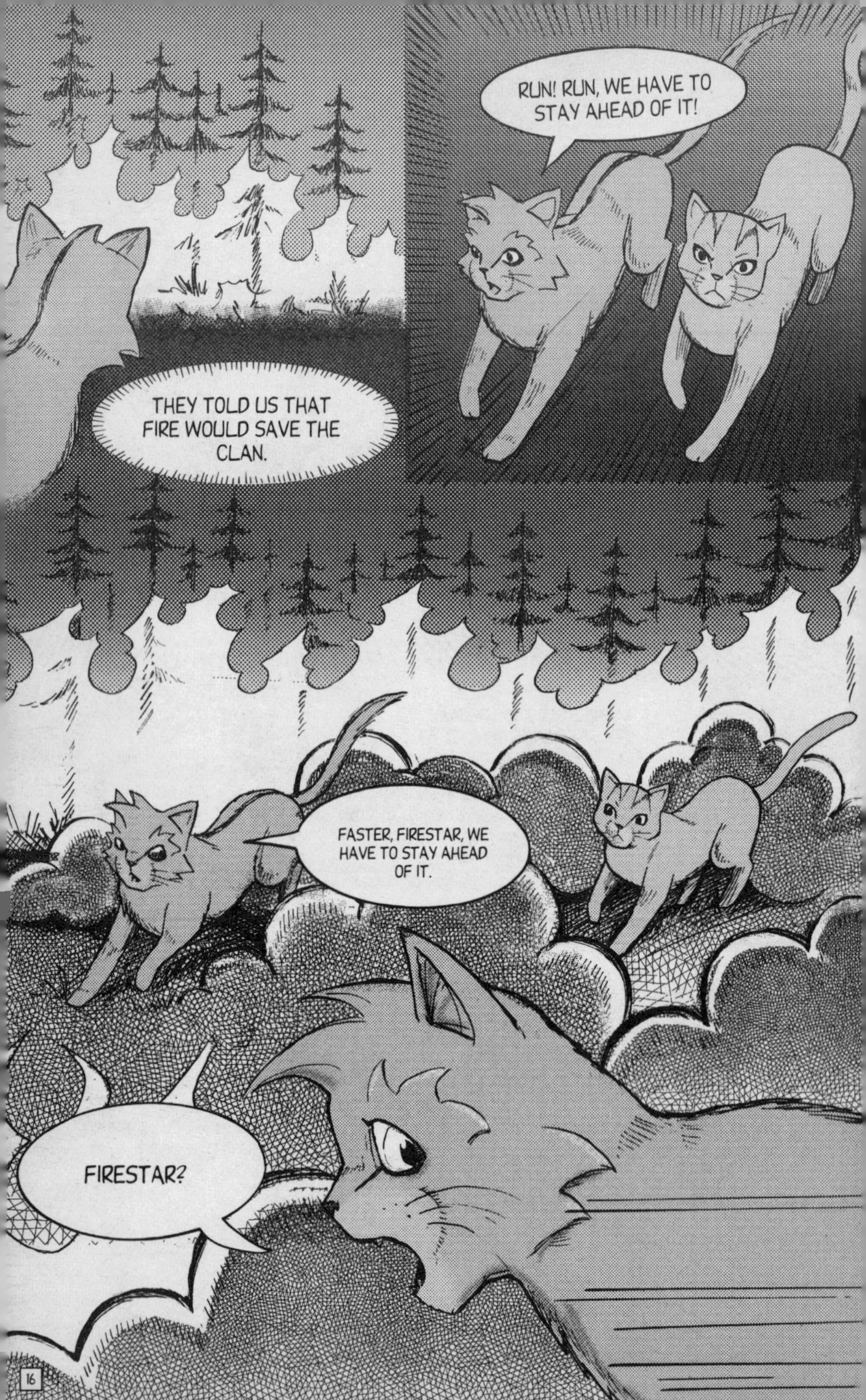
THEY TOLD US THAT FIRE WOULD SAVE THE CLAN.
RUN! RUN, WE HAVE TO STAY AHEAD OF IT!
FASTER, FIRESTAR, WE HAVE TO STAY AHEAD OF IT.
FIRESTAR?

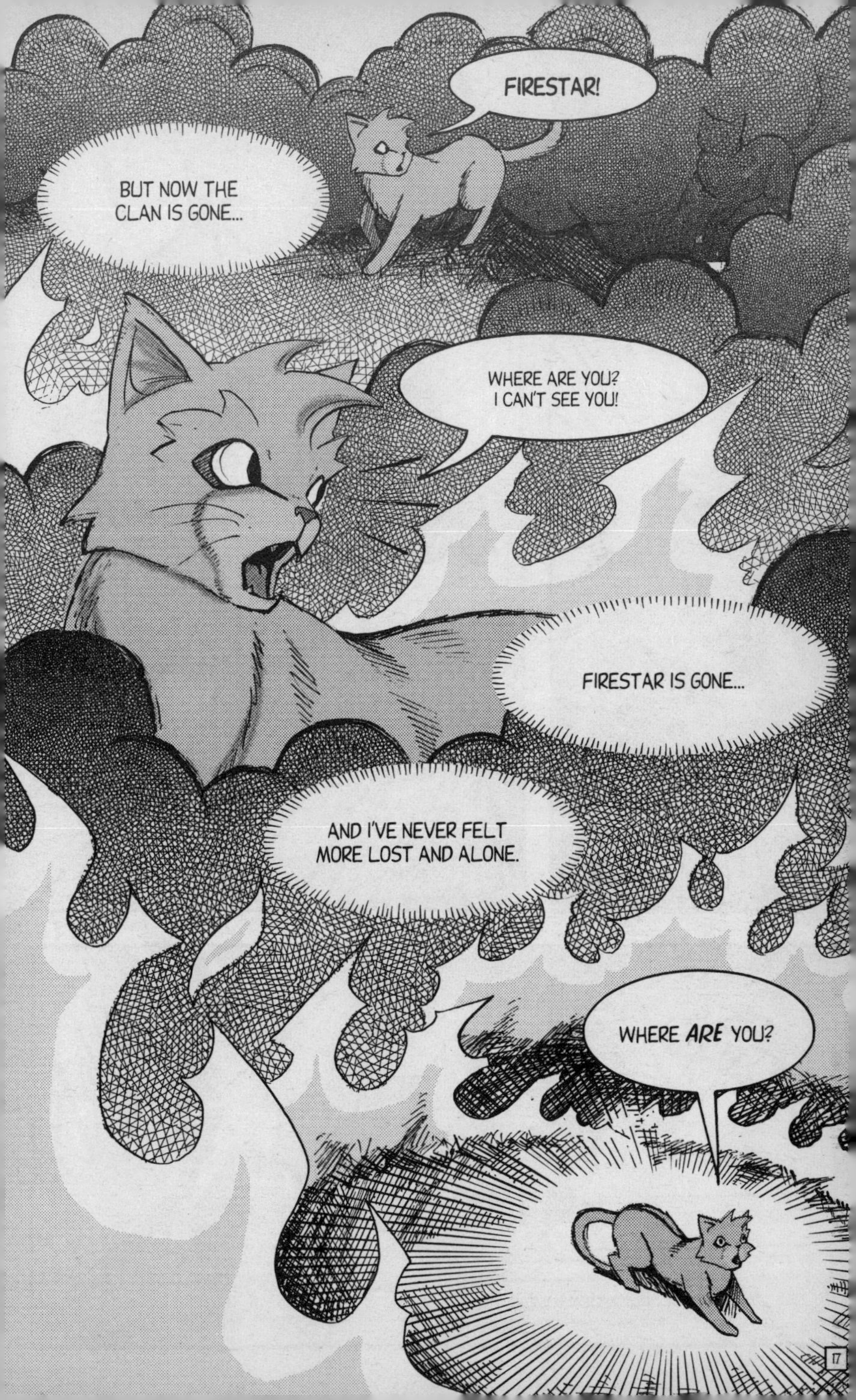
FIRESTAR!
BUT NOW THE CLAN IS GONE...
WHERE ARE YOU? I CAN'T SEE YOU!
FIRESTAR IS GONE...
AND I'VE NEVER FELT MORE LOST AND ALONE.
WHERE *ARE* YOU?

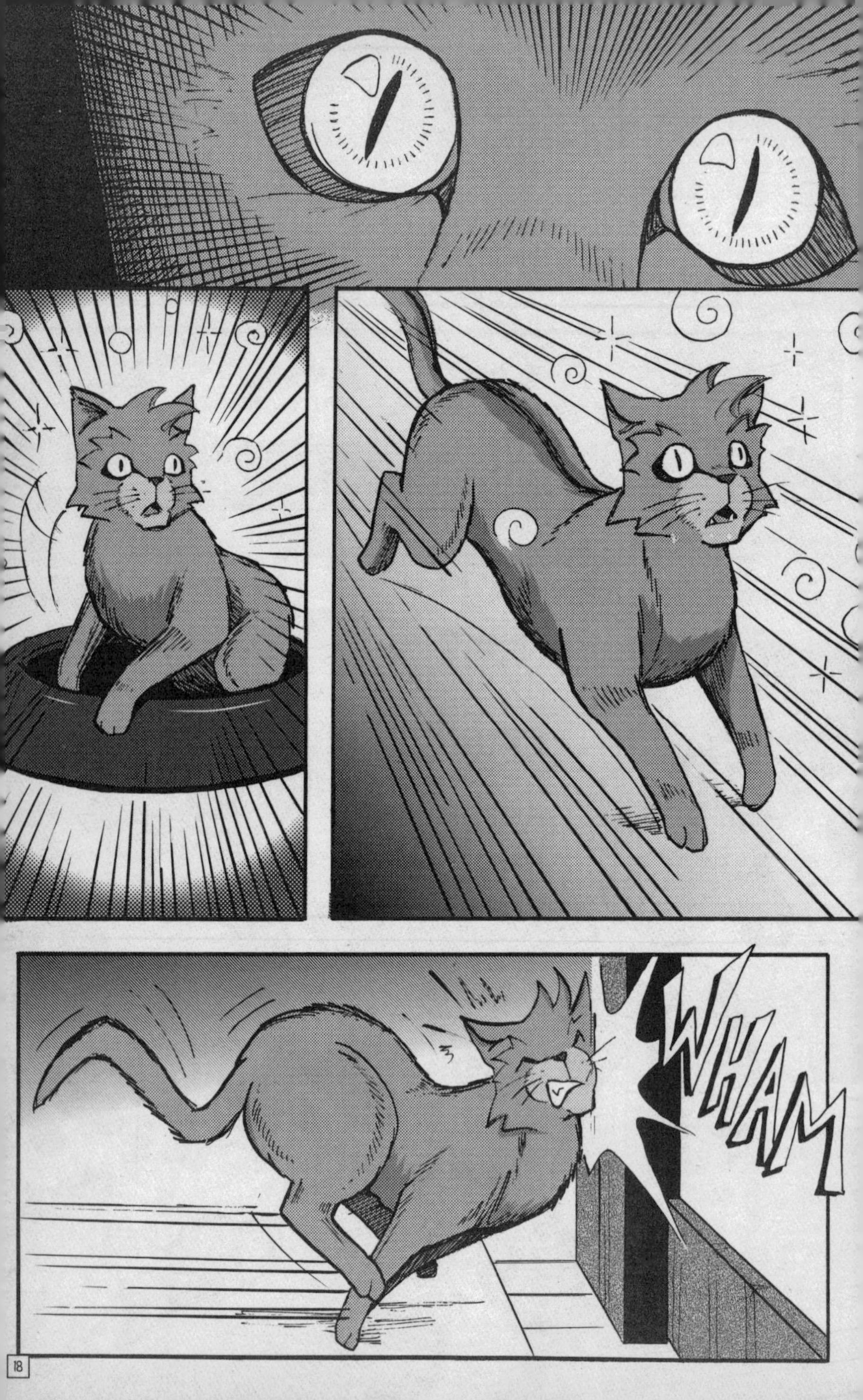
WHAM

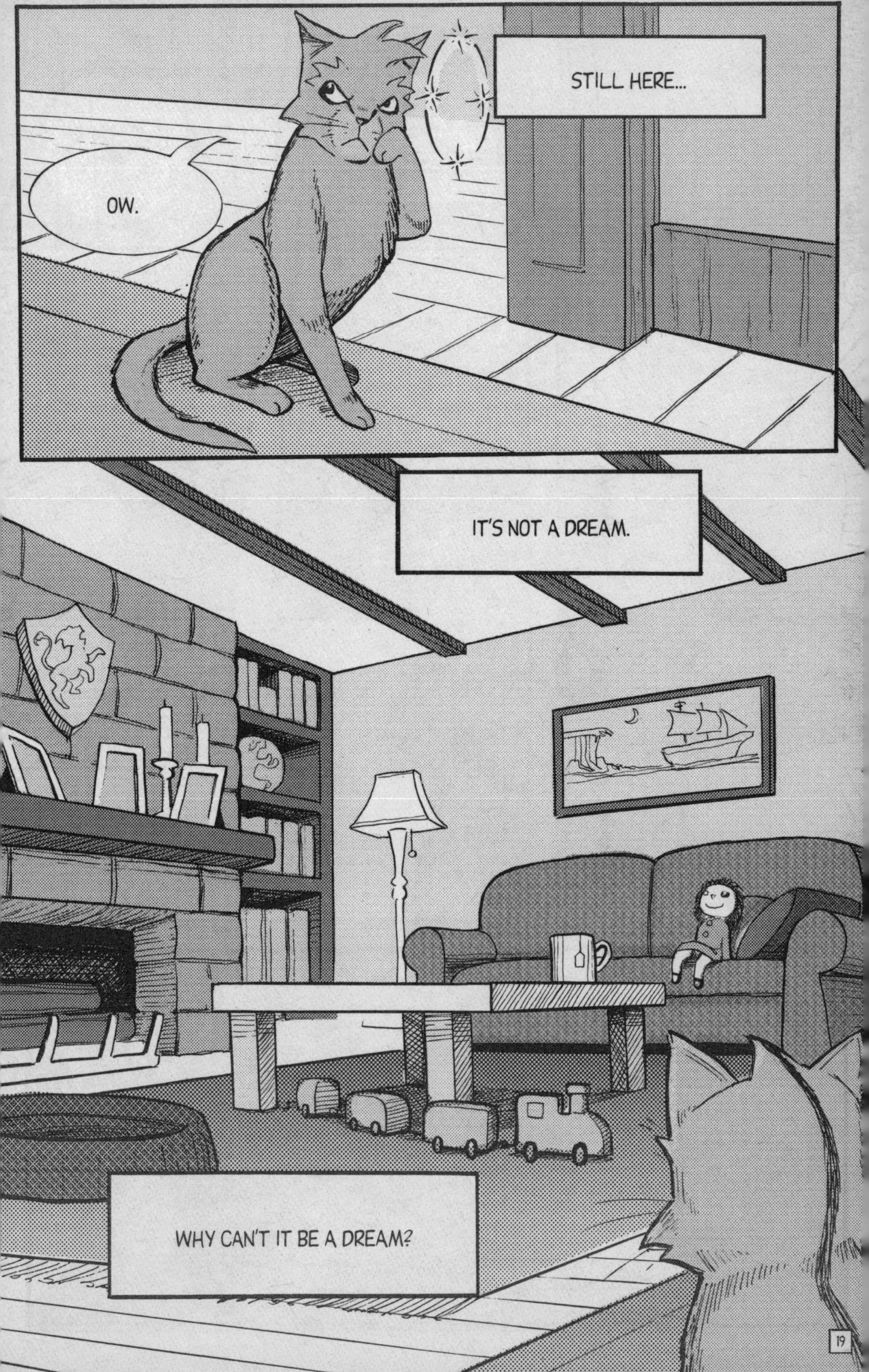
STILL HERE...
OW.
IT'S NOT A DREAM.
WHY CAN'T IT BE A DREAM?

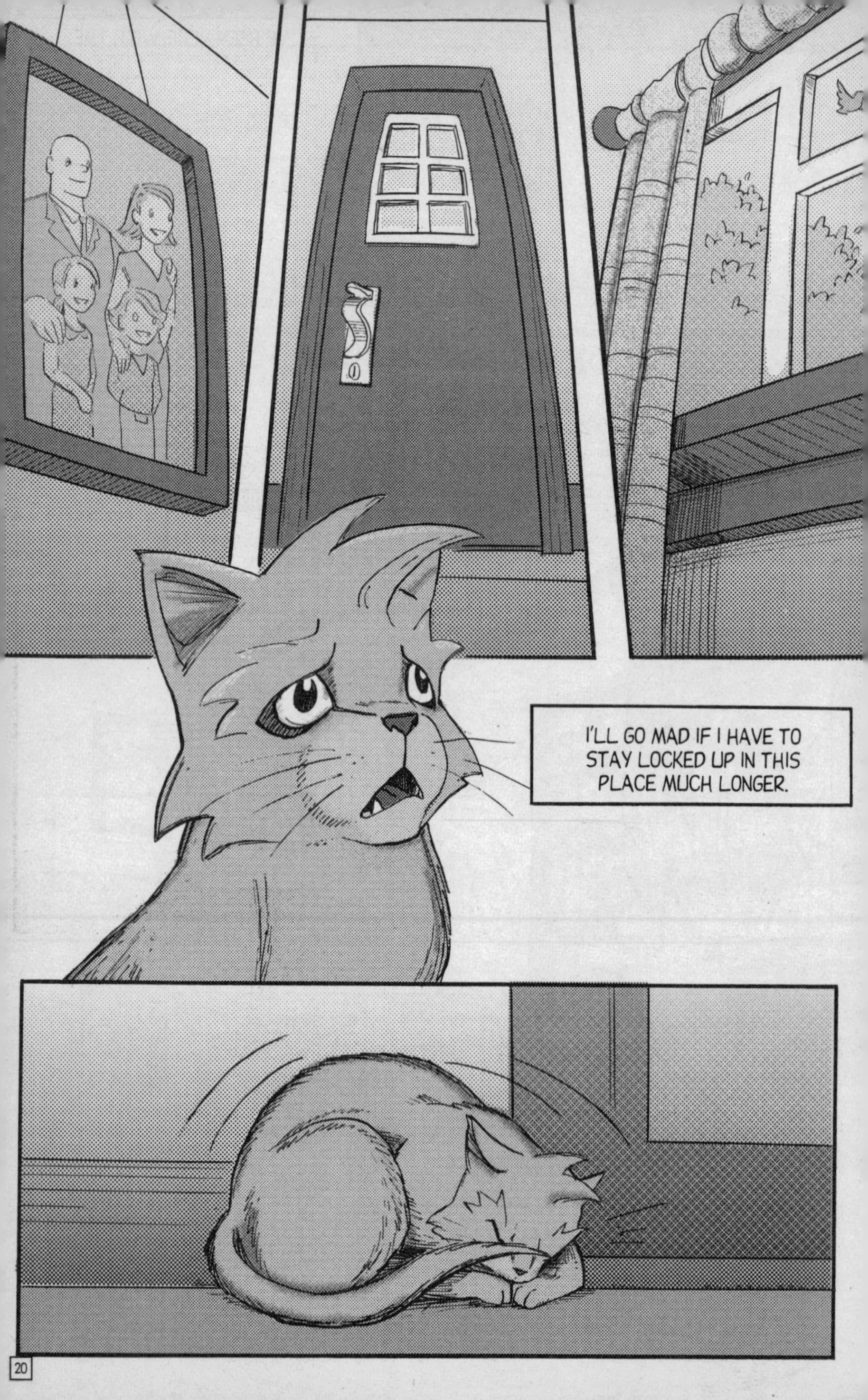
I'LL GO MAD IF I HAVE TO STAY LOCKED UP IN THIS PLACE MUCH LONGER.

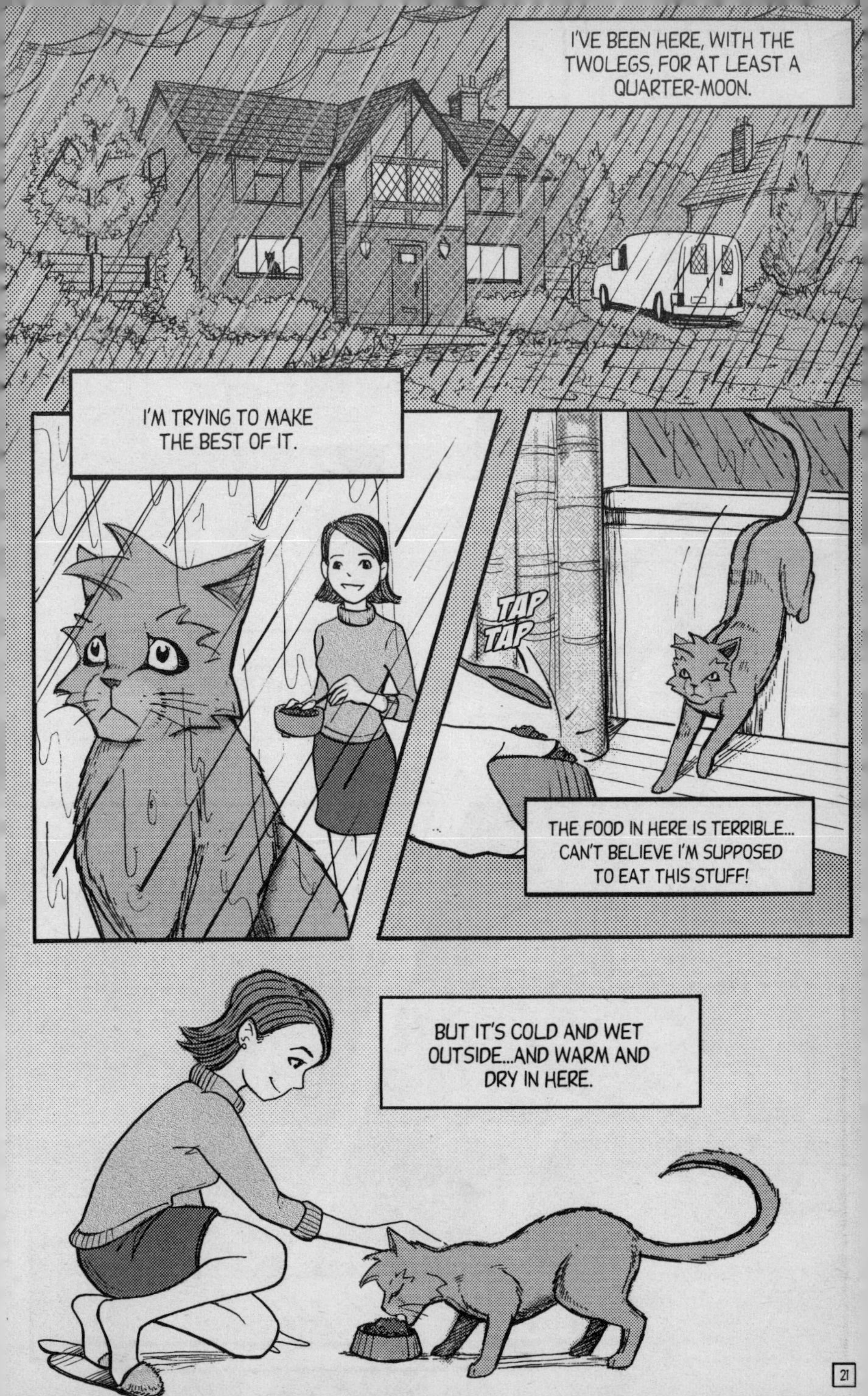
I'VE BEEN HERE, WITH THE TWOLEGS, FOR AT LEAST A QUARTER-MOON.
I'M TRYING TO MAKE THE BEST OF IT.
TAP TAP
THE FOOD IN HERE IS TERRIBLE... CAN'T BELIEVE I'M SUPPOSED TO EAT THIS STUFF!
BUT IT'S COLD AND WET OUTSIDE...AND WARM AND DRY IN HERE.

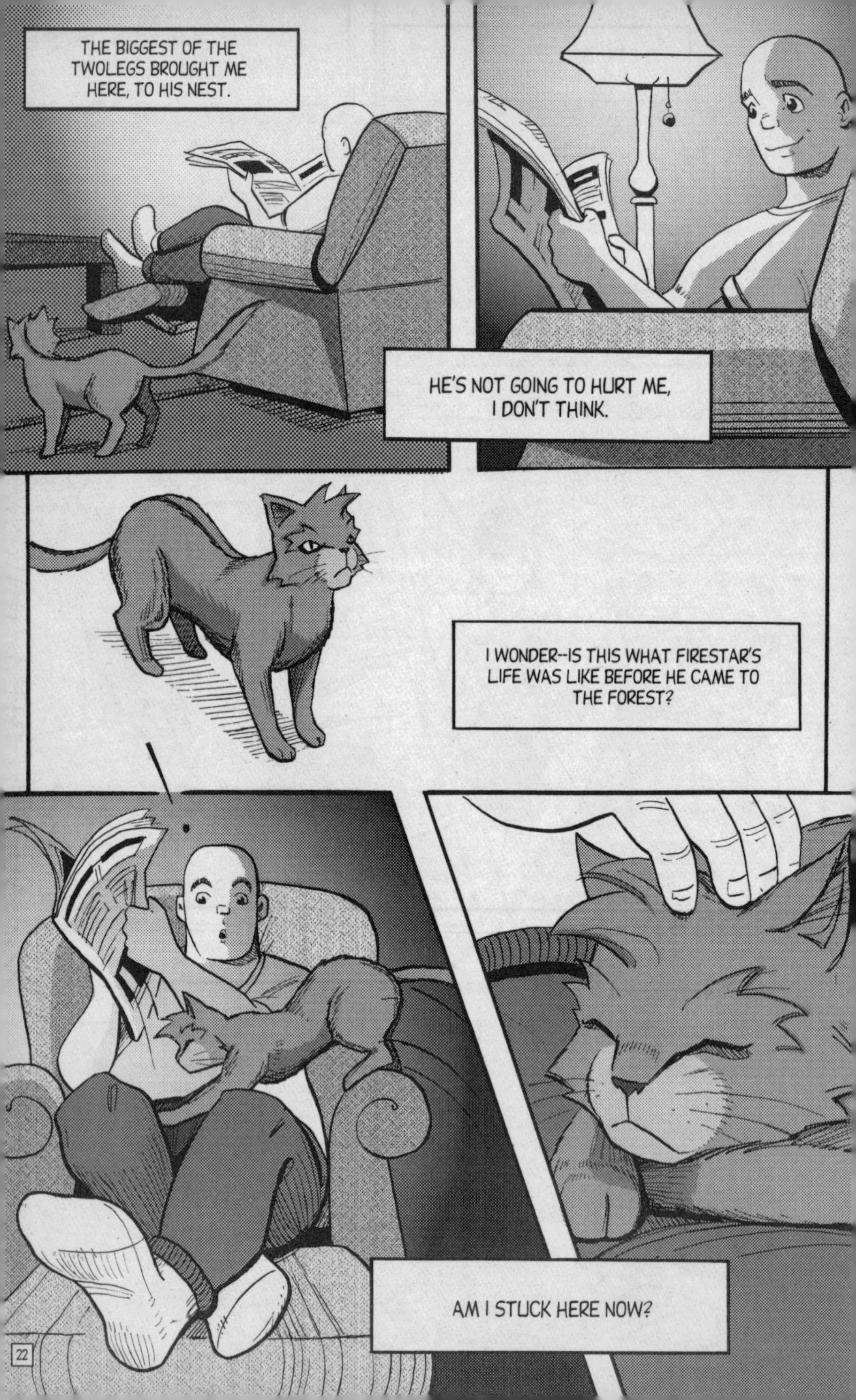
THE BIGGEST OF THE TWOLEGS BROUGHT ME HERE, TO HIS NEST.
HE'S NOT GOING TO HURT ME, I DON'T THINK.
I WONDER--IS THIS WHAT FIRESTAR'S LIFE WAS LIKE BEFORE HE CAME TO THE FOREST?
AM I STUCK HERE NOW?

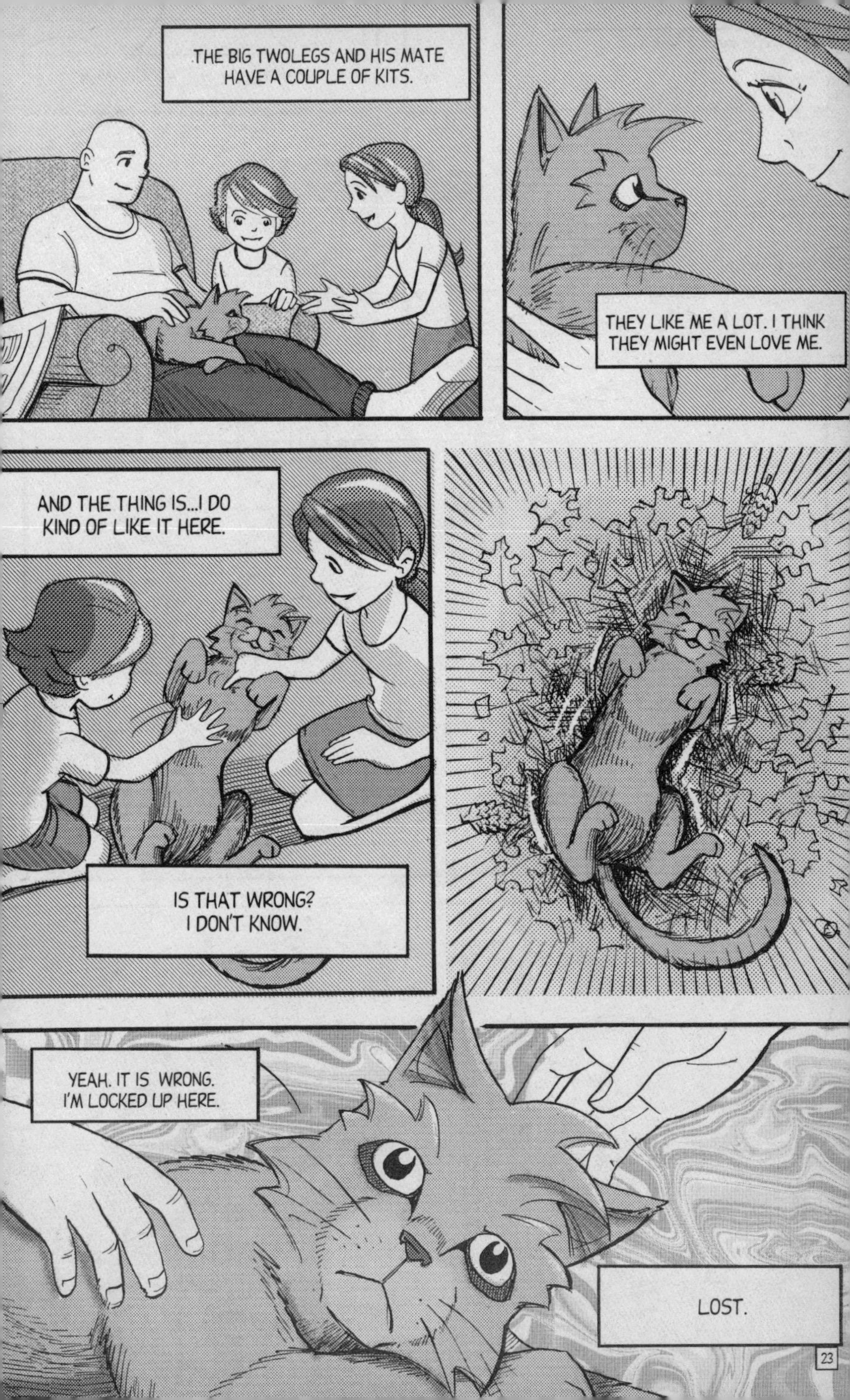
THE BIG TWOLEGS AND HIS MATE HAVE A COUPLE OF KITS.
THEY LIKE ME A LOT. I THINK THEY MIGHT EVEN LOVE ME.
AND THE THING IS...I DO KIND OF LIKE IT HERE.
IS THAT WRONG? I DON'T KNOW.
YEAH. IT IS WRONG. I'M LOCKED UP HERE.
LOST.

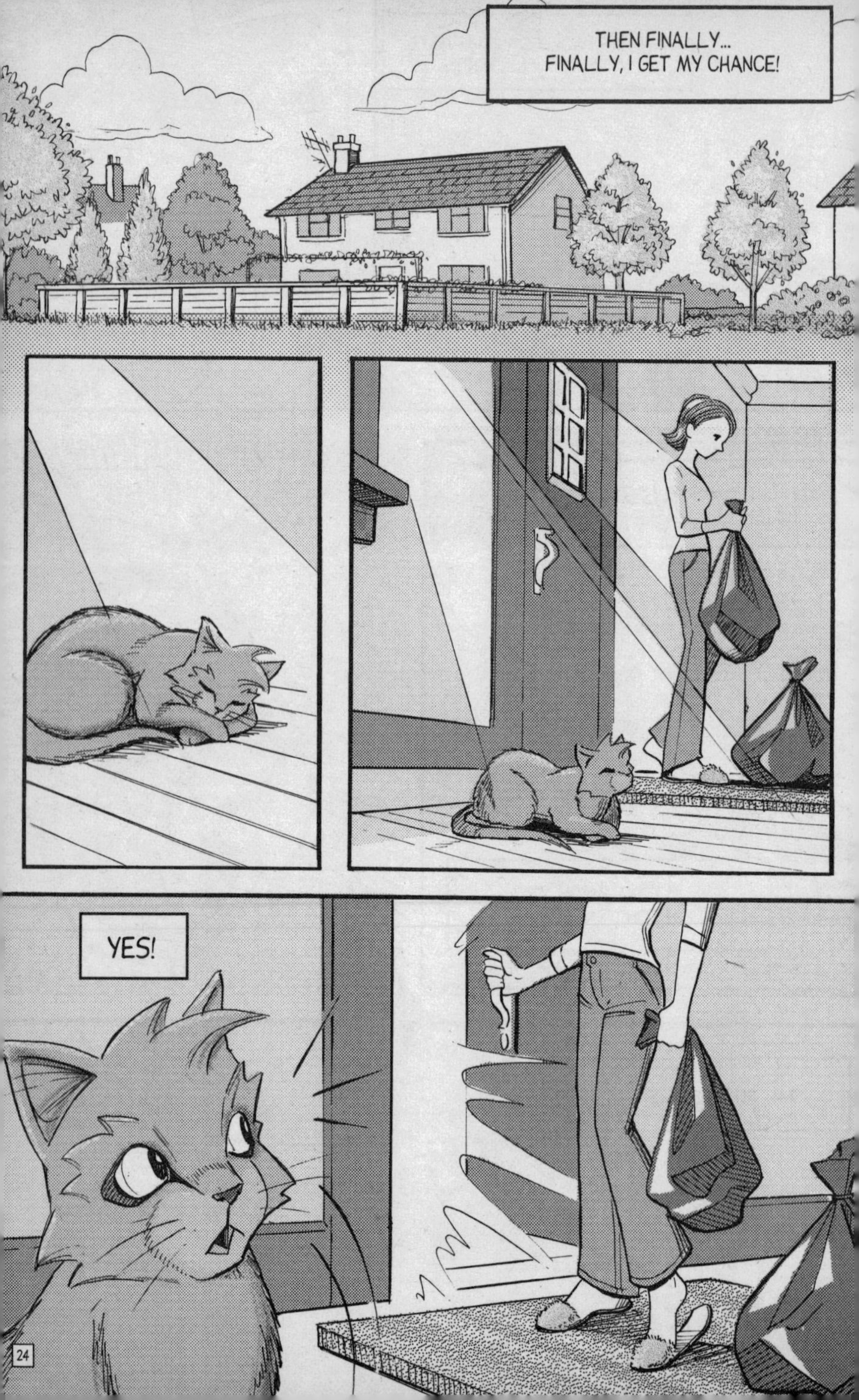
THEN FINALLY...
FINALLY, I GET MY CHANCE!
YES!

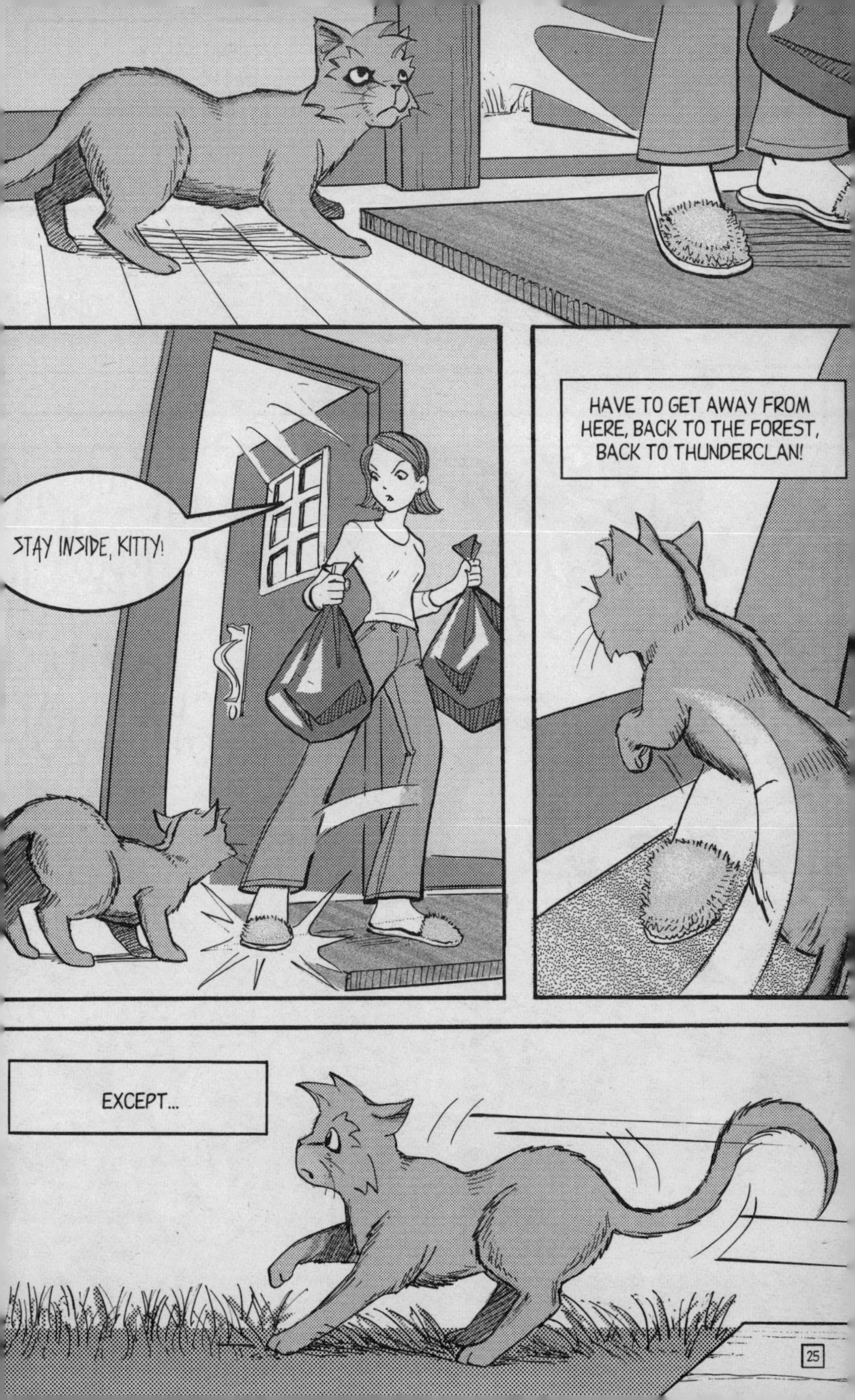
STAY INSIDE, KITTY!
HAVE TO GET AWAY FROM HERE, BACK TO THE FOREST, BACK TO THUNDERCLAN!
EXCEPT...

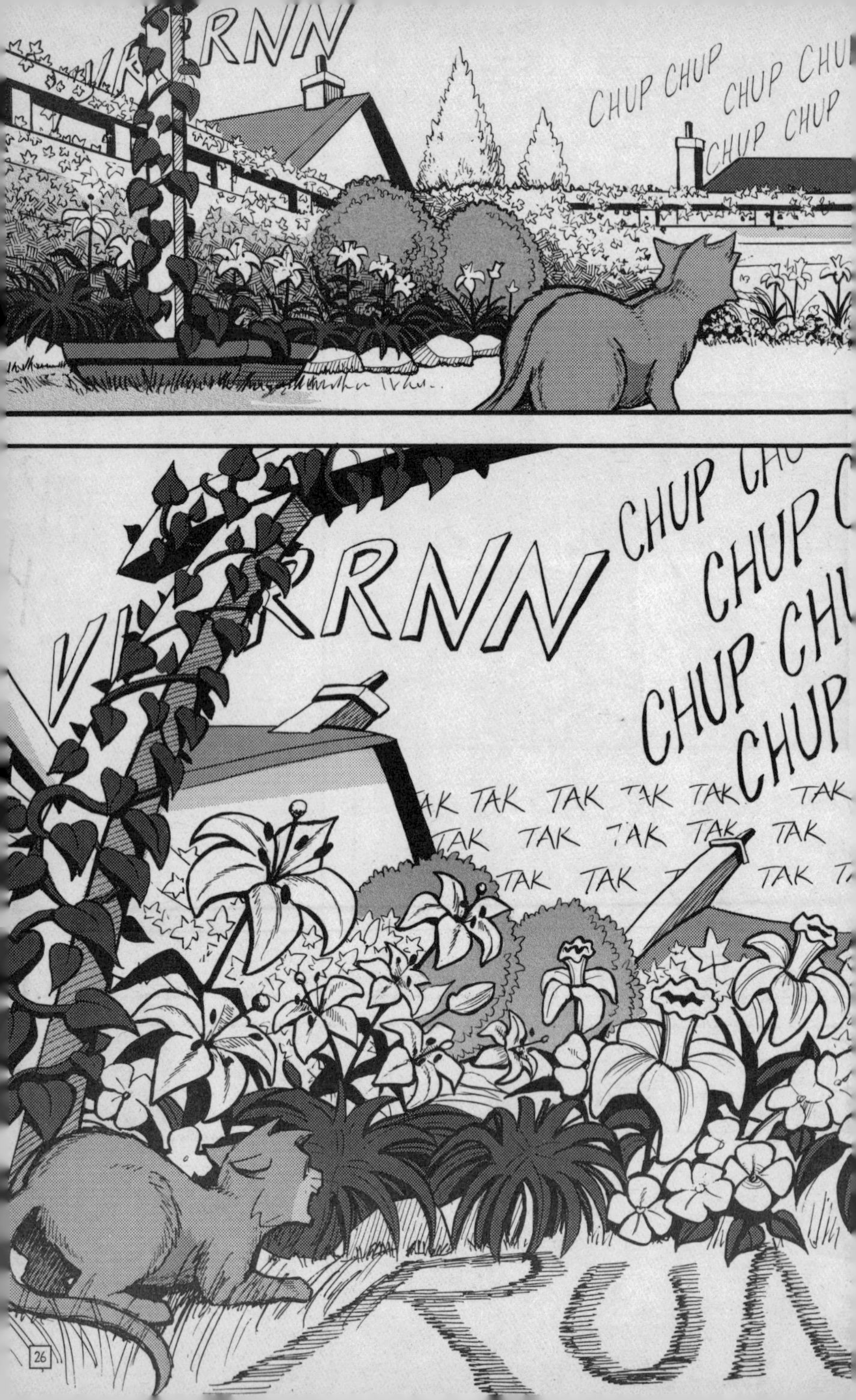
RNN
CHUP CHUP
CHUP CHUP
RNN
CHUP
CHUP
CHUP
CHUP
TAK TAK TAK TAK TAK
TAK TAK TAK TAK
TAK TAK TAK

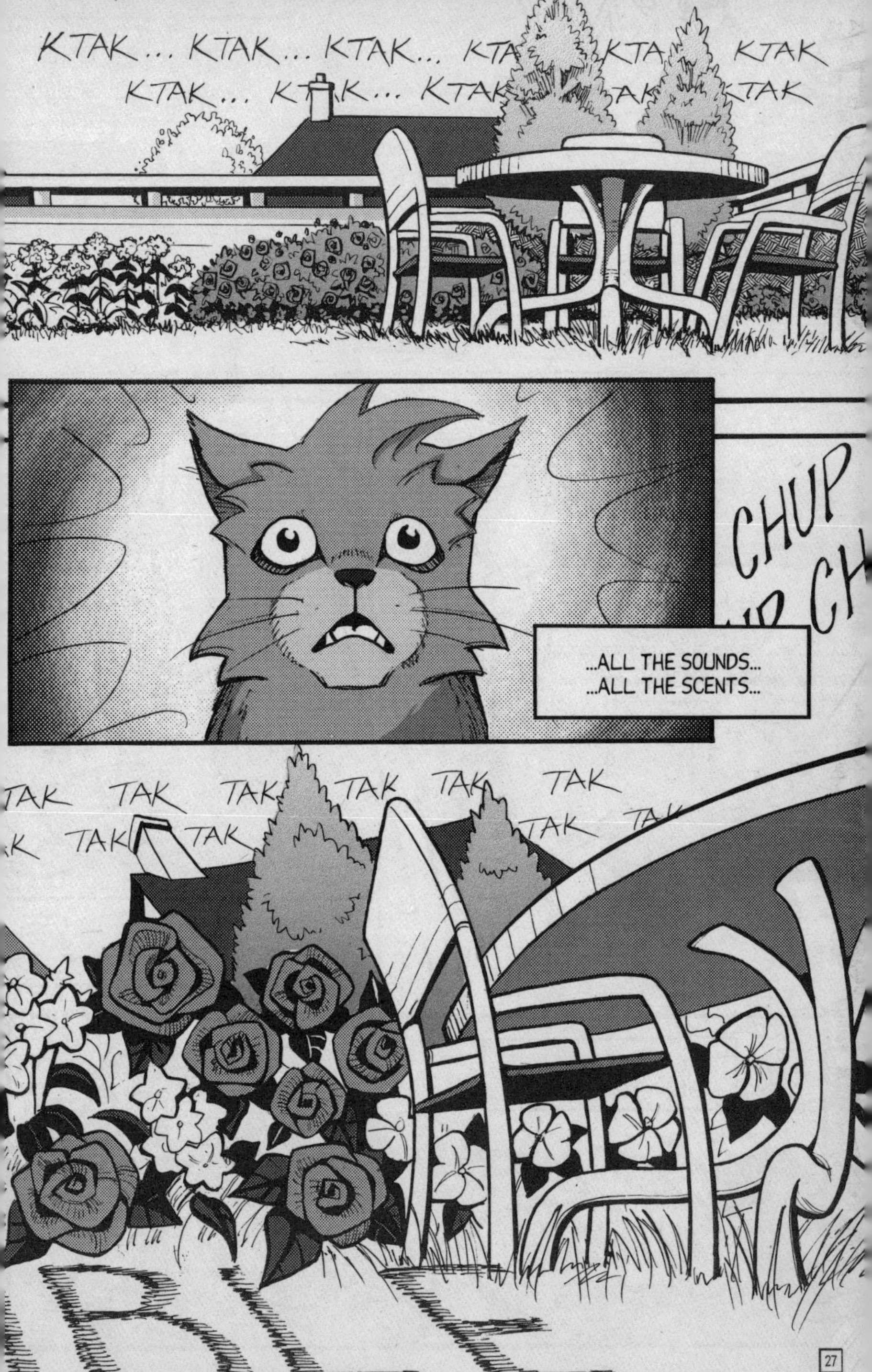
KTAK... KTAK... KTAK... KTA KTA KTAK
KTAK... KTAK... KTAK KTAK
CHUP
CH
...ALL THE SOUNDS...
...ALL THE SCENTS...
TAK TAK TAK TAK TAK TAK
TAK TAK TAK

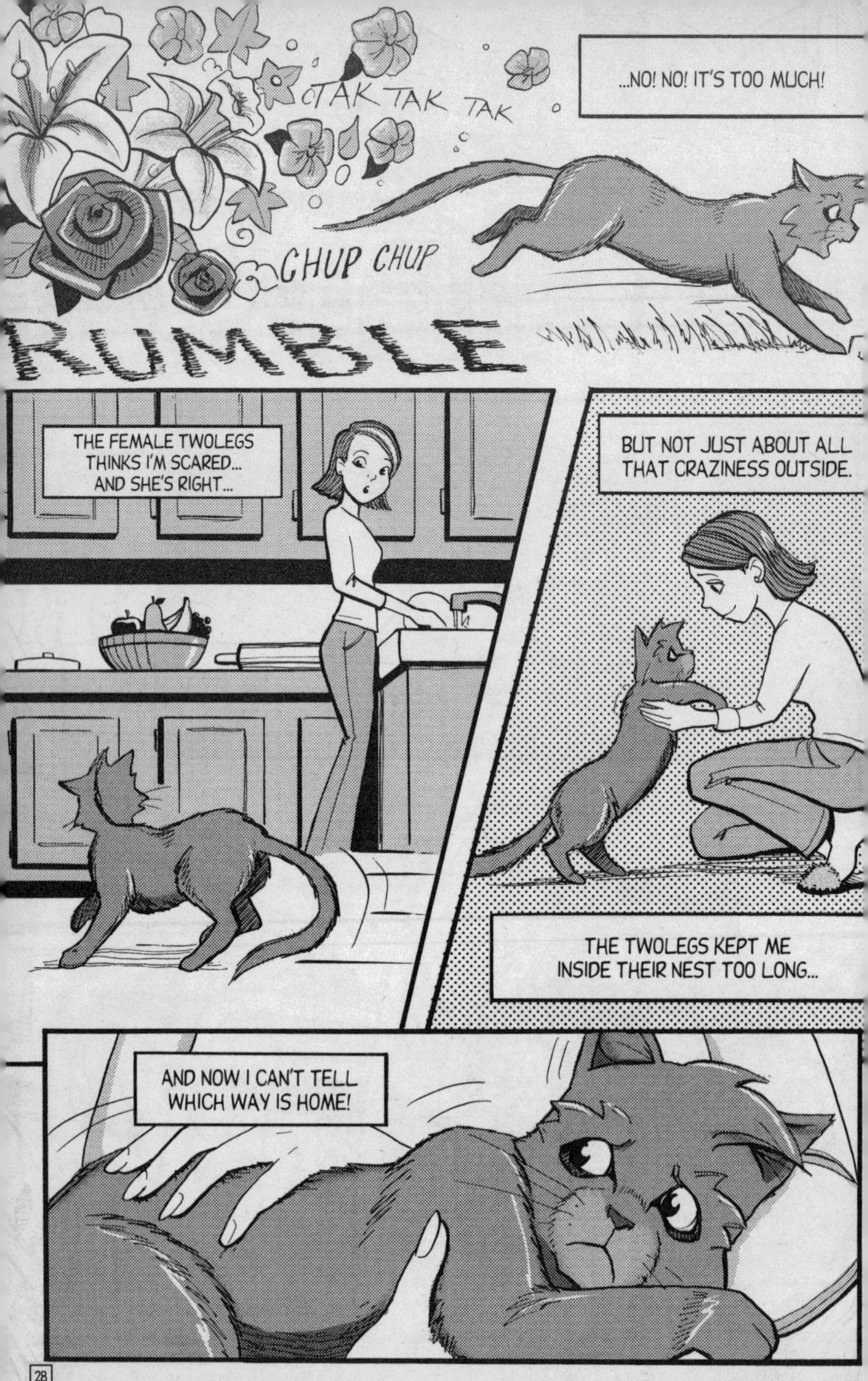
TAK TAK TAK
...NO! NO! IT'S TOO MUCH!
CHUP CHUP
RUMBLE
THE FEMALE TWOLEGS THINKS I'M SCARED... AND SHE'S RIGHT...
BUT NOT JUST ABOUT ALL THAT CRAZINESS OUTSIDE.
THE TWOLEGS KEPT ME INSIDE THEIR NEST TOO LONG...
AND NOW I CAN'T TELL WHICH WAY IS HOME!

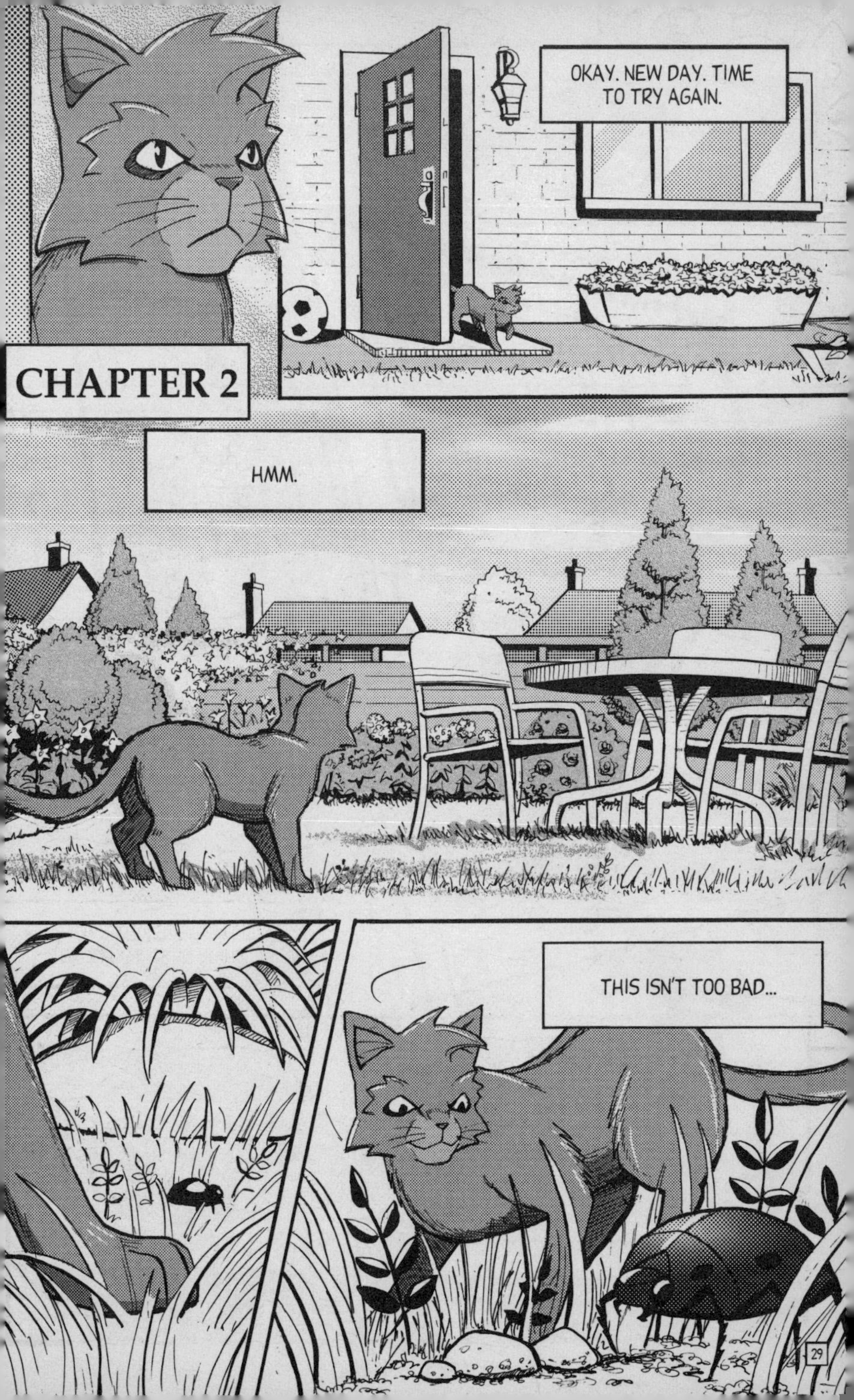

CHAPTER 2
OKAY. NEW DAY. TIME TO TRY AGAIN.
HMM.
THIS ISN'T TOO BAD...

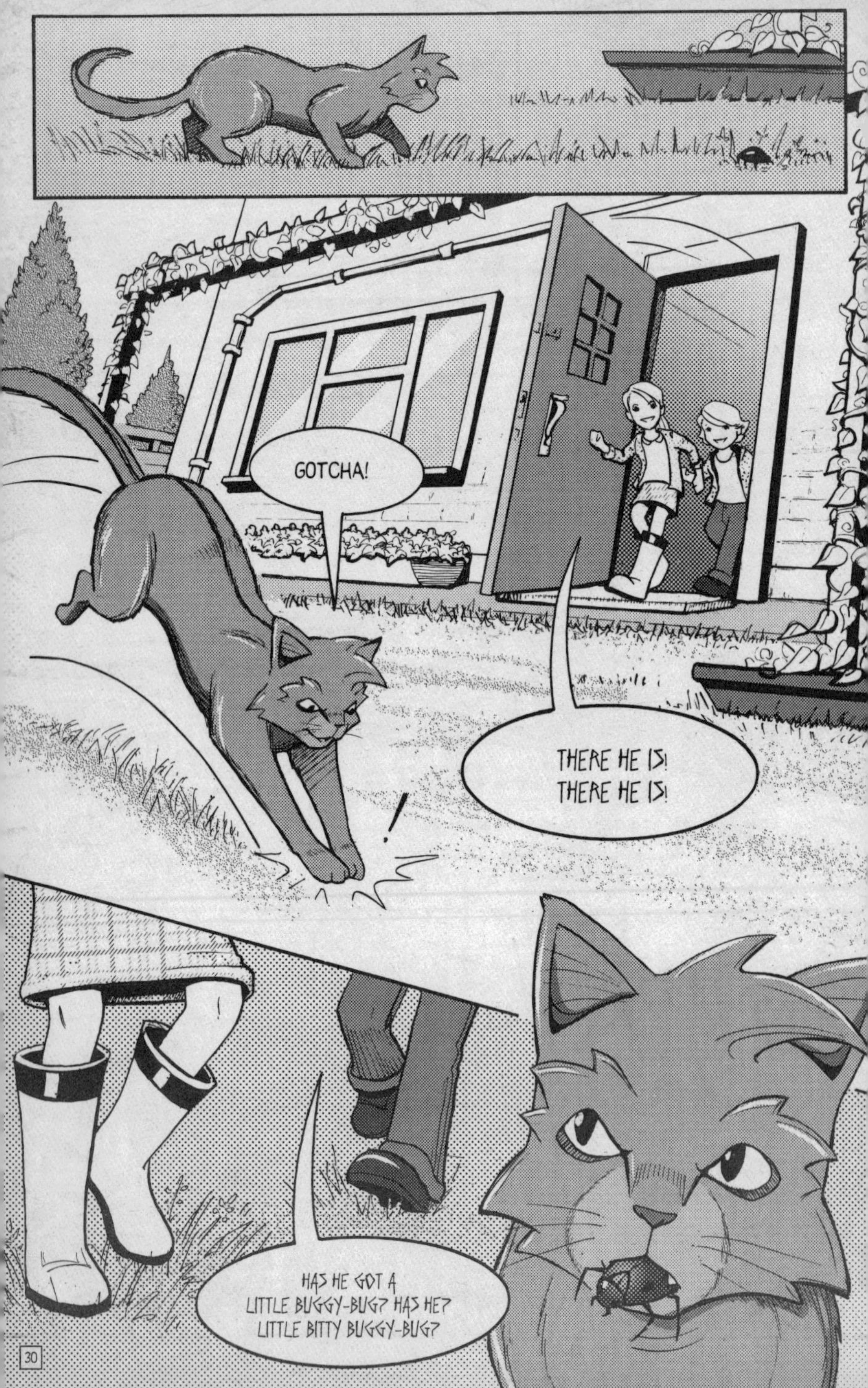
GOTCHA!
THERE HE IS! THERE HE IS!
HAS HE GOT A LITTLE BUGGY-BUG? HAS HE? LITTLE BITTY BUGGY-BUG?

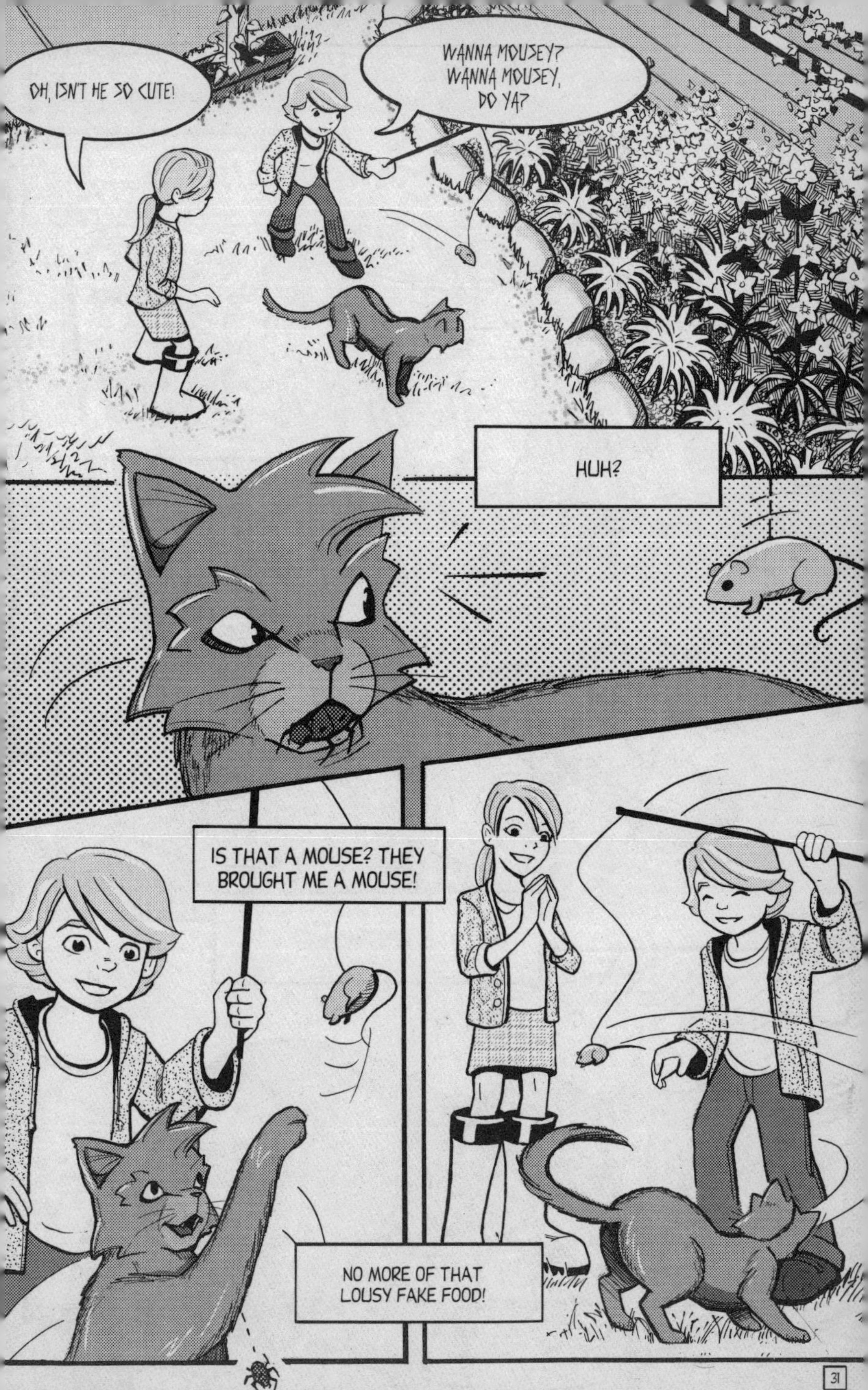

OH, ISN'T HE SO CUTE!
WANNA MOUSEY? WANNA MOUSEY, DO YA?
HUH?
IS THAT A MOUSE? THEY BROUGHT ME A MOUSE!
NO MORE OF THAT LOUSY FAKE FOOD!

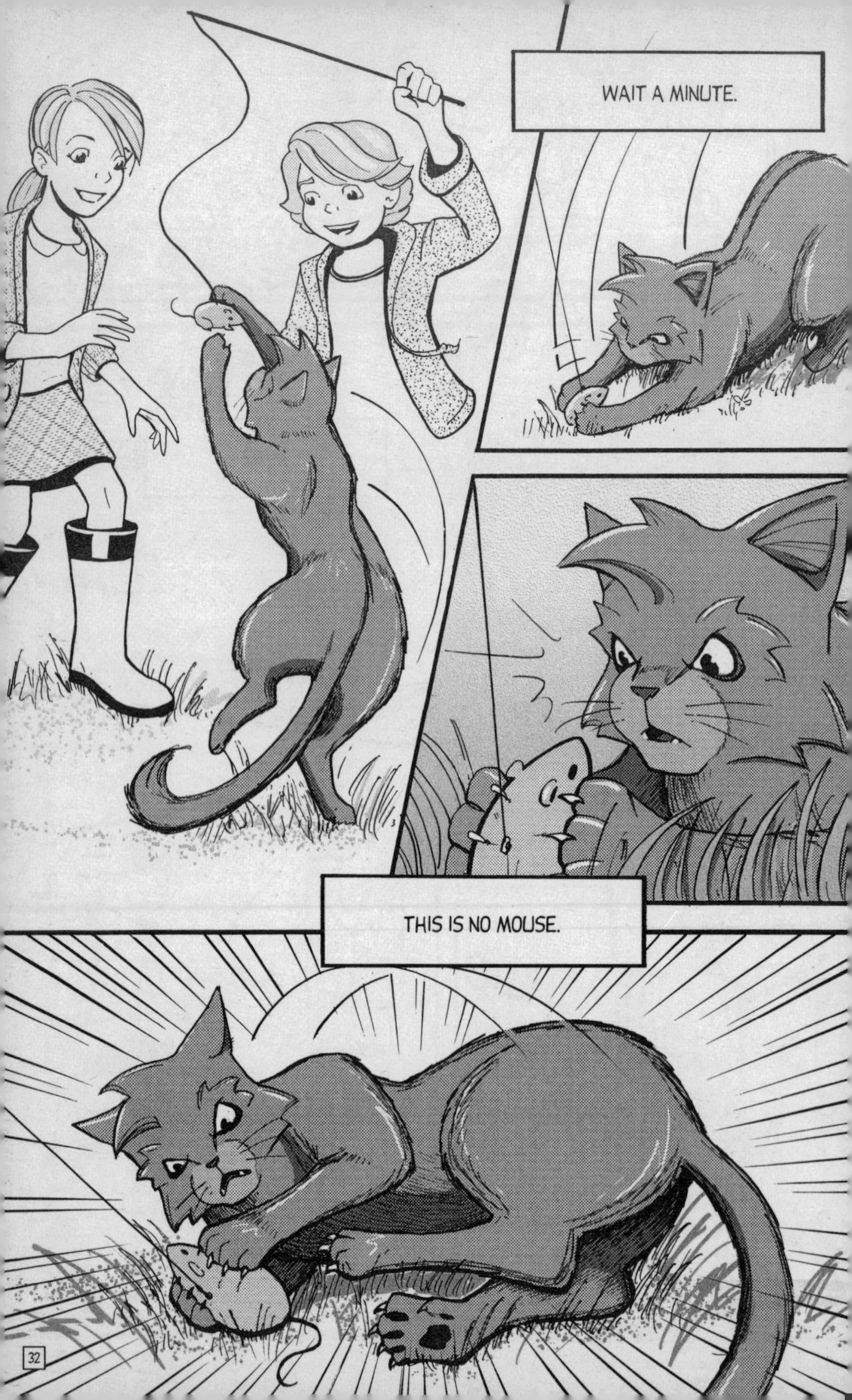
WAIT A MINUTE.
THIS IS NO MOUSE.

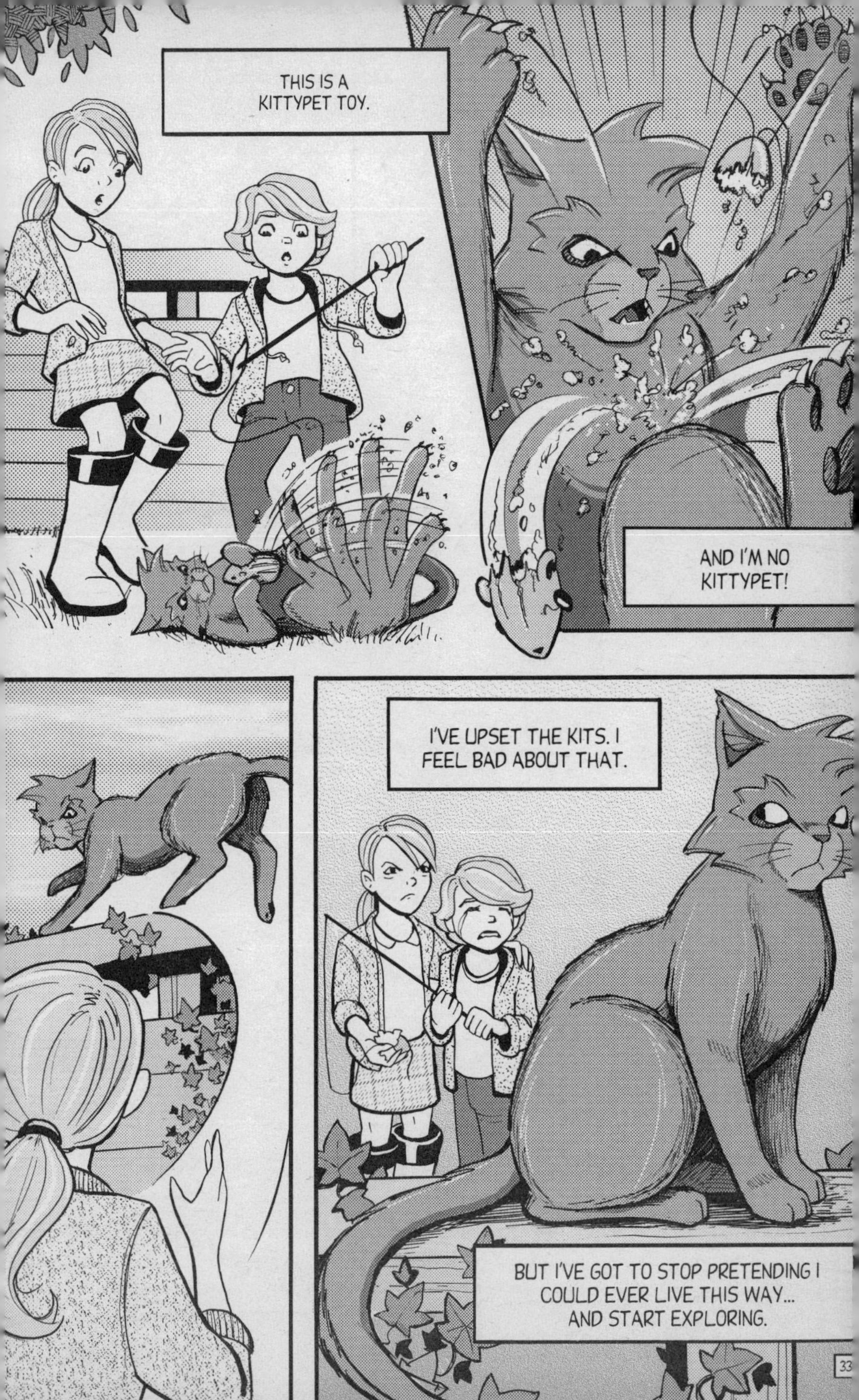
THIS IS A KITTYPET TOY.
AND I'M NO KITTYPET!
I'VE UPSET THE KITS. I FEEL BAD ABOUT THAT.
BUT I'VE GOT TO STOP PRETENDING I COULD EVER LIVE THIS WAY... AND START EXPLORING.

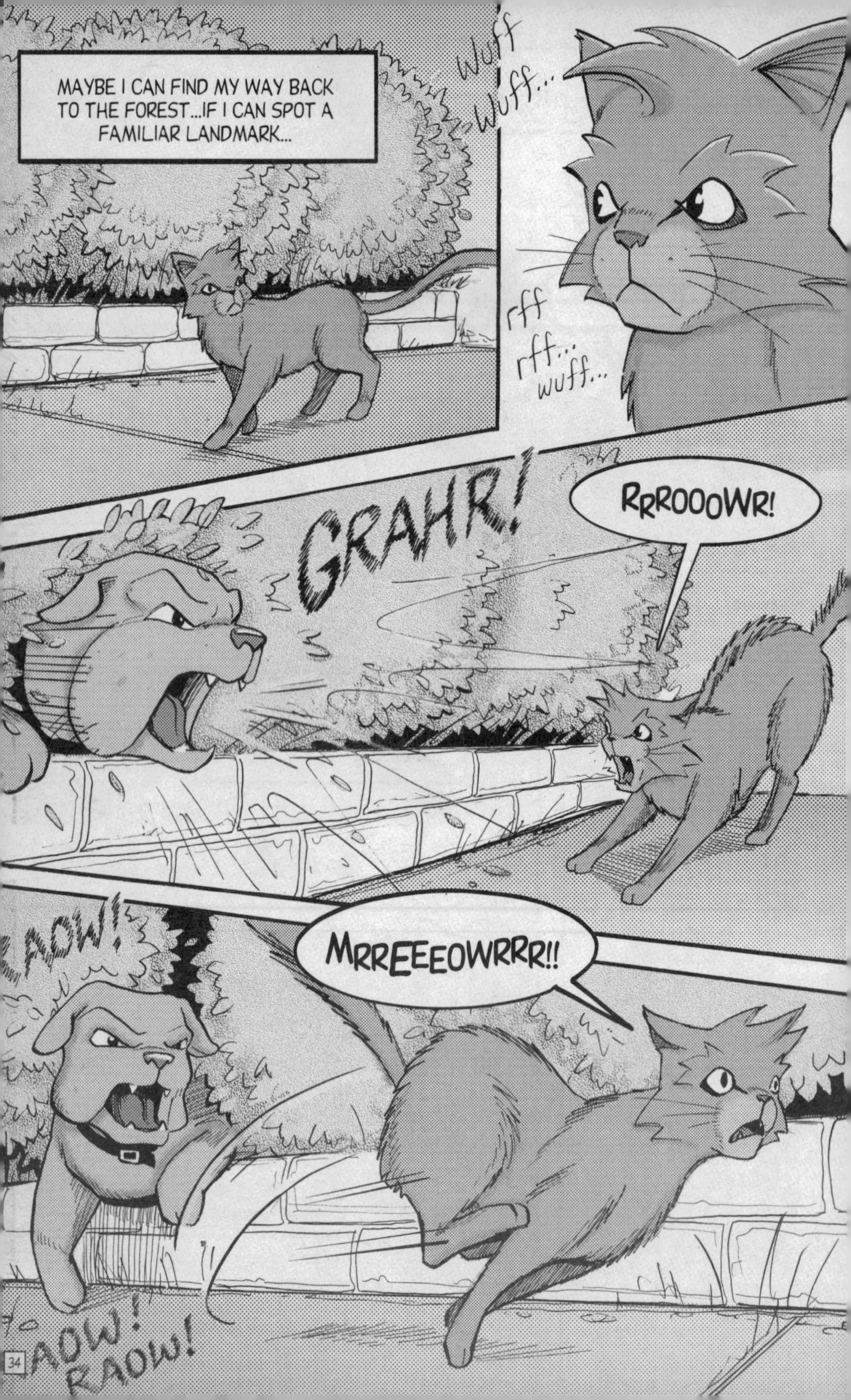
MAYBE I CAN FIND MY WAY BACK TO THE FOREST...IF I CAN SPOT A FAMILIAR LANDMARK...
Wuff Wuff...
rff rff... wuff...
GRAHR!
RRROOOWR!
RAOW!
MRREEEOWRRR!!
AOW! RAOW!

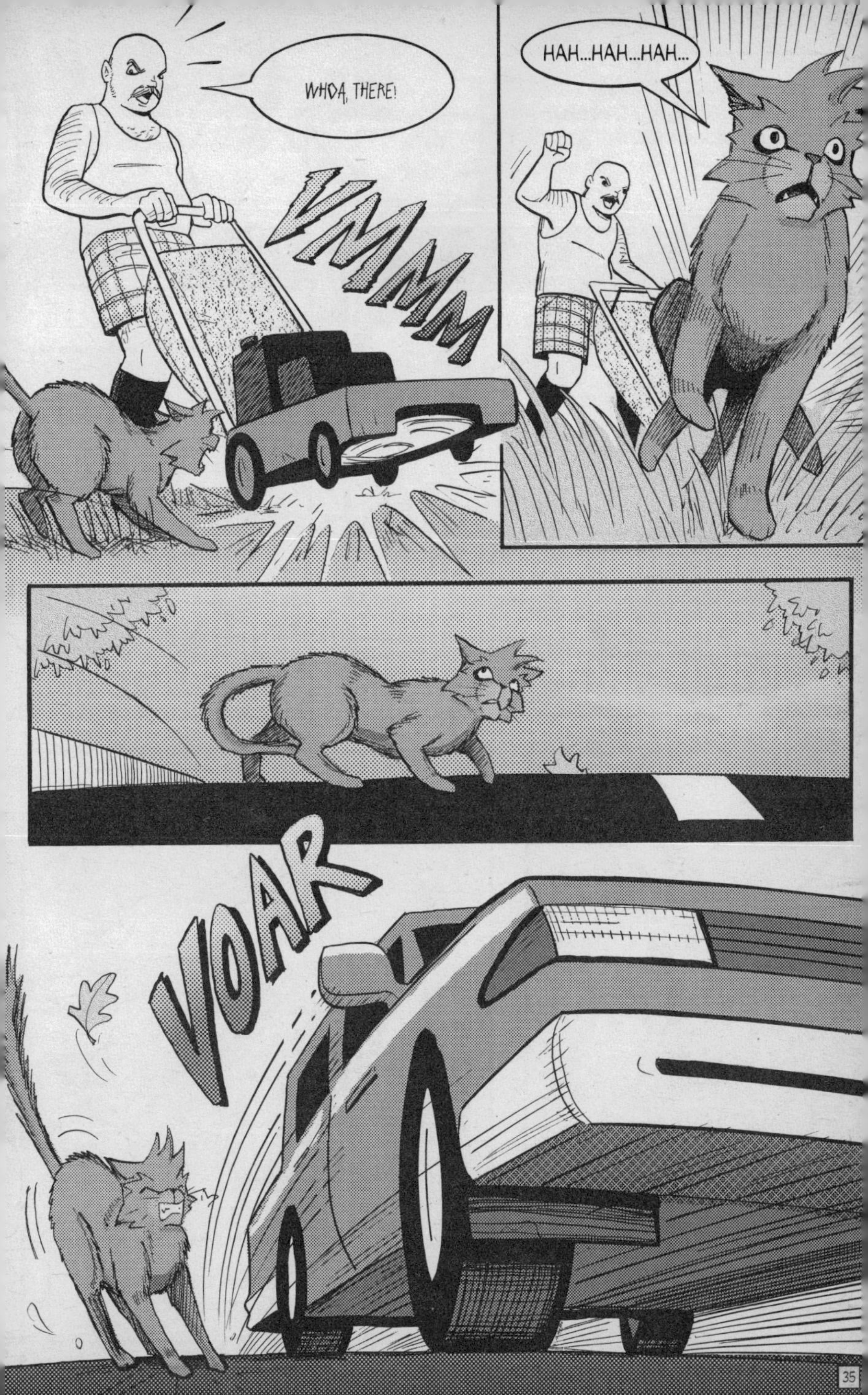
WHOA, THERE!
VMMM
HAH...HAH...HAH...
VOAR

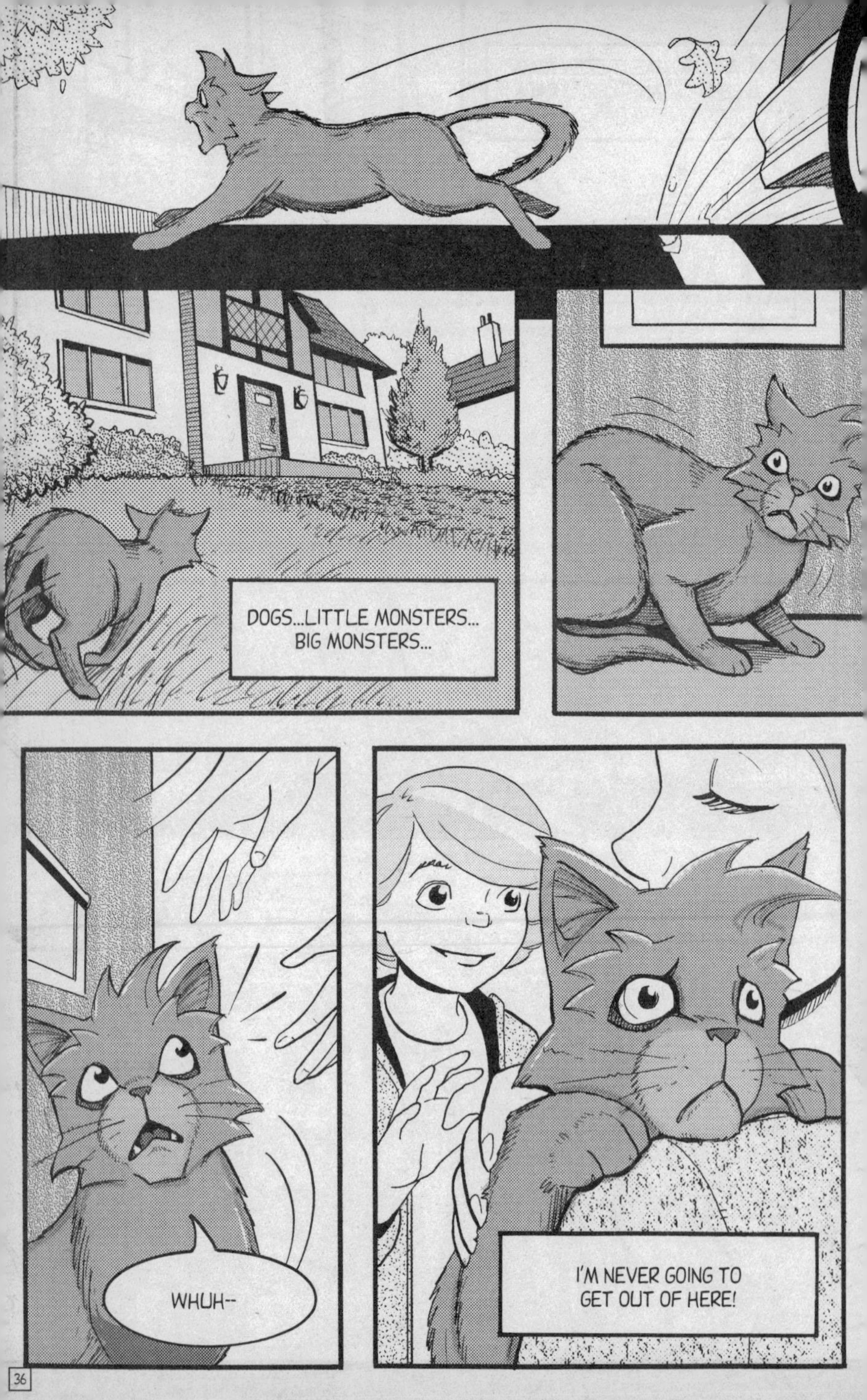
DOGS...LITTLE MONSTERS...
BIG MONSTERS...
WHUH--
I'M NEVER GOING TO
GET OUT OF HERE!

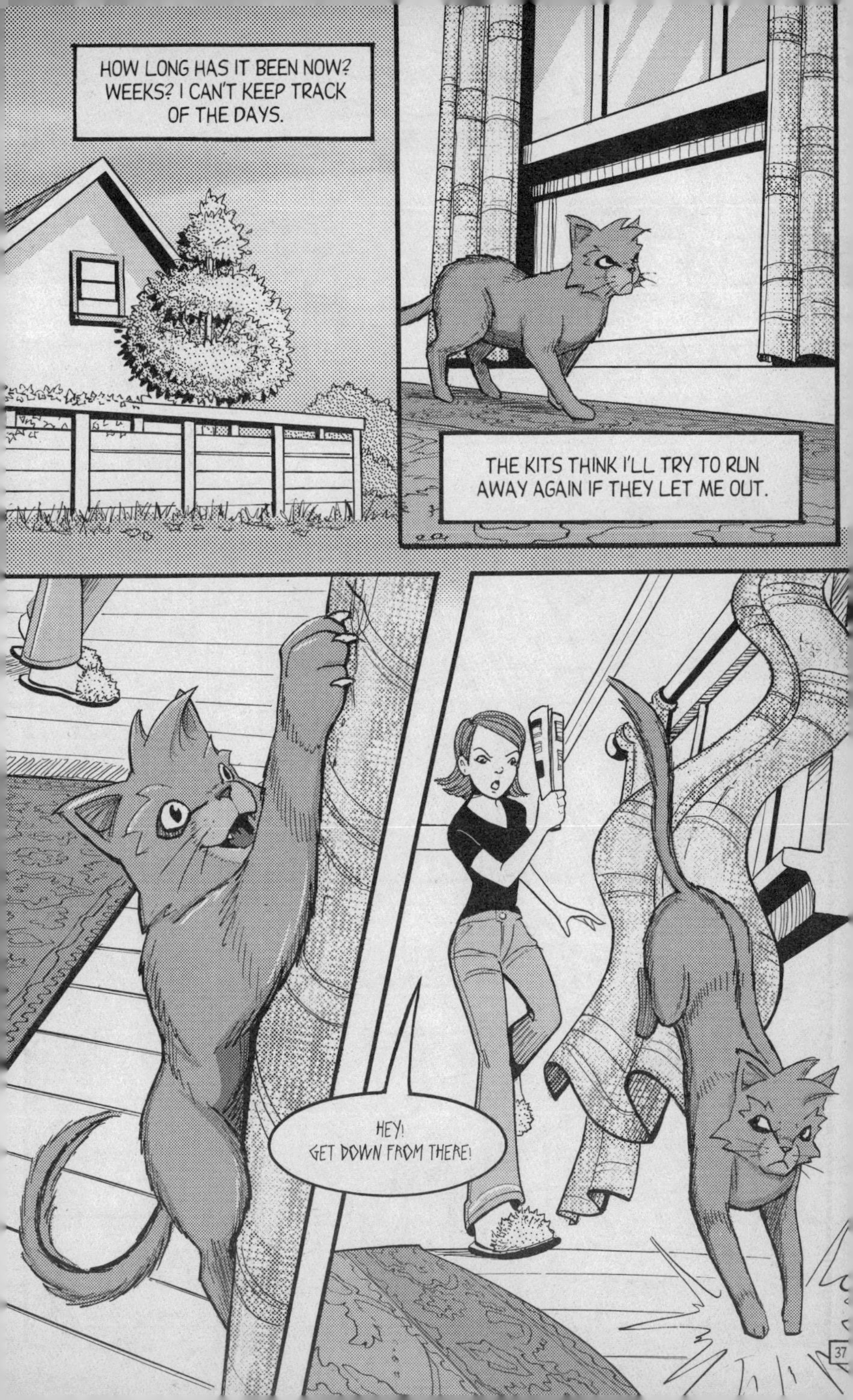
HOW LONG HAS IT BEEN NOW? WEEKS? I CAN'T KEEP TRACK OF THE DAYS.
THE KITS THINK I'LL TRY TO RUN AWAY AGAIN IF THEY LET ME OUT.
HEY! GET DOWN FROM THERE!

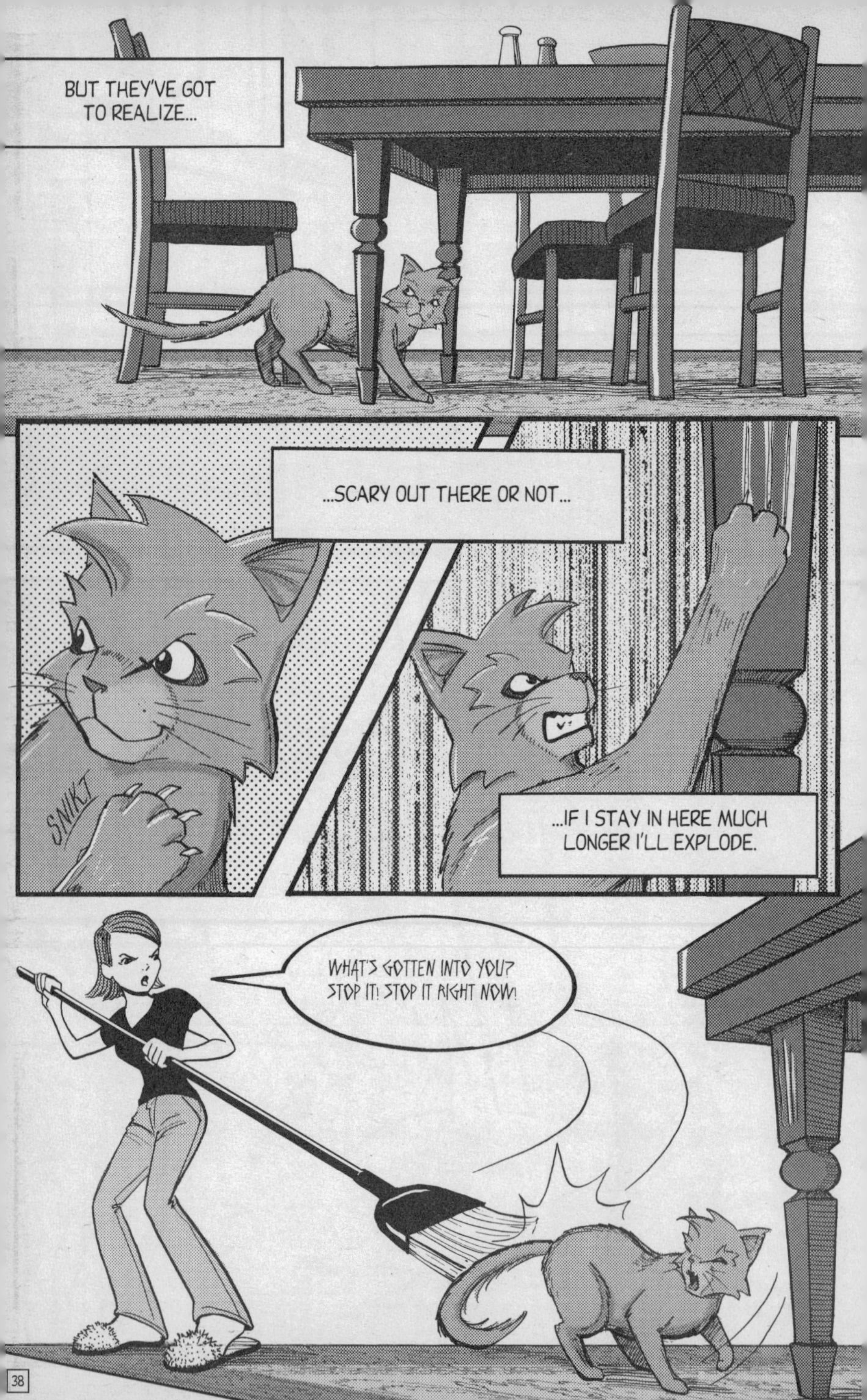
BUT THEY'VE GOT TO REALIZE...
...SCARY OUT THERE OR NOT...
SNIKT
...IF I STAY IN HERE MUCH LONGER I'LL EXPLODE.
WHAT'S GOTTEN INTO YOU? STOP IT! STOP IT RIGHT NOW!

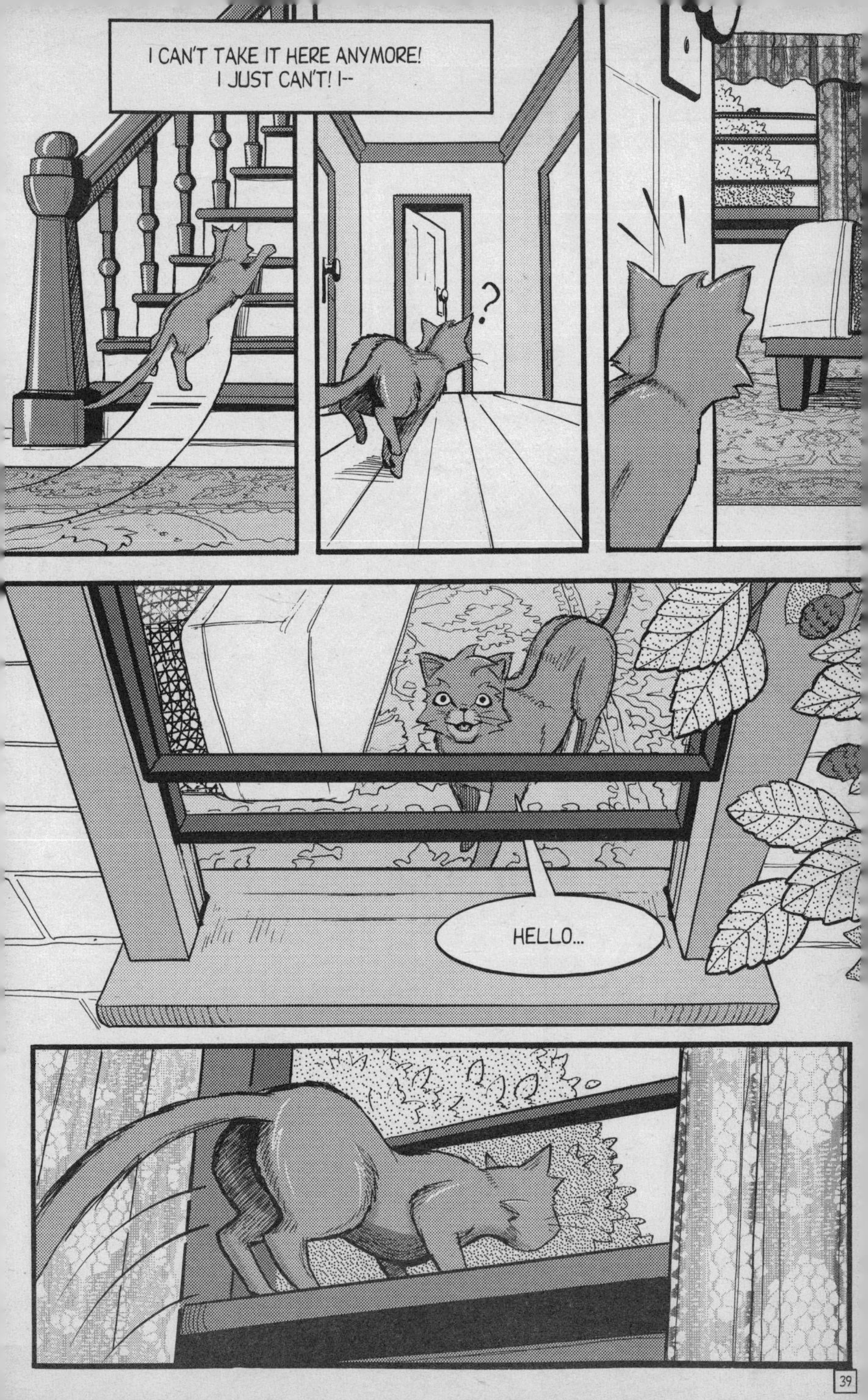
I CAN'T TAKE IT HERE ANYMORE! I JUST CAN'T! I--
?
HELLO...

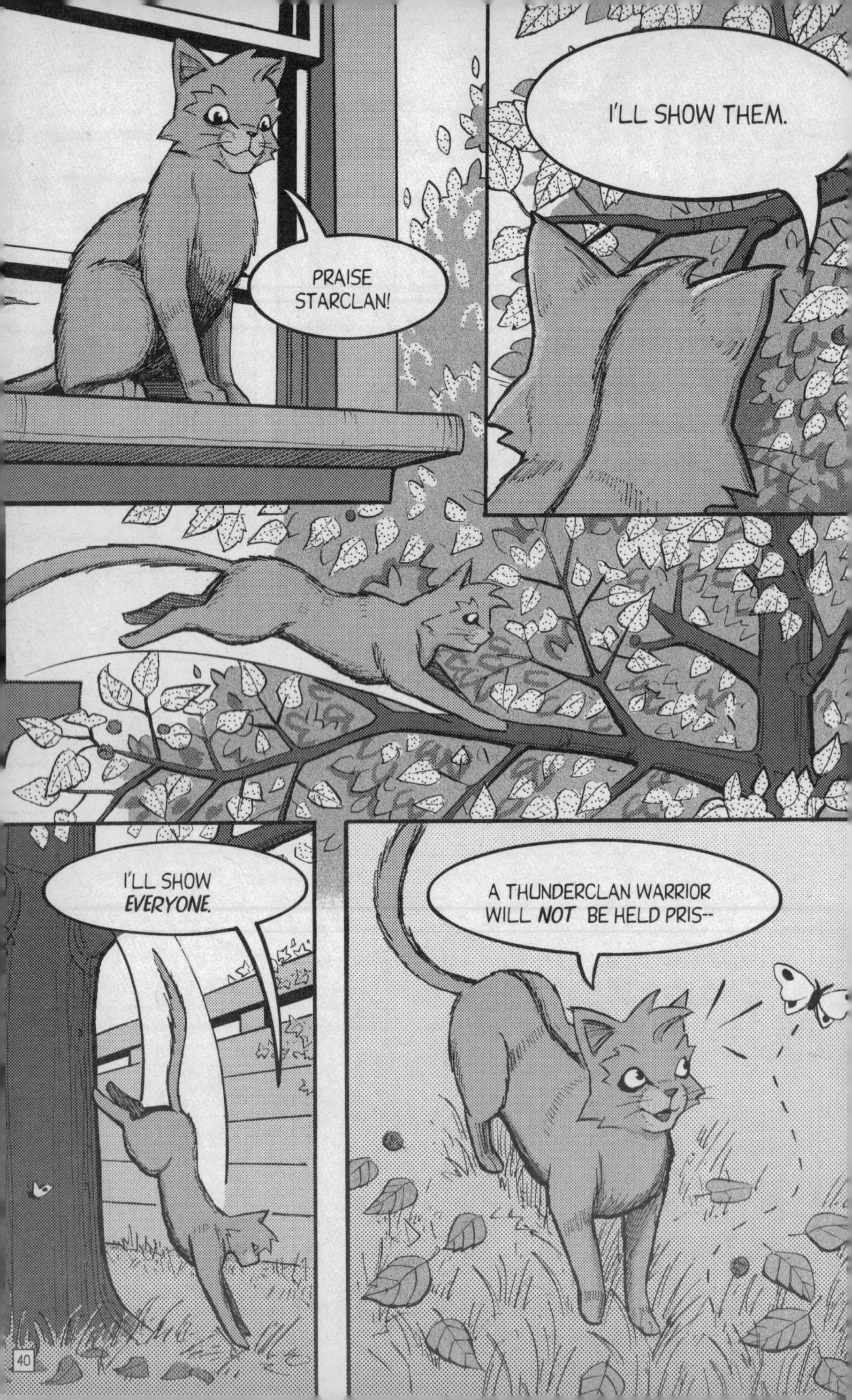
PRAISE STARCLAN!
I'LL SHOW THEM.
I'LL SHOW *EVERYONE.*
A THUNDERCLAN WARRIOR WILL *NOT* BE HELD PRIS--

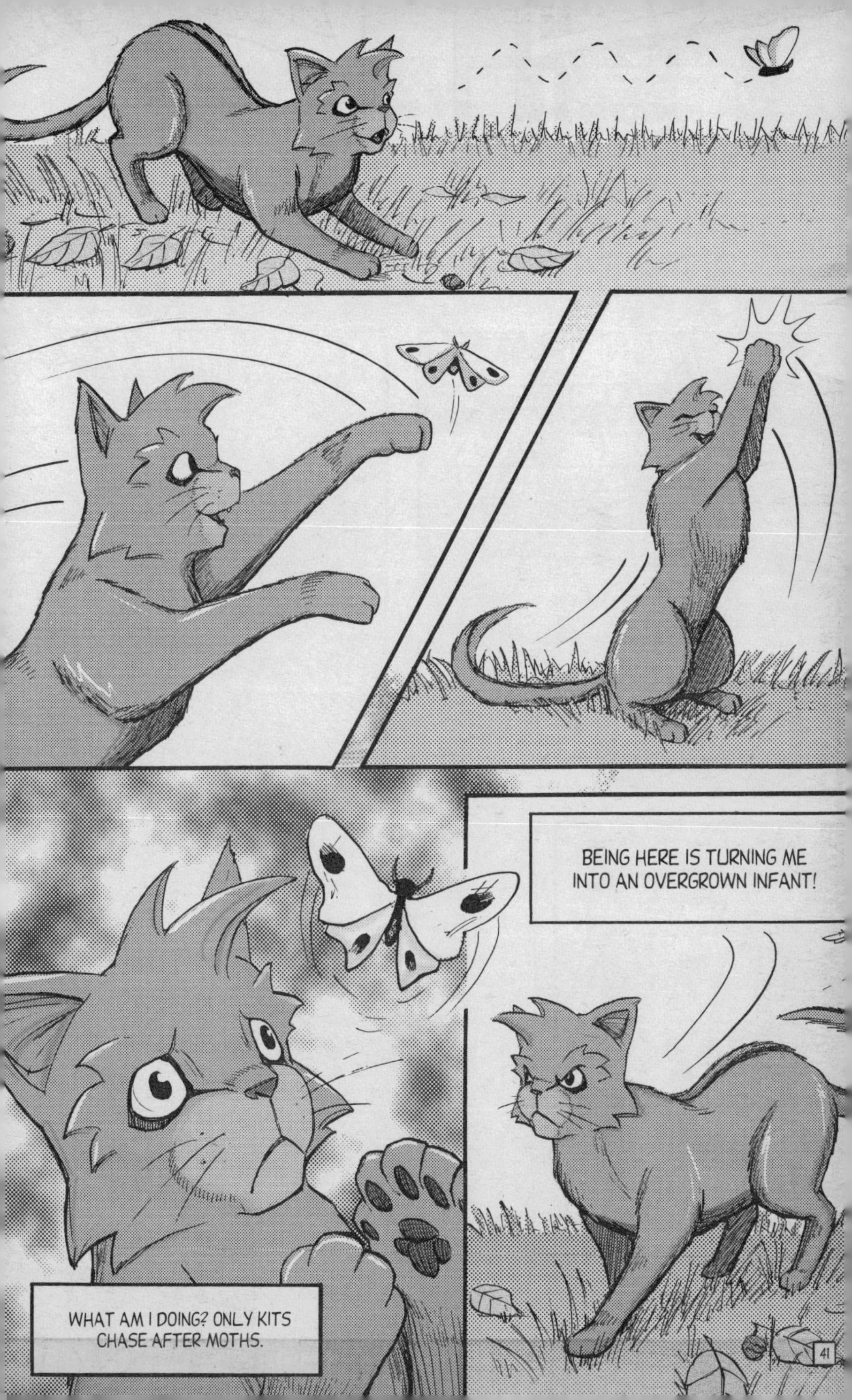
BEING HERE IS TURNING ME INTO AN OVERGROWN INFANT!
WHAT AM I DOING? ONLY KITS CHASE AFTER MOTHS.

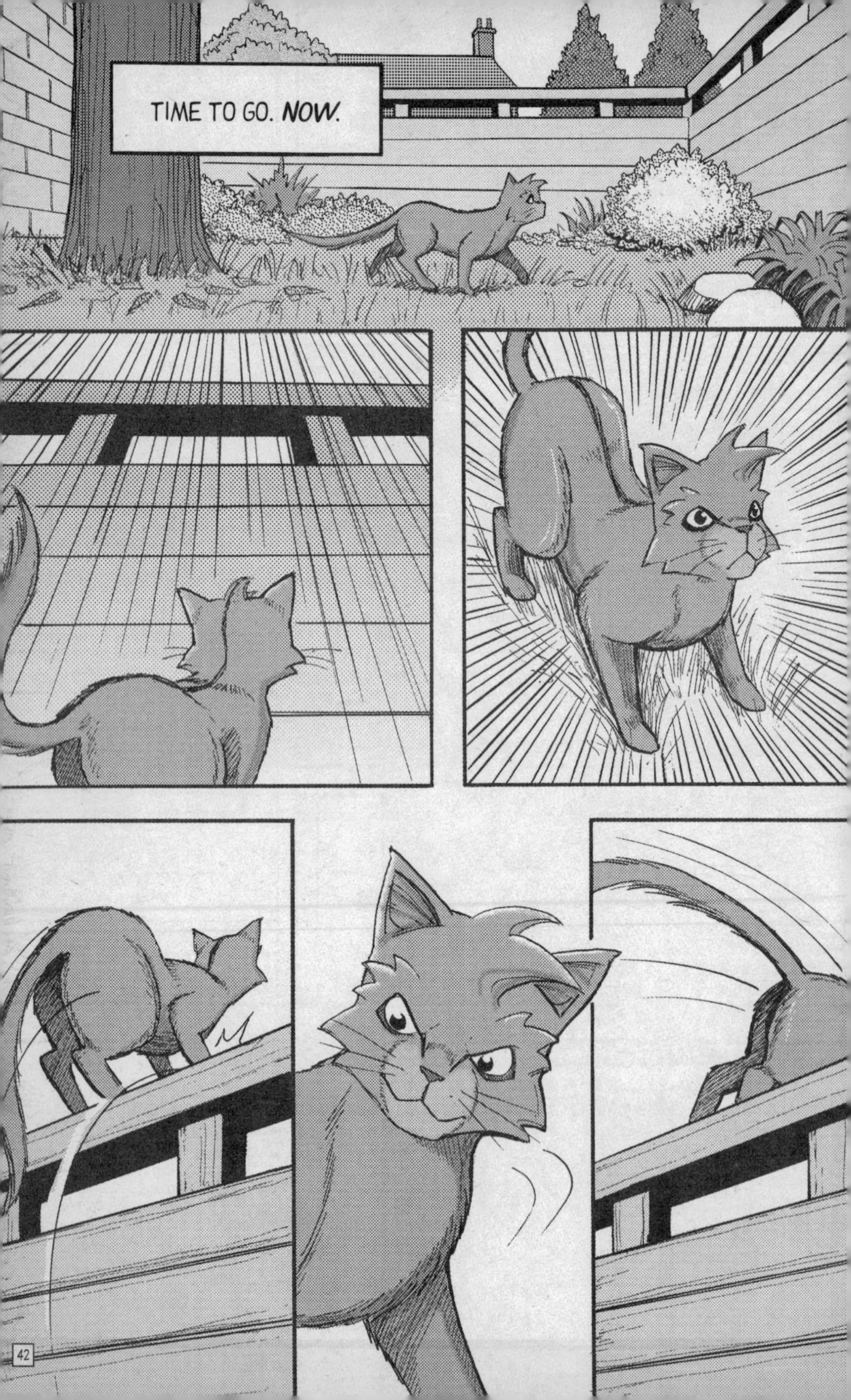
TIME TO GO. NOW.

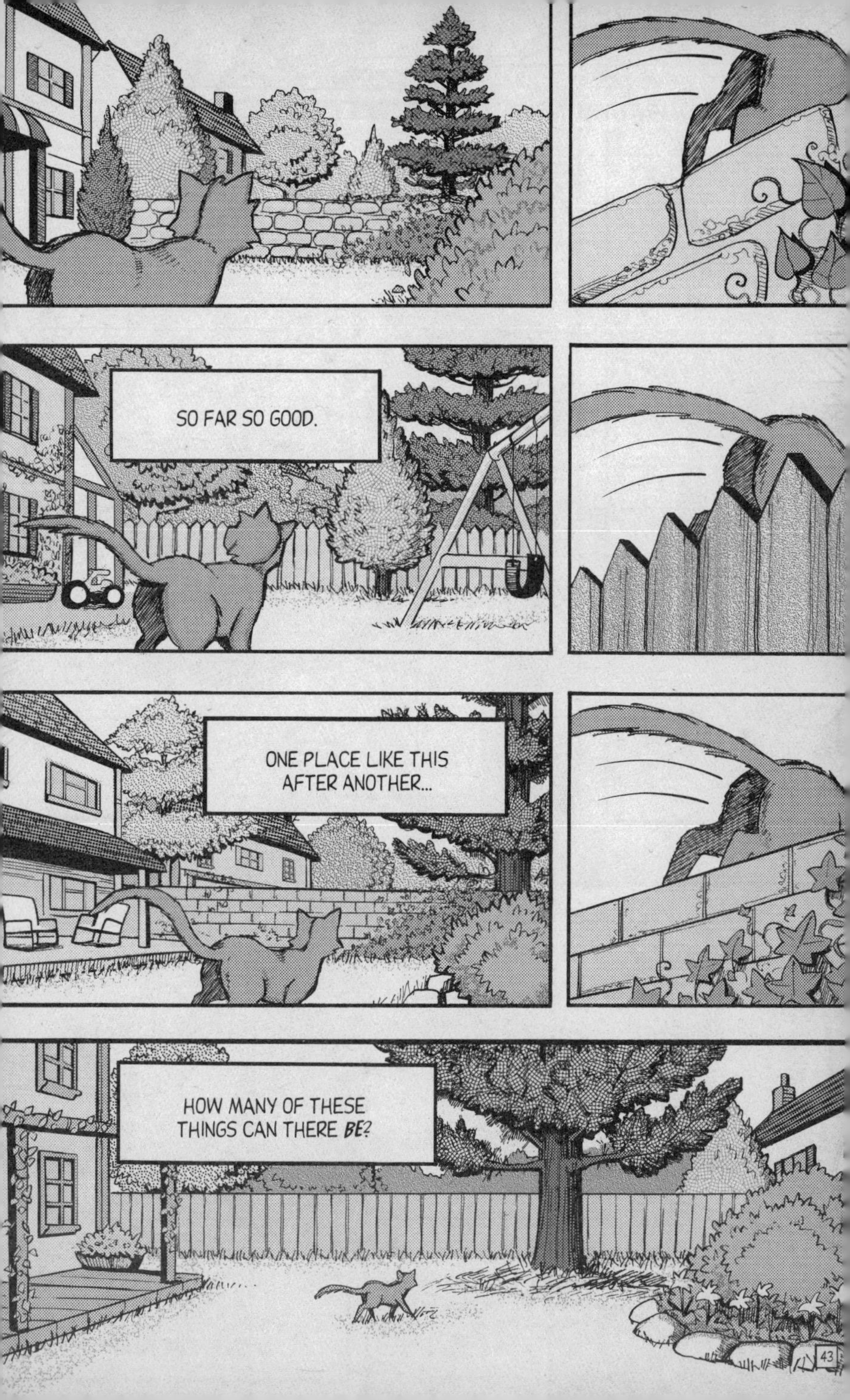
SO FAR SO GOOD.
ONE PLACE LIKE THIS AFTER ANOTHER...
HOW MANY OF THESE THINGS CAN THERE *BE*?

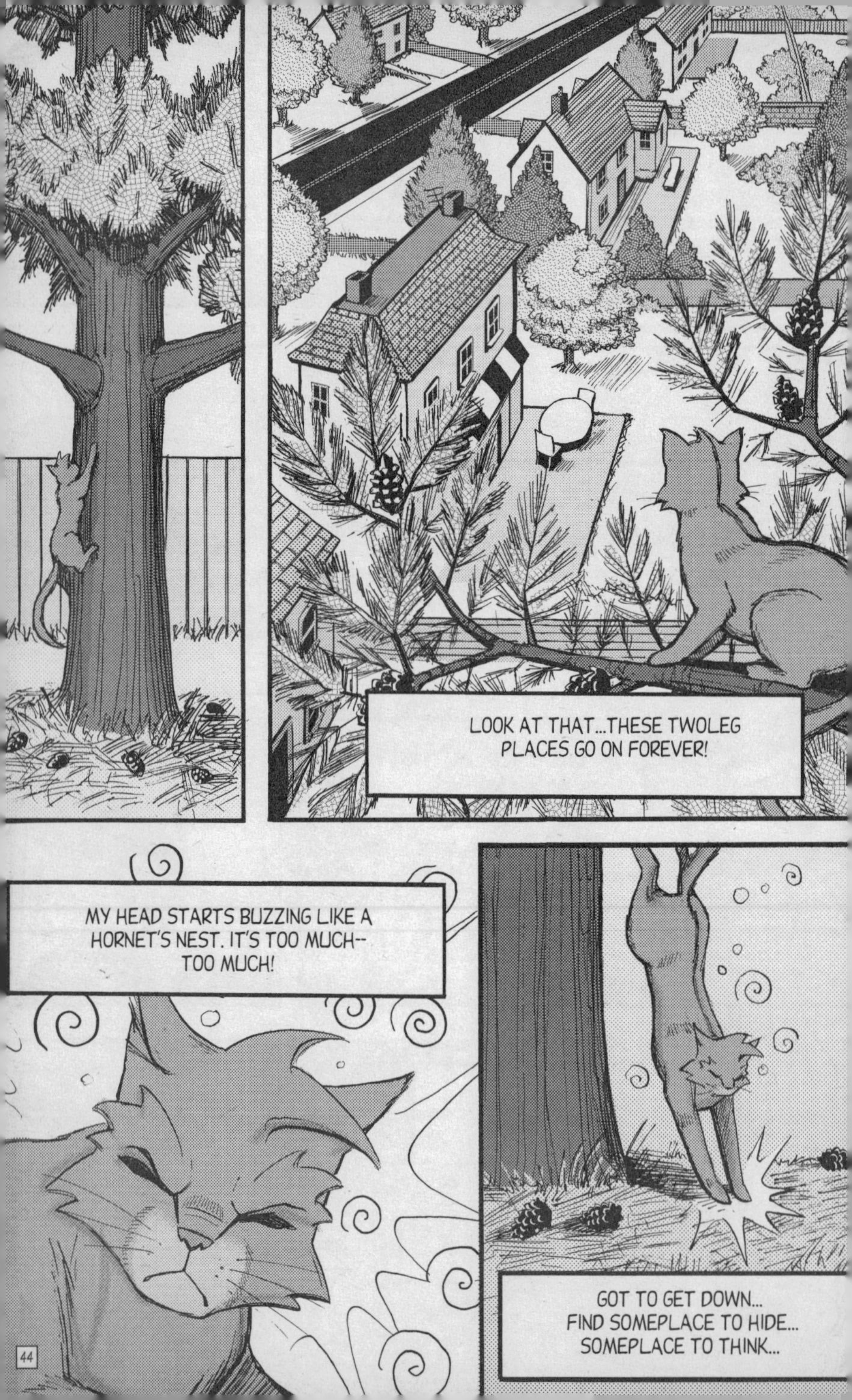
LOOK AT THAT...THESE TWOLEG PLACES GO ON FOREVER!
MY HEAD STARTS BUZZING LIKE A HORNET'S NEST. IT'S TOO MUCH--TOO MUCH!
GOT TO GET DOWN... FIND SOMEPLACE TO HIDE... SOMEPLACE TO THINK...

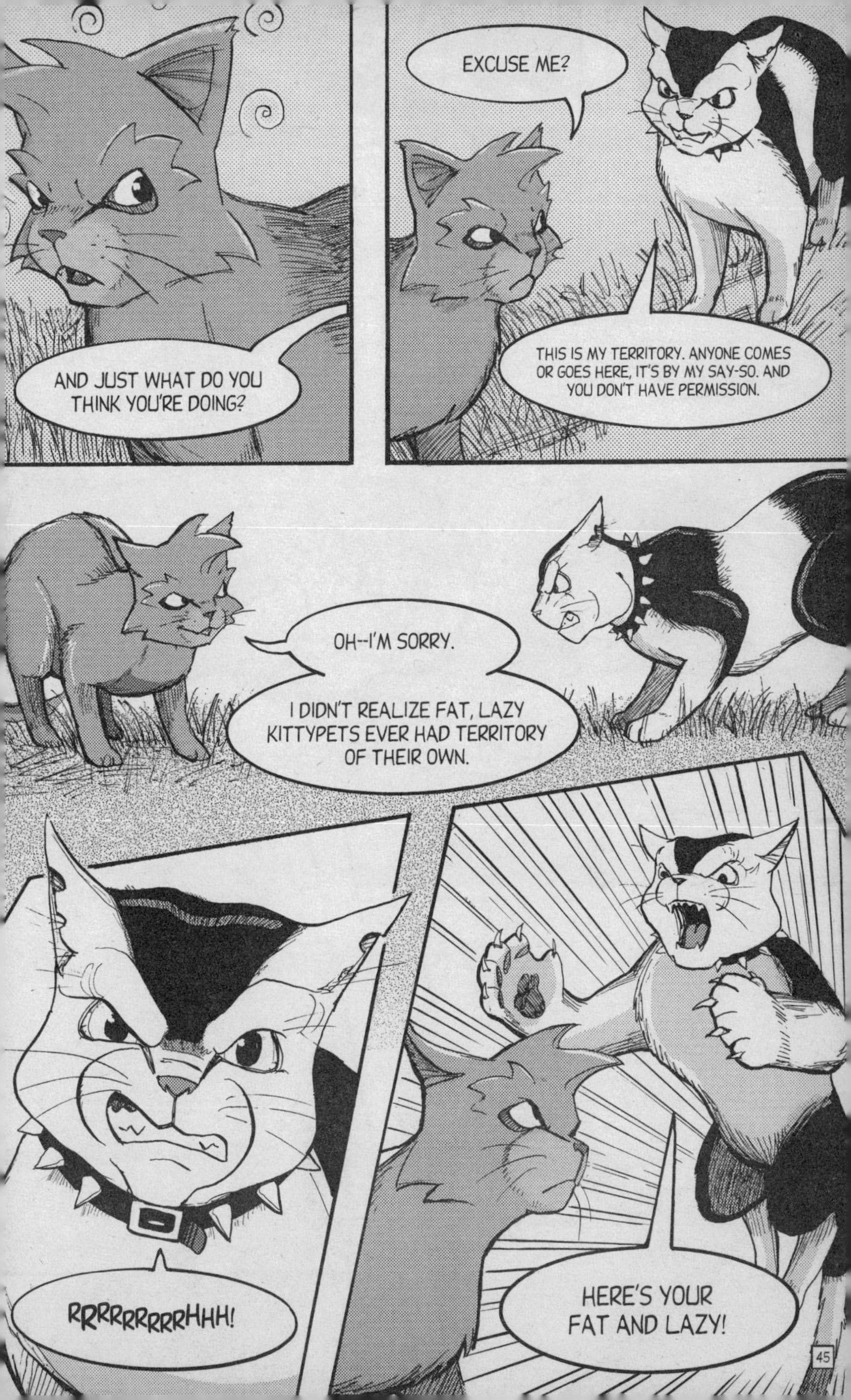
AND JUST WHAT DO YOU THINK YOU'RE DOING?
EXCUSE ME?
THIS IS MY TERRITORY. ANYONE COMES OR GOES HERE, IT'S BY MY SAY-SO. AND YOU DON'T HAVE PERMISSION.
OH--I'M SORRY.
I DIDN'T REALIZE FAT, LAZY KITTYPETS EVER HAD TERRITORY OF THEIR OWN.
RRRRRRRRRHHH!
HERE'S YOUR FAT AND LAZY!

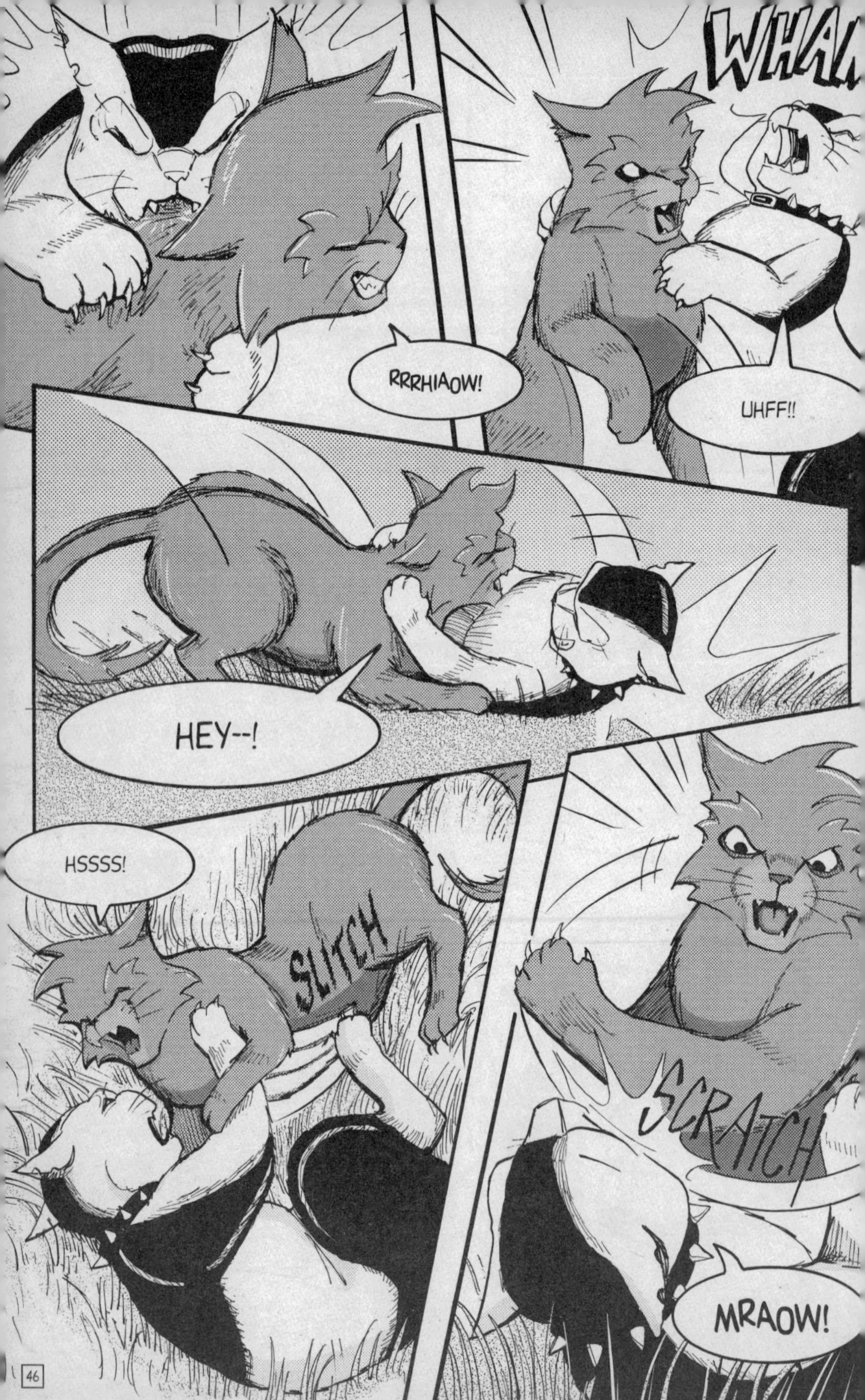
WHAM
RRRHIAOW!
UHFF!!
HEY--!
HSSSS!
SLITCH
SCRATCH
MRAOW!

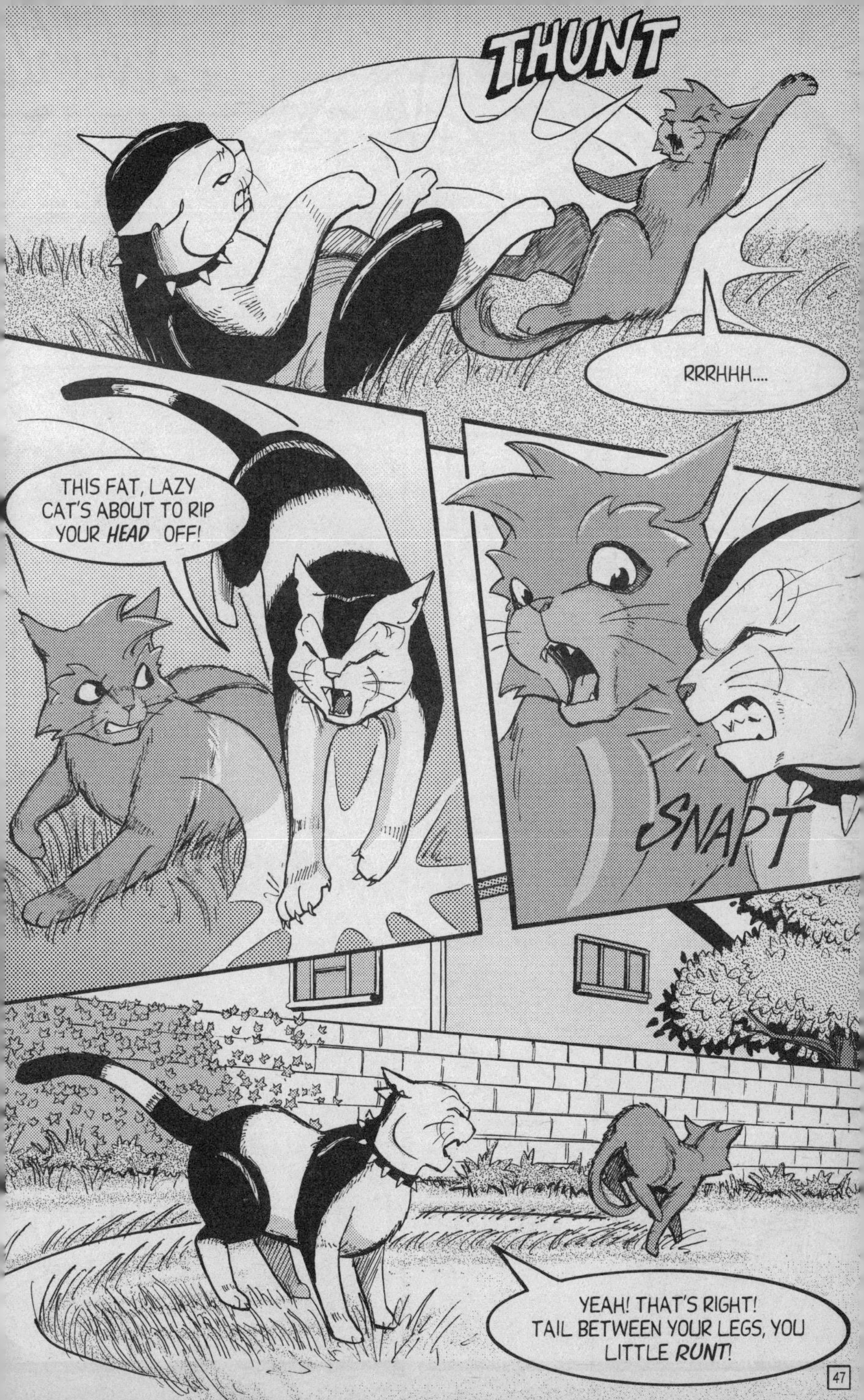
THUNT
RRRHHH....
THIS FAT, LAZY CAT'S ABOUT TO RIP YOUR HEAD OFF!
SNAPT
YEAH! THAT'S RIGHT! TAIL BETWEEN YOUR LEGS, YOU LITTLE RUNT!

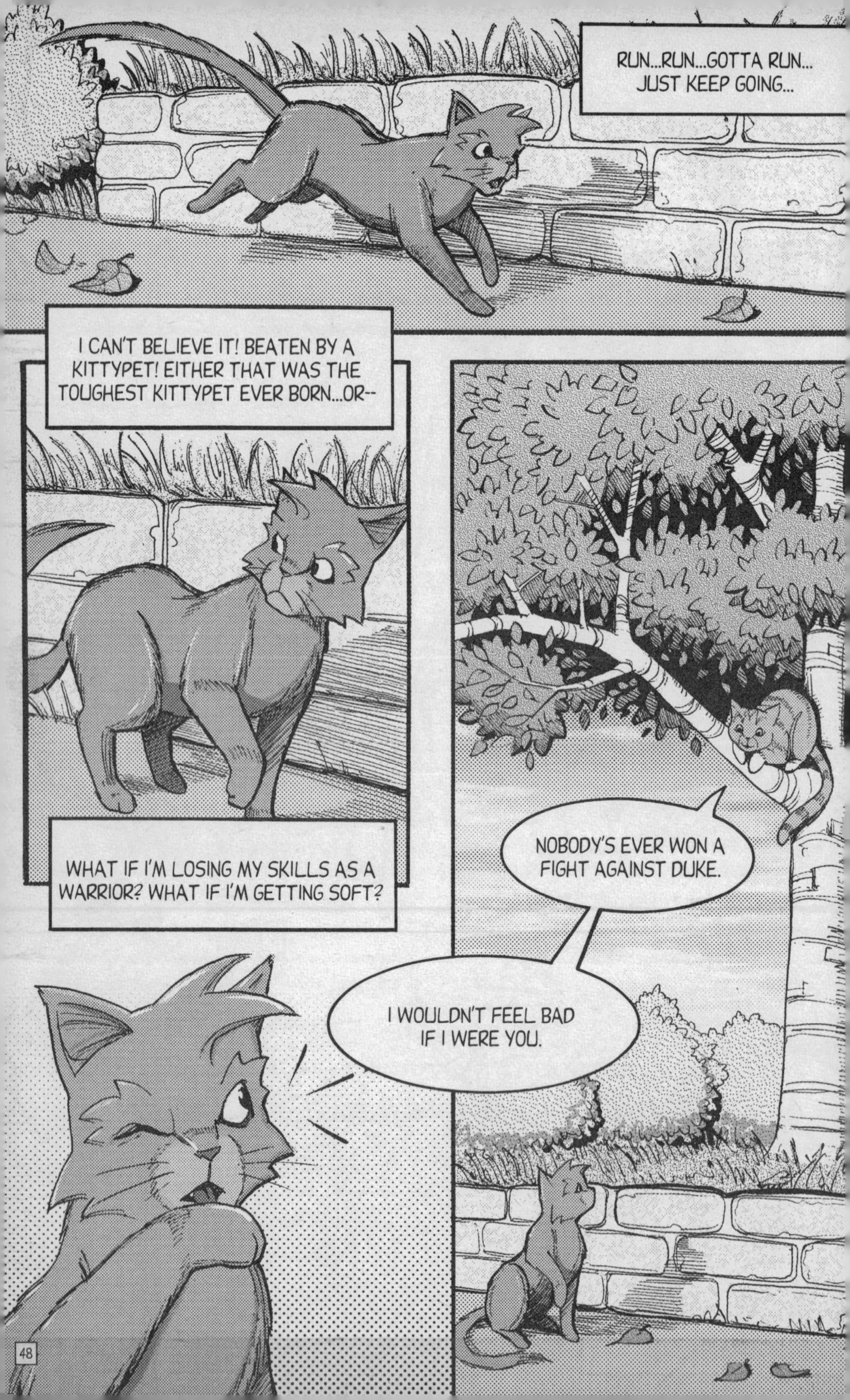
RUN...RUN...GOTTA RUN... JUST KEEP GOING...
I CAN'T BELIEVE IT! BEATEN BY A KITTYPET! EITHER THAT WAS THE TOUGHEST KITTYPET EVER BORN...OR--
WHAT IF I'M LOSING MY SKILLS AS A WARRIOR? WHAT IF I'M GETTING SOFT?
NOBODY'S EVER WON A FIGHT AGAINST DUKE.
I WOULDN'T FEEL BAD IF I WERE YOU.

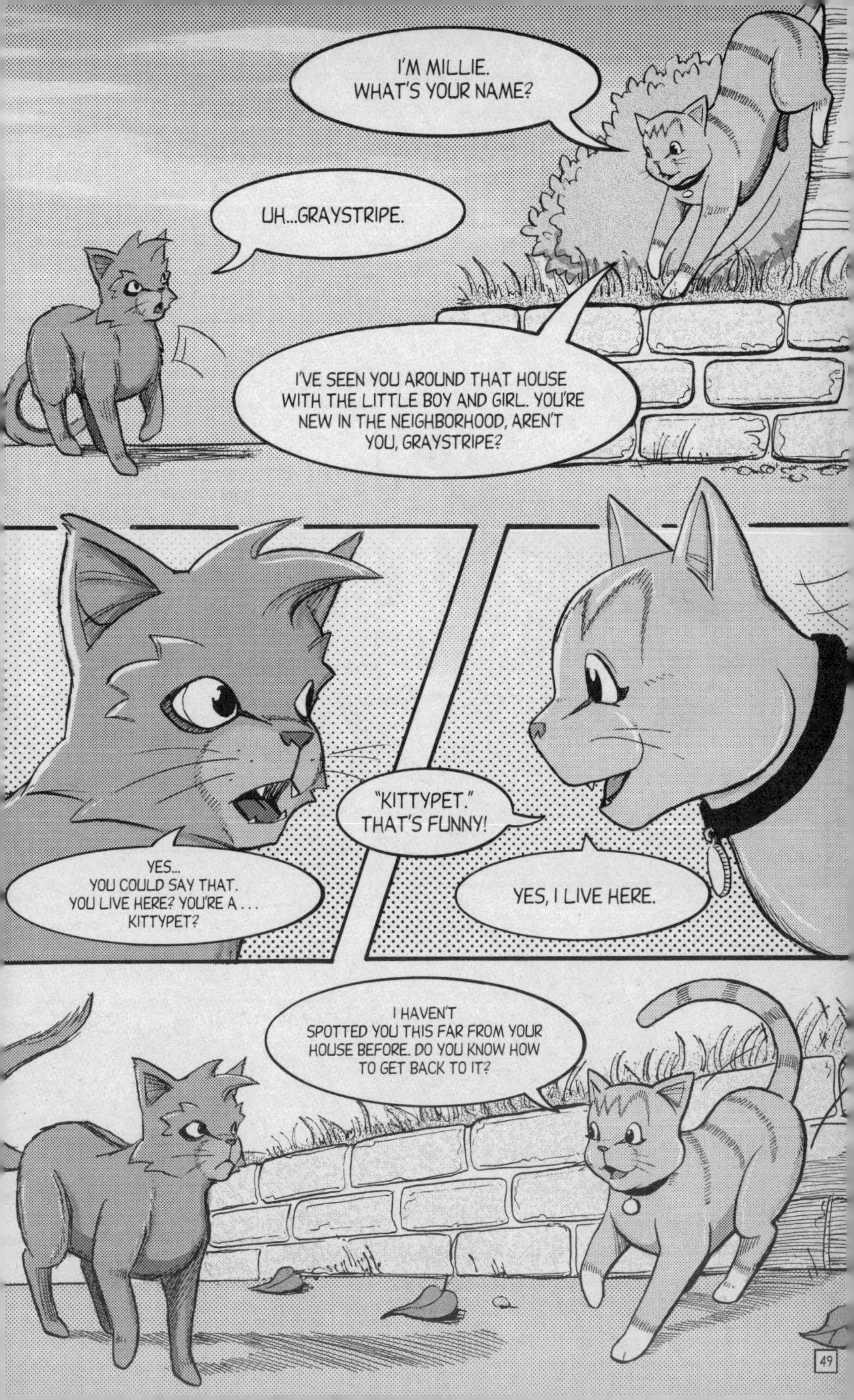
I'M MILLIE.
WHAT'S YOUR NAME?
UH...GRAYSTRIPE.
I'VE SEEN YOU AROUND THAT HOUSE WITH THE LITTLE BOY AND GIRL. YOU'RE NEW IN THE NEIGHBORHOOD, AREN'T YOU, GRAYSTRIPE?
YES... YOU COULD SAY THAT. YOU LIVE HERE? YOU'RE A . . . KITTYPET?
YES, I LIVE HERE.
"KITTYPET." THAT'S FUNNY!
I HAVEN'T SPOTTED YOU THIS FAR FROM YOUR HOUSE BEFORE. DO YOU KNOW HOW TO GET BACK TO IT?

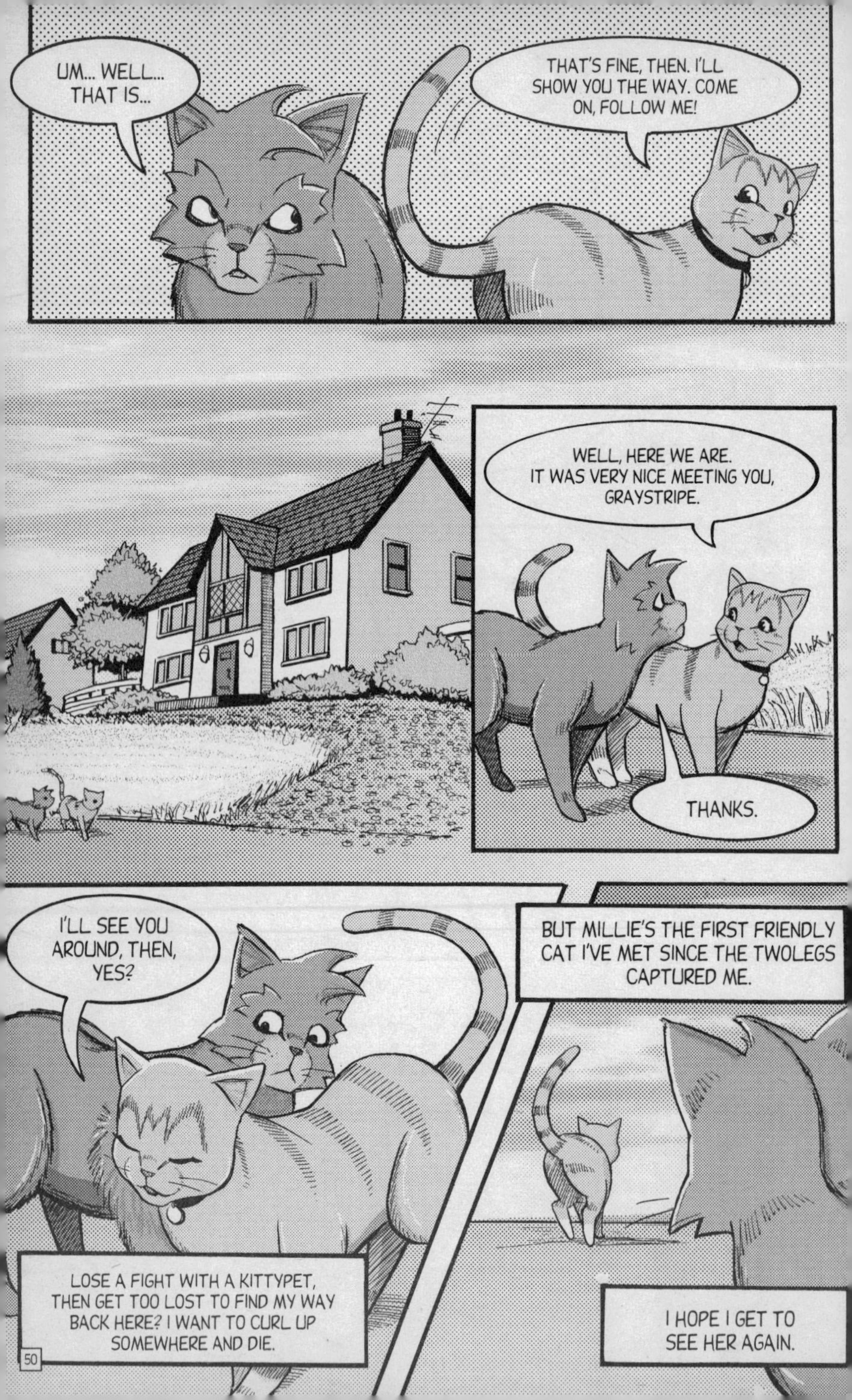
UM... WELL... THAT IS...
THAT'S FINE, THEN. I'LL SHOW YOU THE WAY. COME ON, FOLLOW ME!
WELL, HERE WE ARE. IT WAS VERY NICE MEETING YOU, GRAYSTRIPE.
THANKS.
I'LL SEE YOU AROUND, THEN, YES?
LOSE A FIGHT WITH A KITTYPET, THEN GET TOO LOST TO FIND MY WAY BACK HERE? I WANT TO CURL UP SOMEWHERE AND DIE.
BUT MILLIE'S THE FIRST FRIENDLY CAT I'VE MET SINCE THE TWOLEGS CAPTURED ME.
I HOPE I GET TO SEE HER AGAIN.

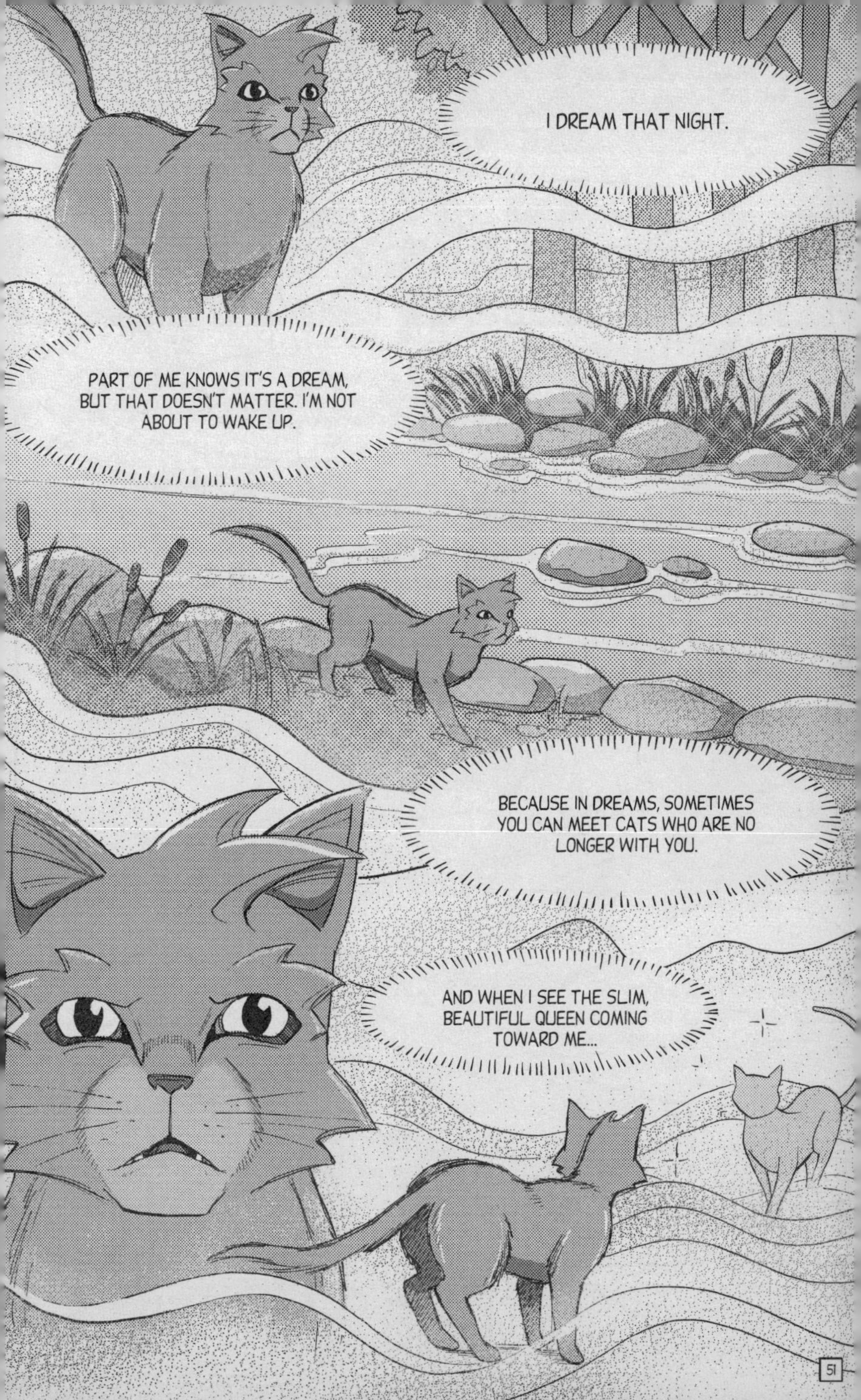
I DREAM THAT NIGHT.
PART OF ME KNOWS IT'S A DREAM, BUT THAT DOESN'T MATTER. I'M NOT ABOUT TO WAKE UP.
BECAUSE IN DREAMS, SOMETIMES YOU CAN MEET CATS WHO ARE NO LONGER WITH YOU.
AND WHEN I SEE THE SLIM, BEAUTIFUL QUEEN COMING TOWARD ME...

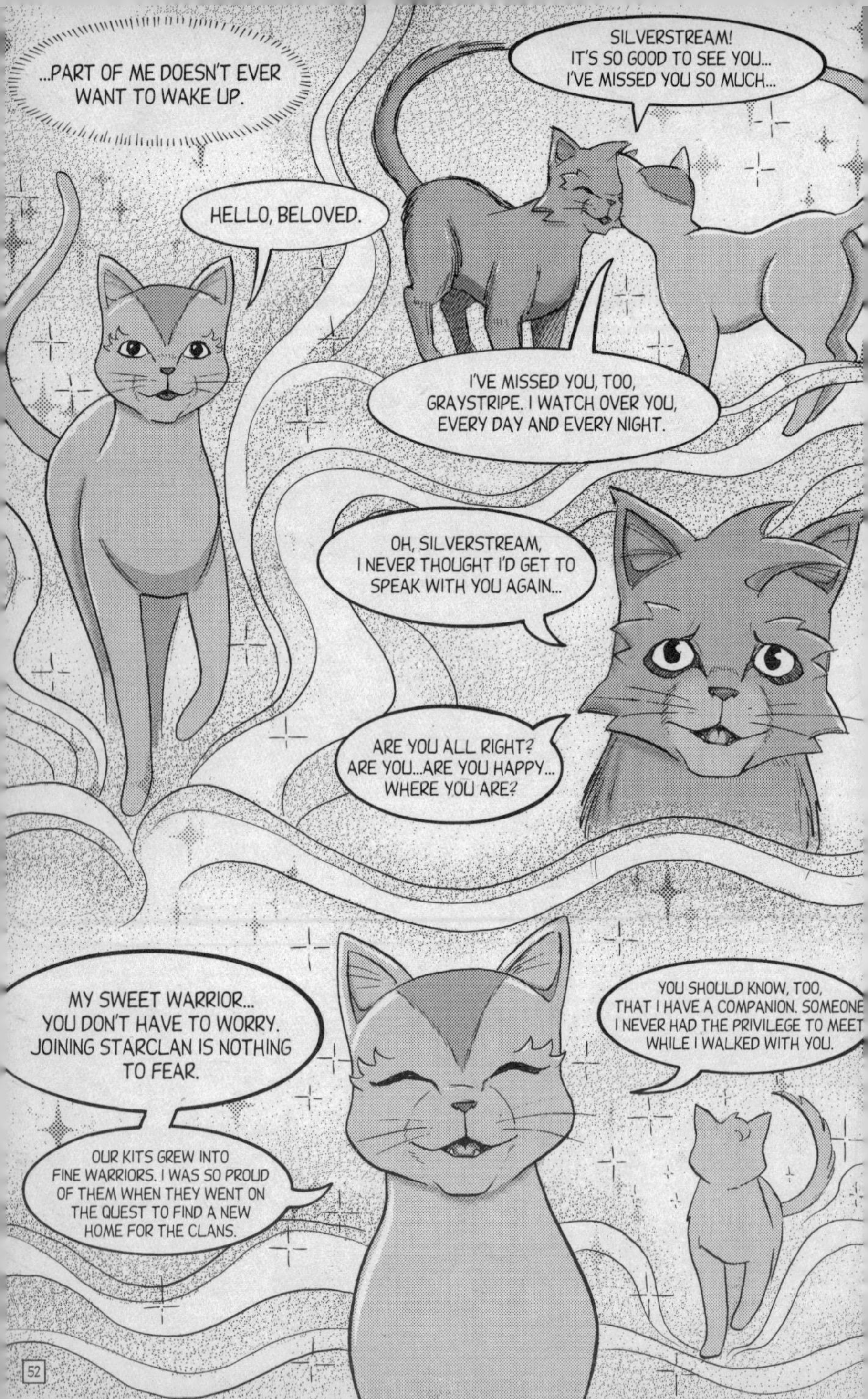
...PART OF ME DOESN'T EVER WANT TO WAKE UP.
SILVERSTREAM! IT'S SO GOOD TO SEE YOU... I'VE MISSED YOU SO MUCH...
HELLO, BELOVED.
I'VE MISSED YOU, TOO, GRAYSTRIPE. I WATCH OVER YOU, EVERY DAY AND EVERY NIGHT.
OH, SILVERSTREAM, I NEVER THOUGHT I'D GET TO SPEAK WITH YOU AGAIN...
ARE YOU ALL RIGHT? ARE YOU...ARE YOU HAPPY... WHERE YOU ARE?
MY SWEET WARRIOR... YOU DON'T HAVE TO WORRY. JOINING STARCLAN IS NOTHING TO FEAR.
OUR KITS GREW INTO FINE WARRIORS. I WAS SO PROUD OF THEM WHEN THEY WENT ON THE QUEST TO FIND A NEW HOME FOR THE CLANS.
YOU SHOULD KNOW, TOO, THAT I HAVE A COMPANION. SOMEONE I NEVER HAD THE PRIVILEGE TO MEET WHILE I WALKED WITH YOU.

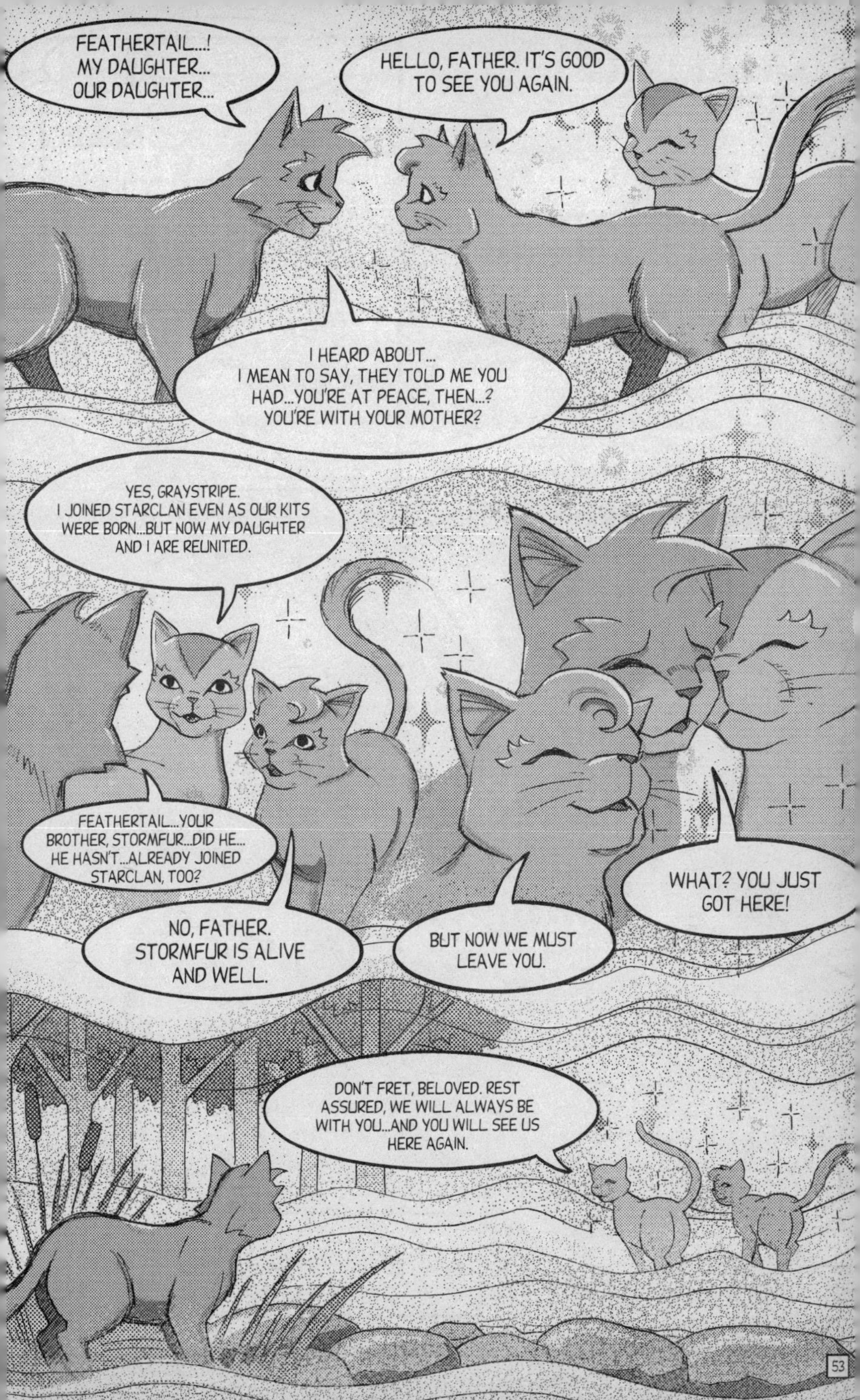
FEATHERTAIL...! MY DAUGHTER... OUR DAUGHTER...
HELLO, FATHER. IT'S GOOD TO SEE YOU AGAIN.
I HEARD ABOUT... I MEAN TO SAY, THEY TOLD ME YOU HAD...YOU'RE AT PEACE, THEN...? YOU'RE WITH YOUR MOTHER?
YES, GRAYSTRIPE. I JOINED STARCLAN EVEN AS OUR KITS WERE BORN...BUT NOW MY DAUGHTER AND I ARE REUNITED.
FEATHERTAIL...YOUR BROTHER, STORMFUR...DID HE... HE HASN'T...ALREADY JOINED STARCLAN, TOO?
NO, FATHER. STORMFUR IS ALIVE AND WELL.
BUT NOW WE MUST LEAVE YOU.
WHAT? YOU JUST GOT HERE!
DON'T FRET, BELOVED. REST ASSURED, WE WILL ALWAYS BE WITH YOU...AND YOU WILL SEE US HERE AGAIN.

CHAPTER 3

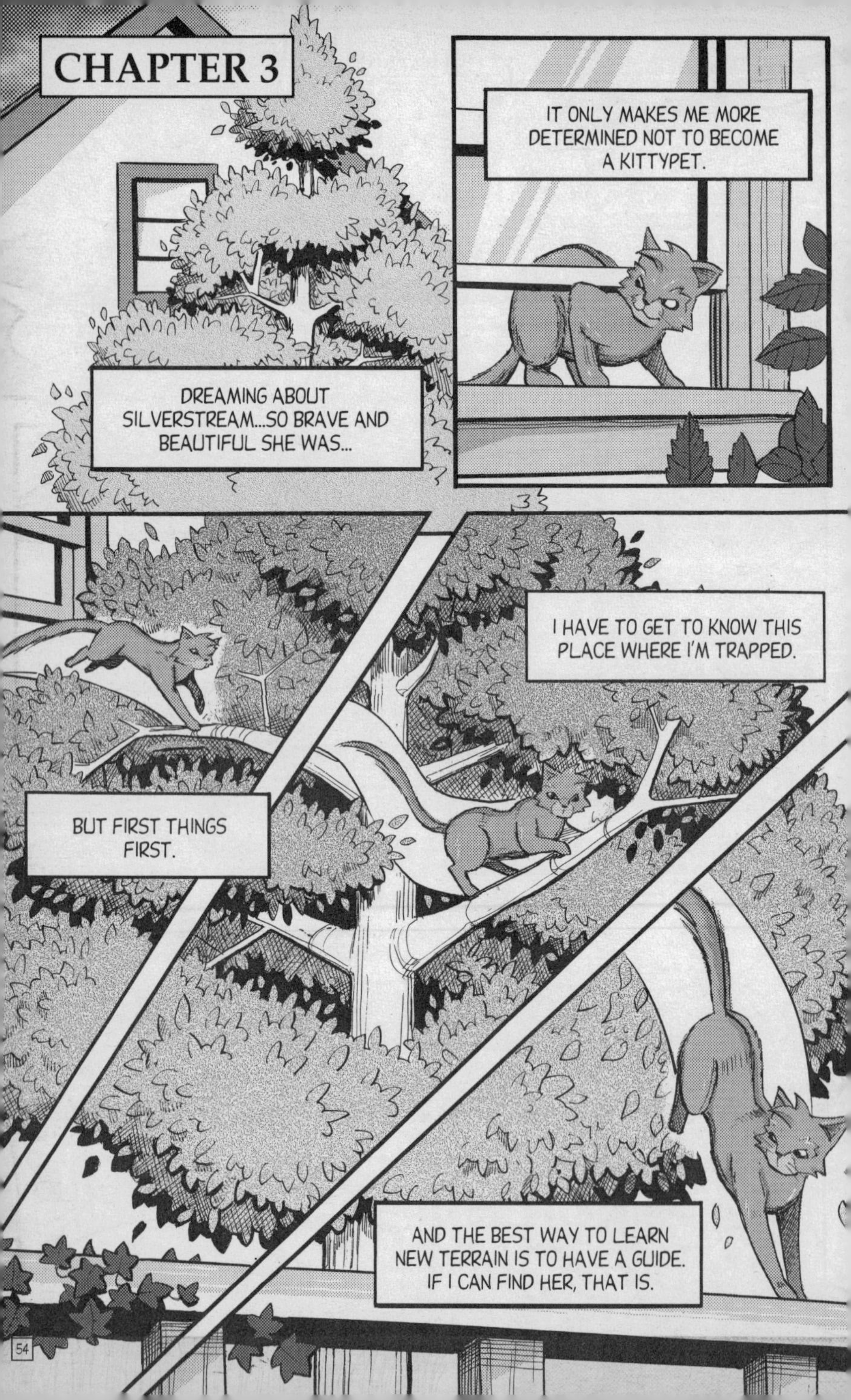
DREAMING ABOUT SILVERSTREAM...SO BRAVE AND BEAUTIFUL SHE WAS...
IT ONLY MAKES ME MORE DETERMINED NOT TO BECOME A KITTYPET.
I HAVE TO GET TO KNOW THIS PLACE WHERE I'M TRAPPED.
BUT FIRST THINGS FIRST.
AND THE BEST WAY TO LEARN NEW TERRAIN IS TO HAVE A GUIDE. IF I CAN FIND HER, THAT IS.

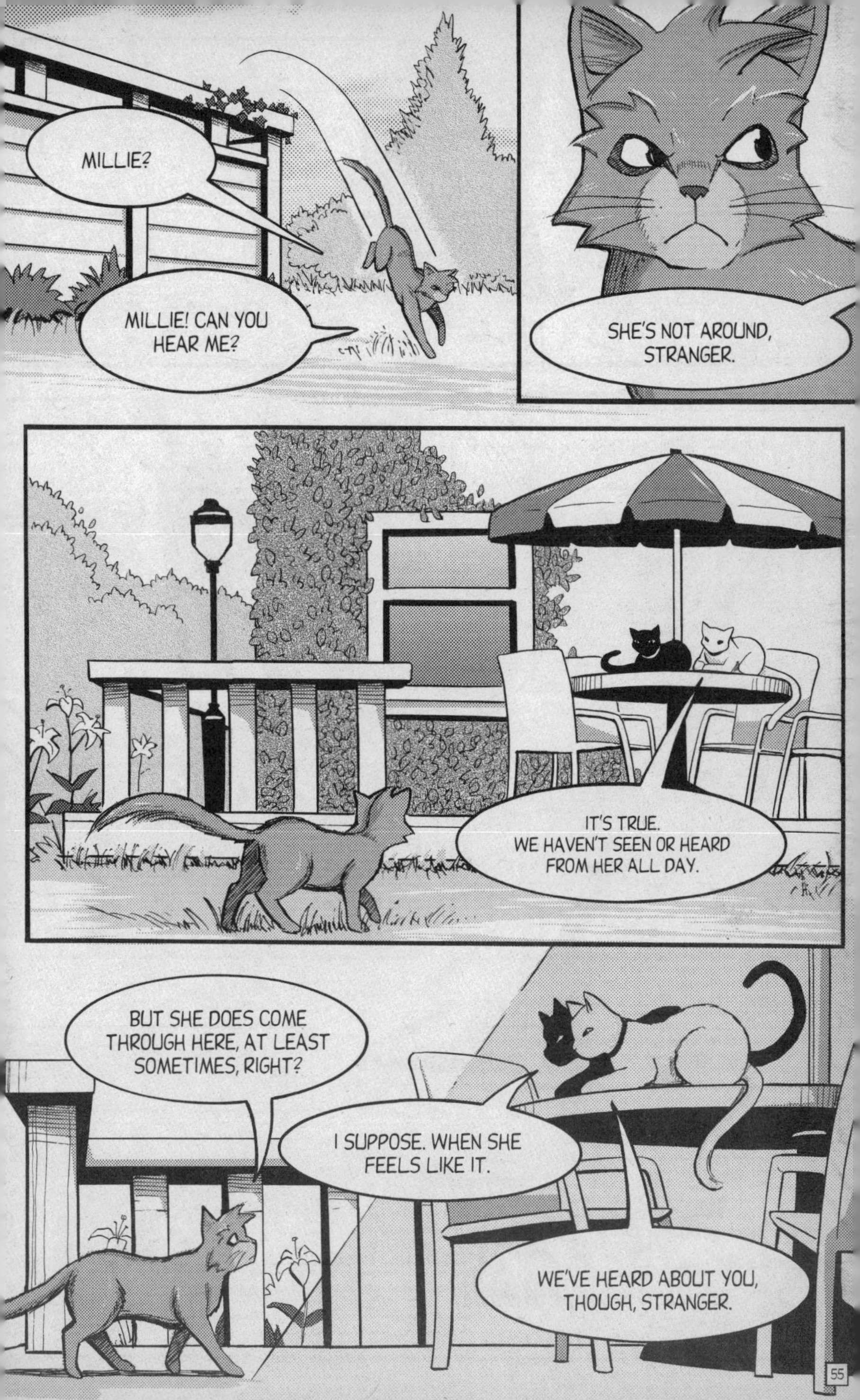
MILLIE?
MILLIE! CAN YOU HEAR ME?
SHE'S NOT AROUND, STRANGER.
IT'S TRUE. WE HAVEN'T SEEN OR HEARD FROM HER ALL DAY.
BUT SHE DOES COME THROUGH HERE, AT LEAST SOMETIMES, RIGHT?
I SUPPOSE. WHEN SHE FEELS LIKE IT.
WE'VE HEARD ABOUT YOU, THOUGH, STRANGER.

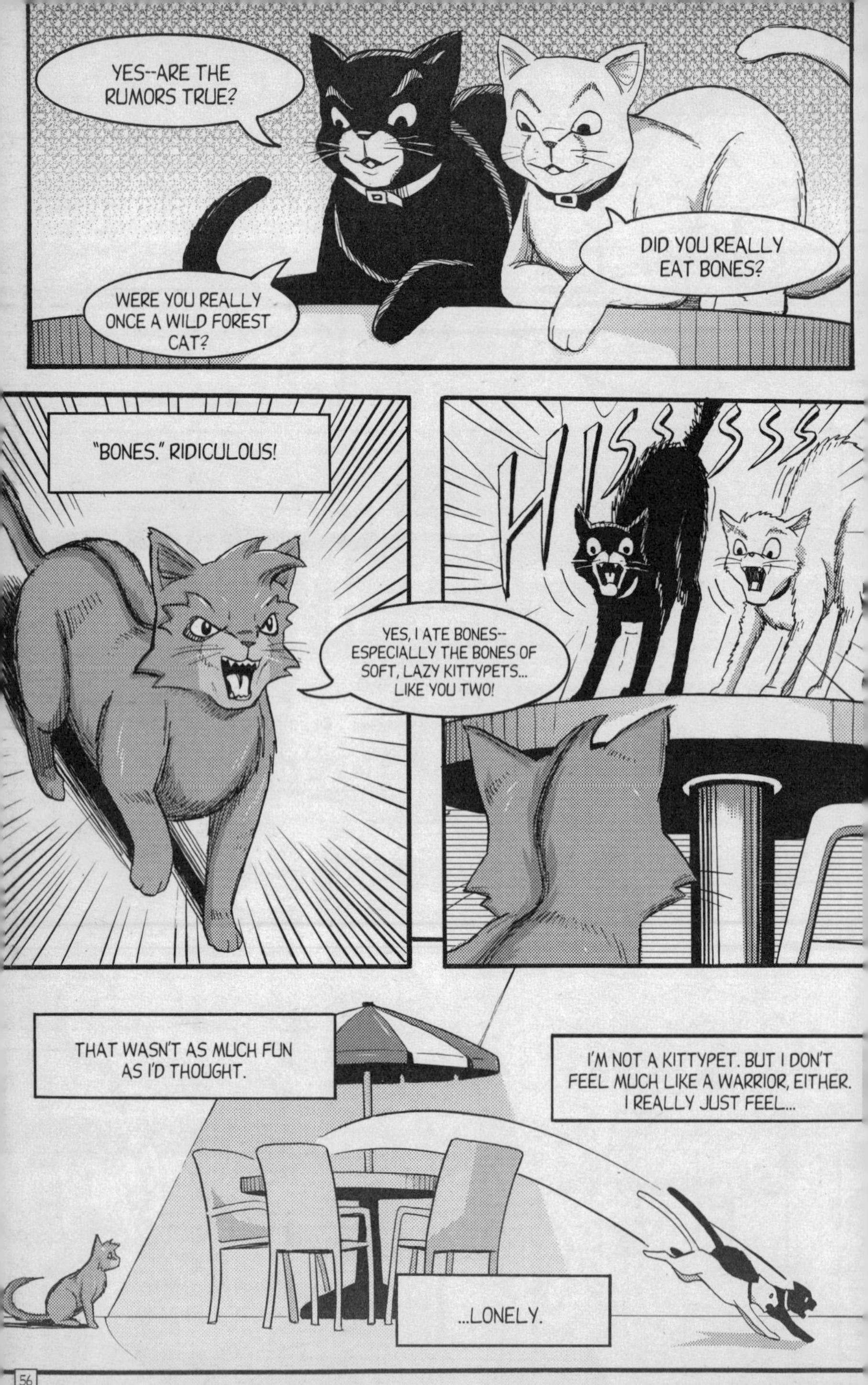
YES--ARE THE RUMORS TRUE?
WERE YOU REALLY ONCE A WILD FOREST CAT?
DID YOU REALLY EAT BONES?
"BONES." RIDICULOUS!
YES, I ATE BONES-- ESPECIALLY THE BONES OF SOFT, LAZY KITTYPETS... LIKE YOU TWO!
HISSSSS
THAT WASN'T AS MUCH FUN AS I'D THOUGHT.
I'M NOT A KITTYPET. BUT I DON'T FEEL MUCH LIKE A WARRIOR, EITHER. I REALLY JUST FEEL...
...LONELY.

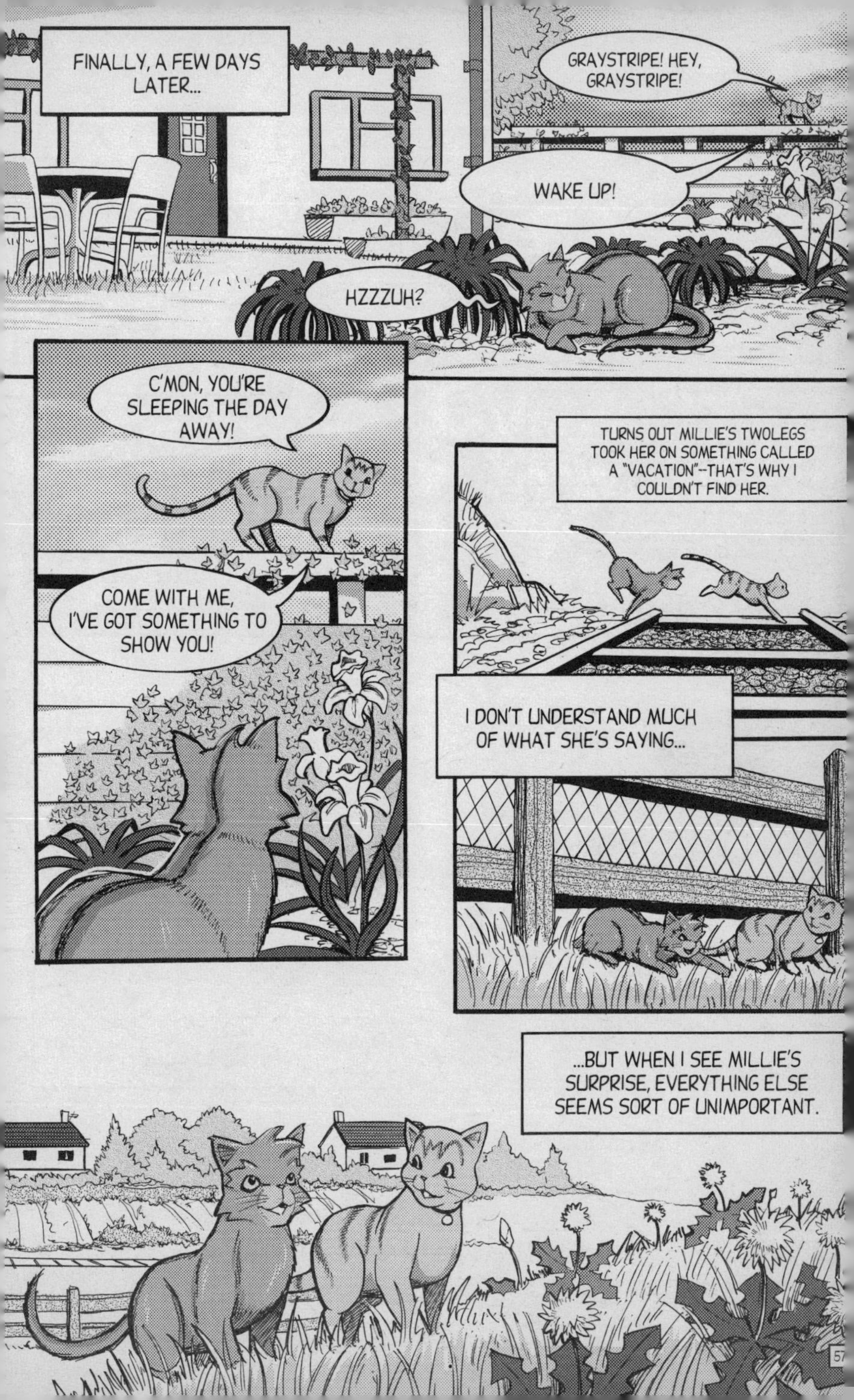
FINALLY, A FEW DAYS LATER...
GRAYSTRIPE! HEY, GRAYSTRIPE!
WAKE UP!
HZZZUH?
C'MON, YOU'RE SLEEPING THE DAY AWAY!
COME WITH ME, I'VE GOT SOMETHING TO SHOW YOU!
TURNS OUT MILLIE'S TWOLEGS TOOK HER ON SOMETHING CALLED A "VACATION"--THAT'S WHY I COULDN'T FIND HER.
I DON'T UNDERSTAND MUCH OF WHAT SHE'S SAYING...
...BUT WHEN I SEE MILLIE'S SURPRISE, EVERYTHING ELSE SEEMS SORT OF UNIMPORTANT.

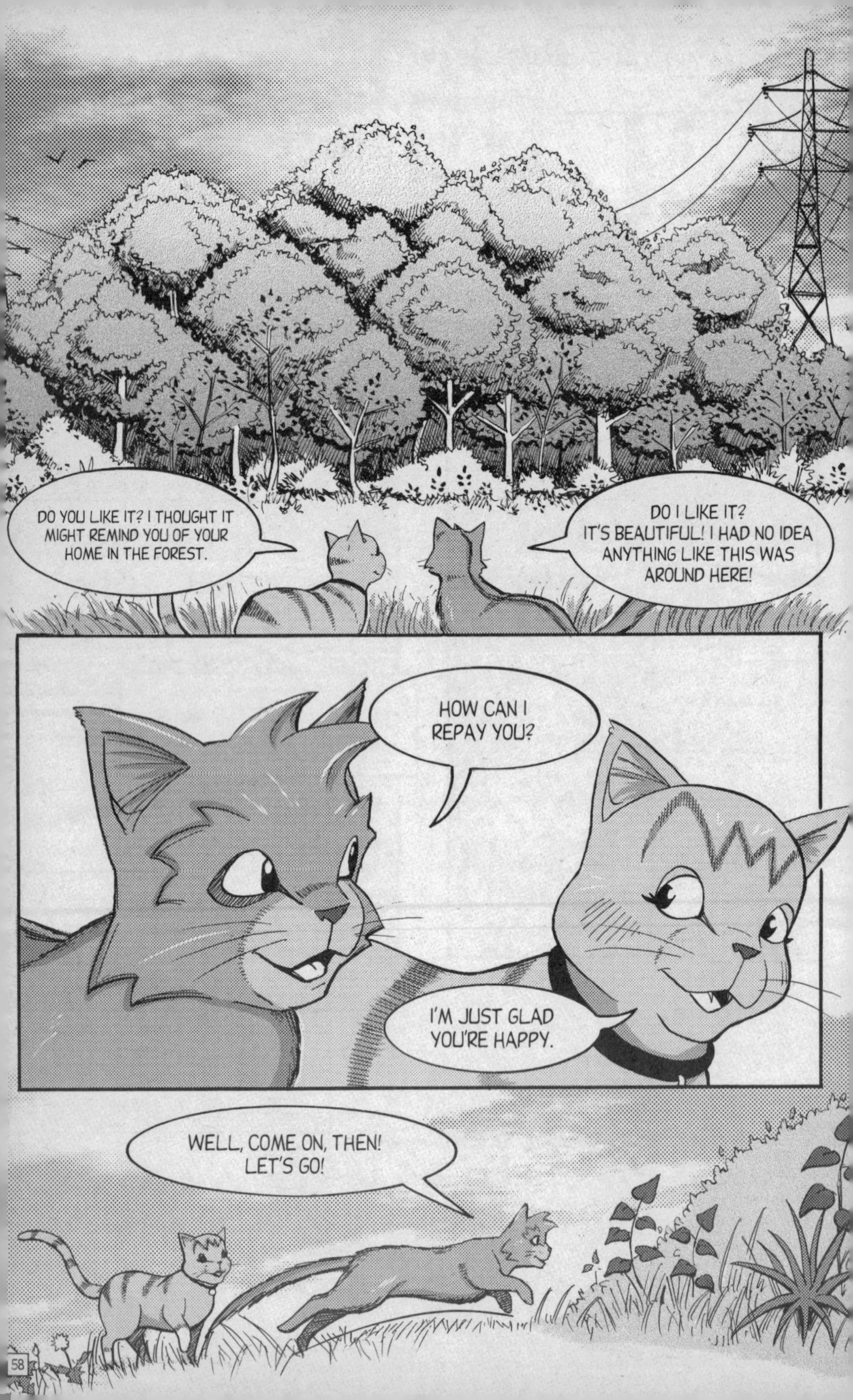
DO YOU LIKE IT? I THOUGHT IT MIGHT REMIND YOU OF YOUR HOME IN THE FOREST.
DO I LIKE IT? IT'S BEAUTIFUL! I HAD NO IDEA ANYTHING LIKE THIS WAS AROUND HERE!
HOW CAN I REPAY YOU?
I'M JUST GLAD YOU'RE HAPPY.
WELL, COME ON, THEN! LET'S GO!

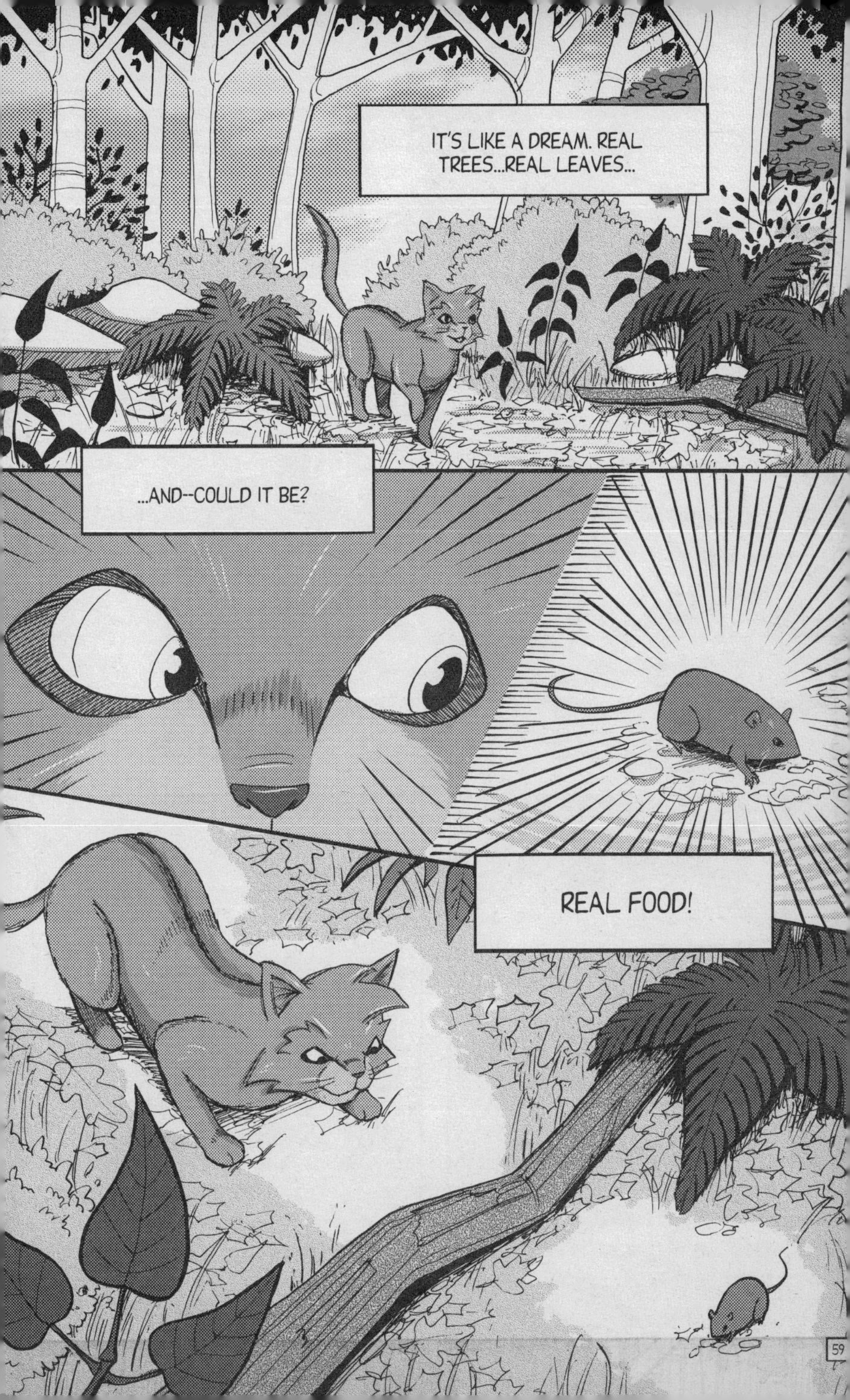
IT'S LIKE A DREAM. REAL TREES...REAL LEAVES...
...AND--COULD IT BE?
REAL FOOD!

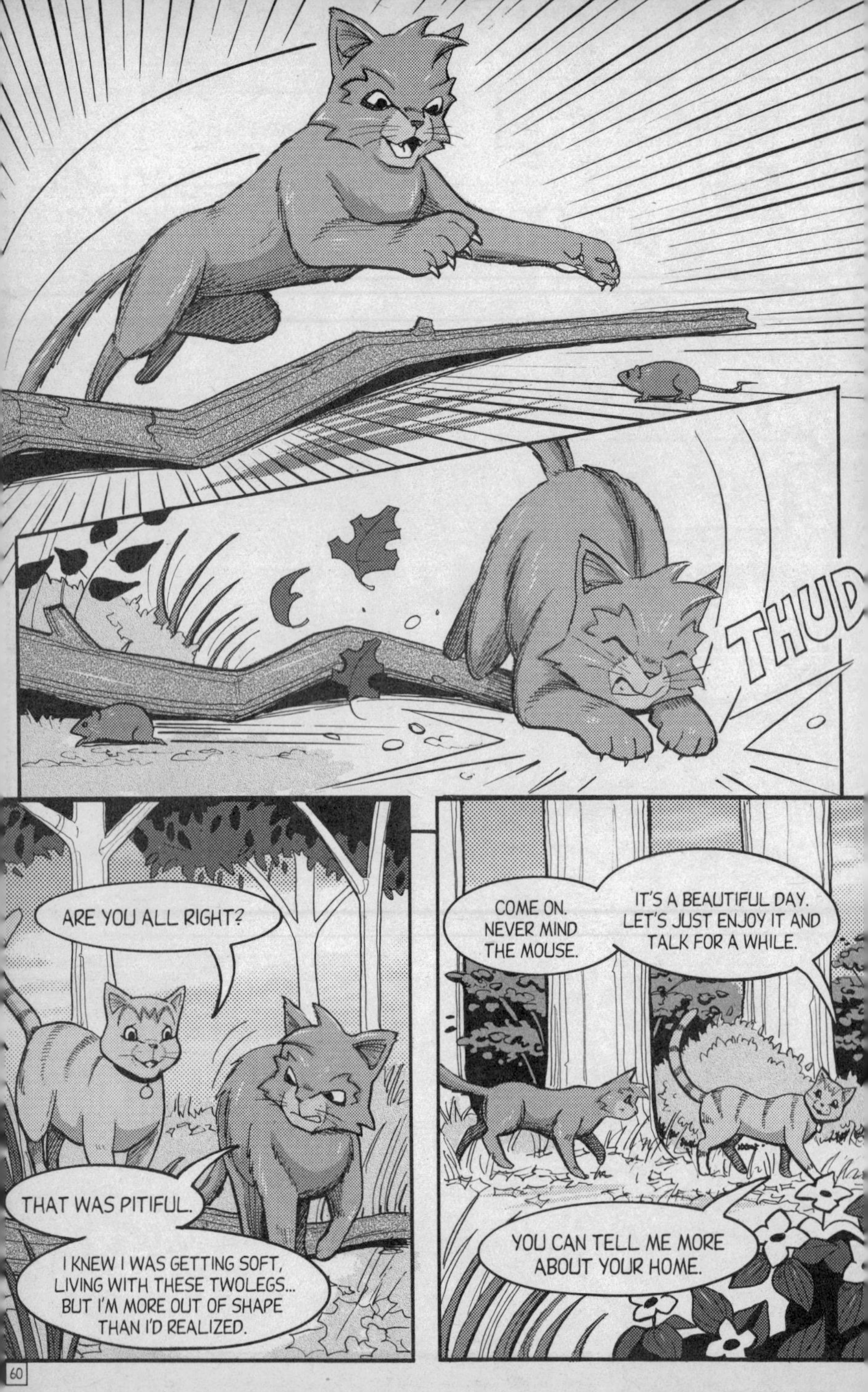
THUD
ARE YOU ALL RIGHT?
THAT WAS PITIFUL.
I KNEW I WAS GETTING SOFT, LIVING WITH THESE TWOLEGS... BUT I'M MORE OUT OF SHAPE THAN I'D REALIZED.
COME ON. NEVER MIND THE MOUSE.
IT'S A BEAUTIFUL DAY. LET'S JUST ENJOY IT AND TALK FOR A WHILE.
YOU CAN TELL ME MORE ABOUT YOUR HOME.

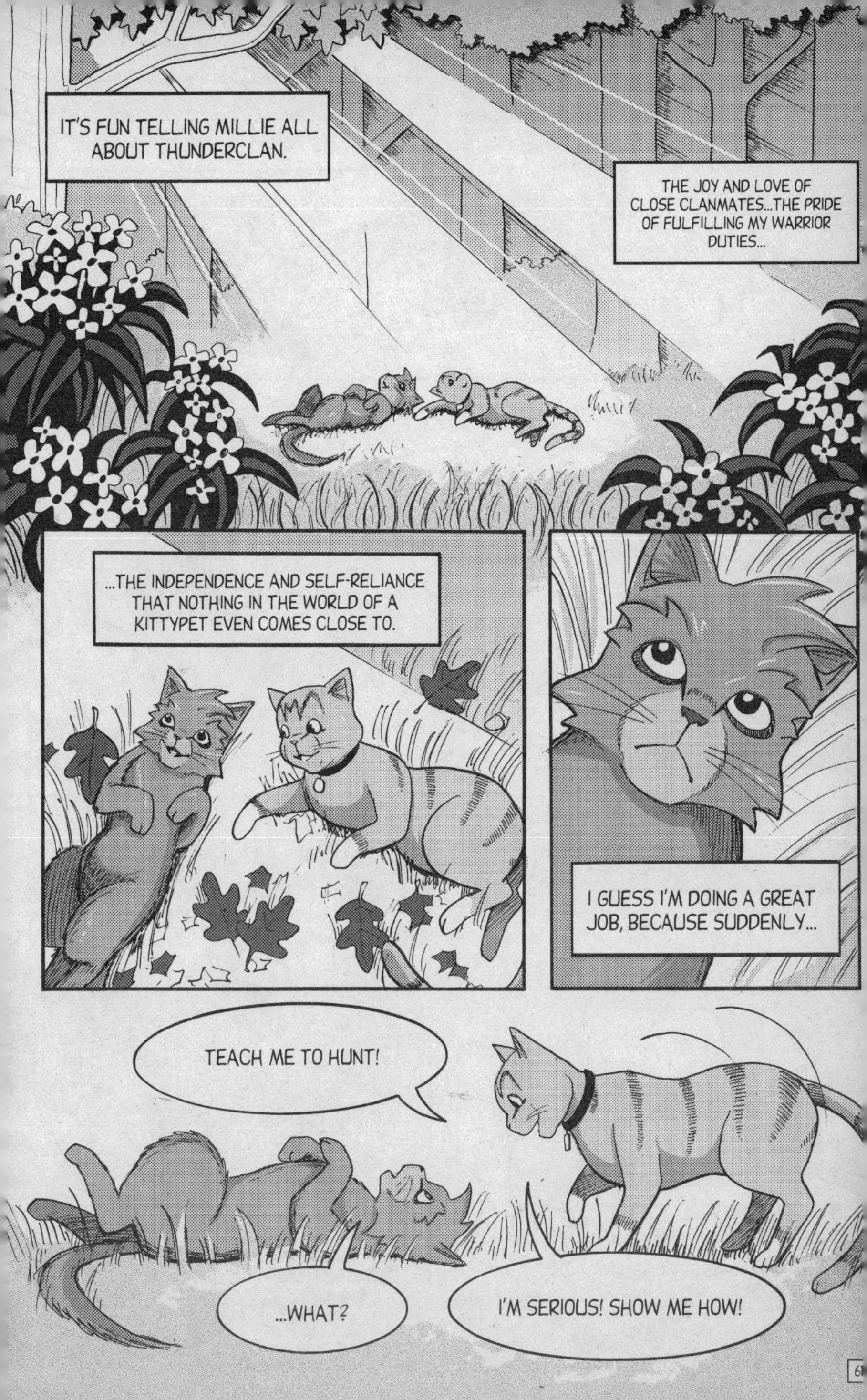

IT'S FUN TELLING MILLIE ALL ABOUT THUNDERCLAN.
THE JOY AND LOVE OF CLOSE CLANMATES...THE PRIDE OF FULFILLING MY WARRIOR DUTIES...
...THE INDEPENDENCE AND SELF-RELIANCE THAT NOTHING IN THE WORLD OF A KITTYPET EVEN COMES CLOSE TO.
I GUESS I'M DOING A GREAT JOB, BECAUSE SUDDENLY...
TEACH ME TO HUNT!
...WHAT?
I'M SERIOUS! SHOW ME HOW!

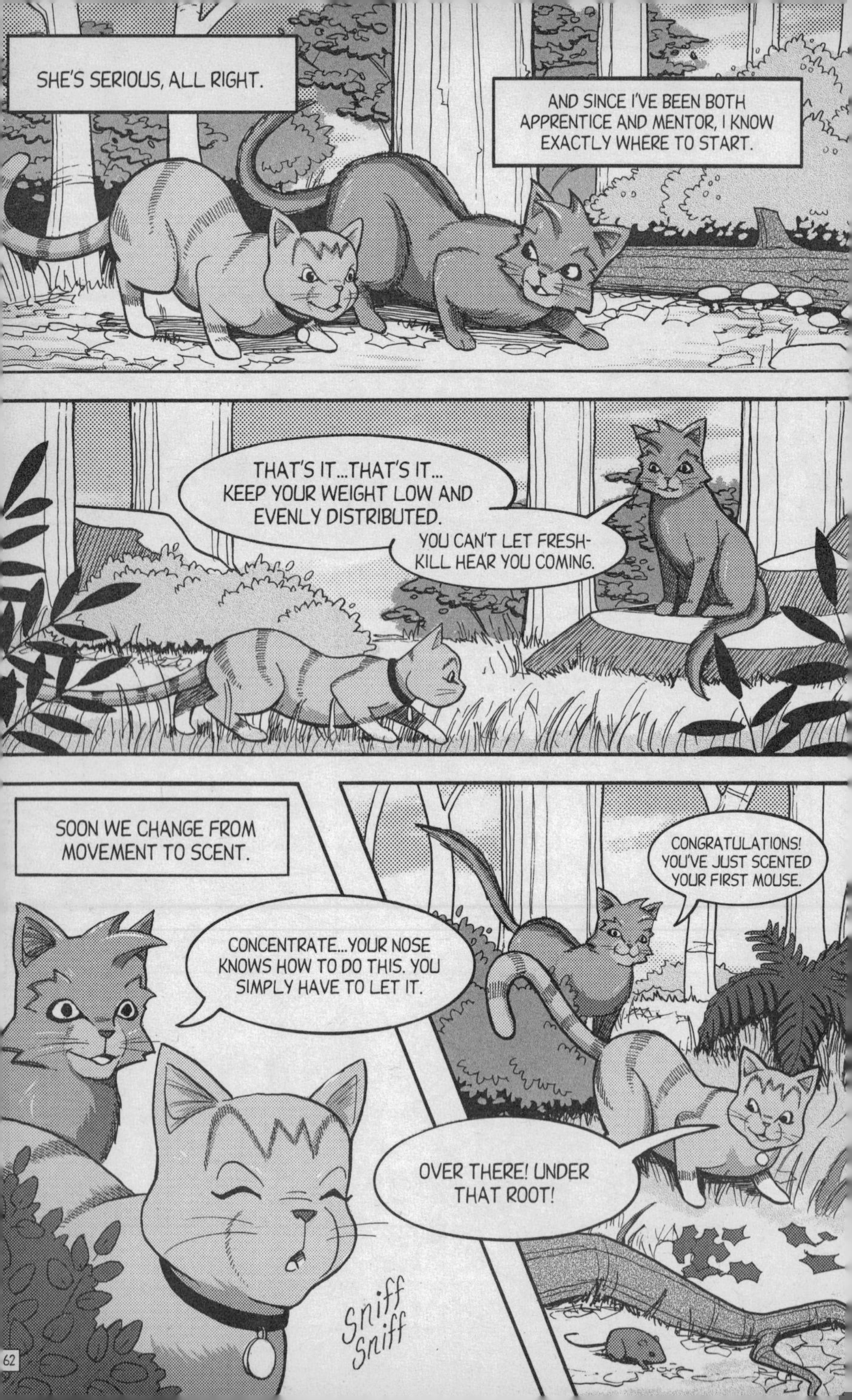

SHE'S SERIOUS, ALL RIGHT.
AND SINCE I'VE BEEN BOTH APPRENTICE AND MENTOR, I KNOW EXACTLY WHERE TO START.
THAT'S IT...THAT'S IT... KEEP YOUR WEIGHT LOW AND EVENLY DISTRIBUTED.
YOU CAN'T LET FRESH-KILL HEAR YOU COMING.
SOON WE CHANGE FROM MOVEMENT TO SCENT.
CONCENTRATE...YOUR NOSE KNOWS HOW TO DO THIS. YOU SIMPLY HAVE TO LET IT.
Sniff Sniff
OVER THERE! UNDER THAT ROOT!
CONGRATULATIONS! YOU'VE JUST SCENTED YOUR FIRST MOUSE.

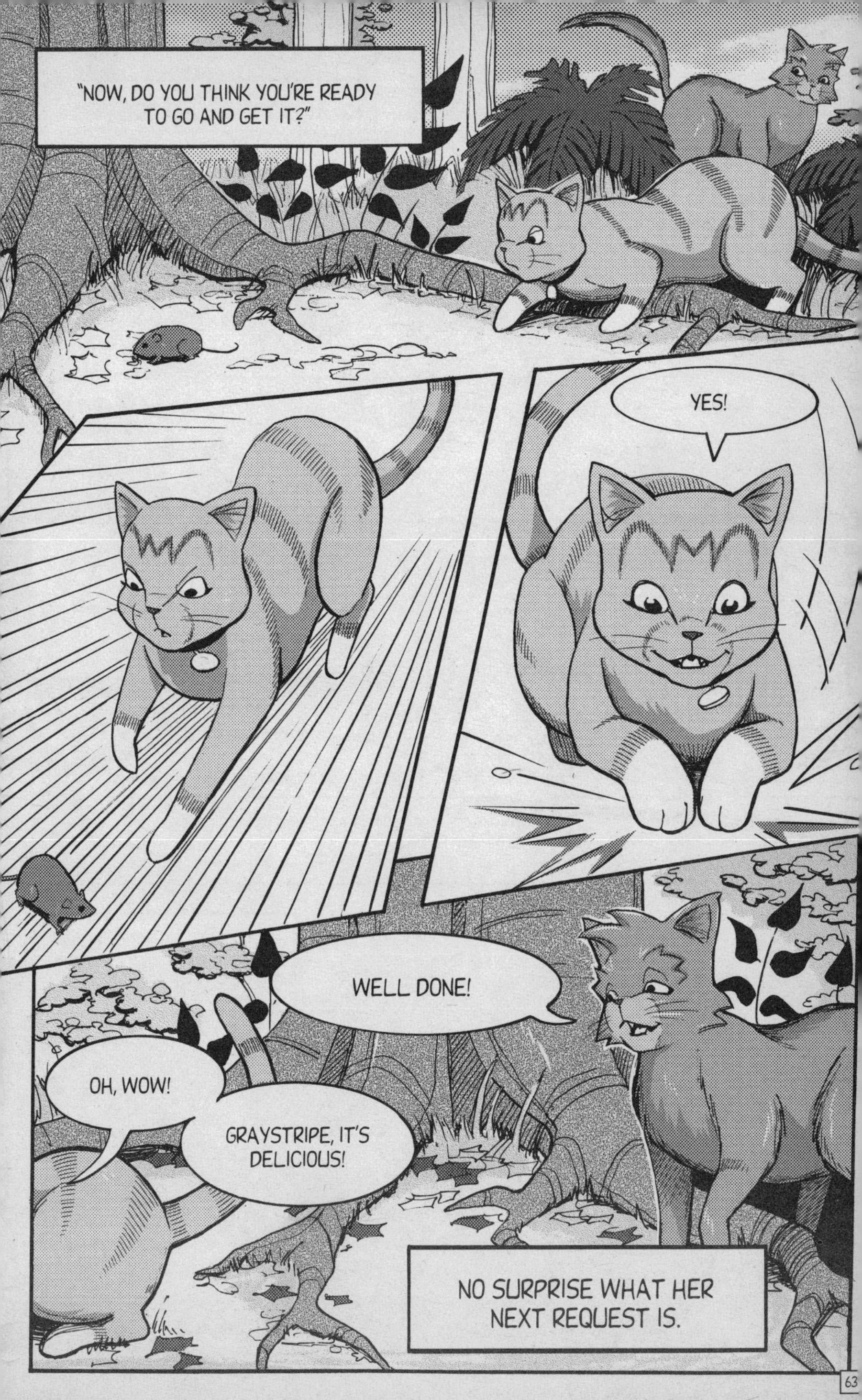
"NOW, DO YOU THINK YOU'RE READY TO GO AND GET IT?"
YES!
WELL DONE!
OH, WOW!
GRAYSTRIPE, IT'S DELICIOUS!
NO SURPRISE WHAT HER NEXT REQUEST IS.

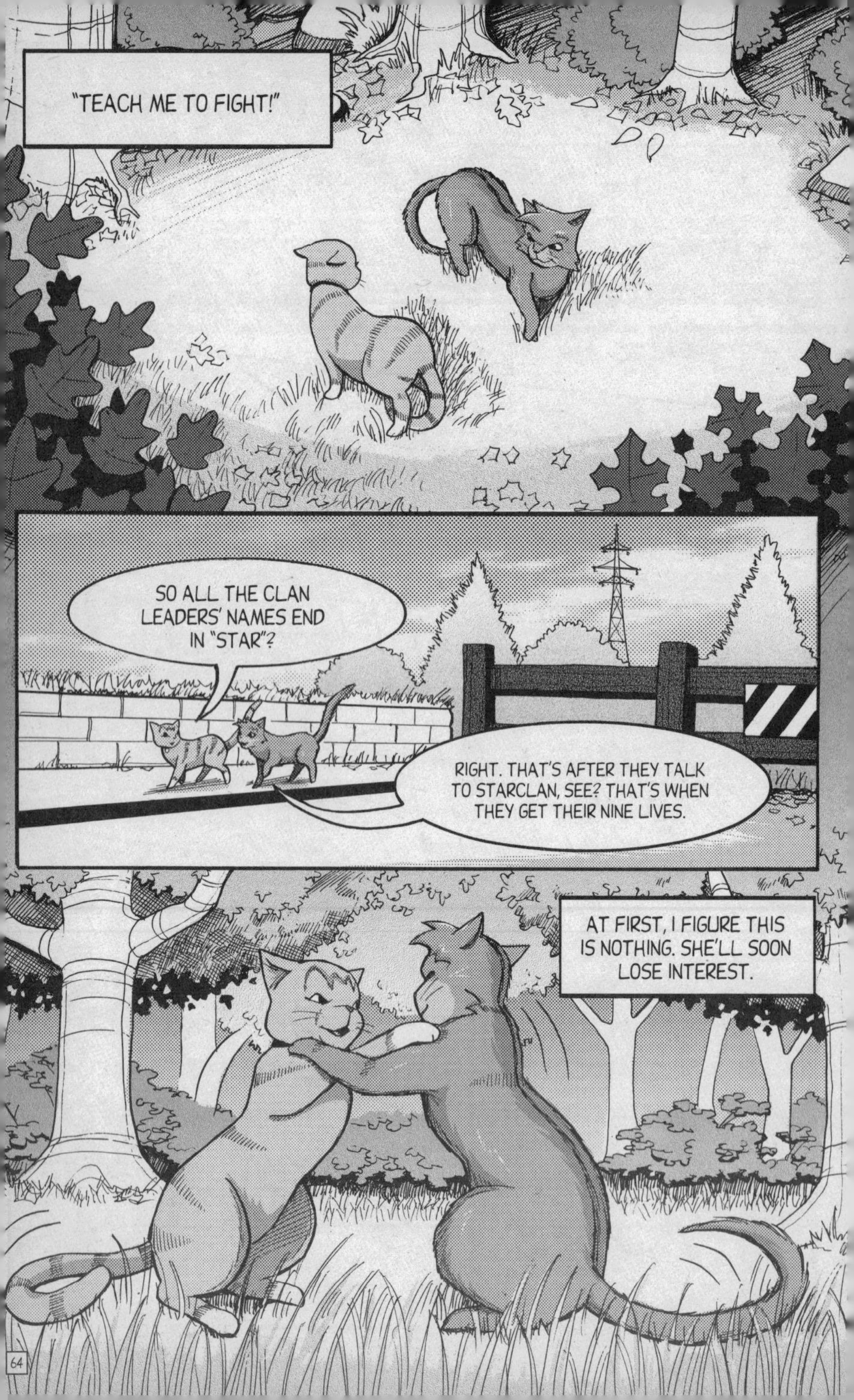
"TEACH ME TO FIGHT!"
SO ALL THE CLAN LEADERS' NAMES END IN "STAR"?
RIGHT. THAT'S AFTER THEY TALK TO STARCLAN, SEE? THAT'S WHEN THEY GET THEIR NINE LIVES.
AT FIRST, I FIGURE THIS IS NOTHING. SHE'LL SOON LOSE INTEREST.

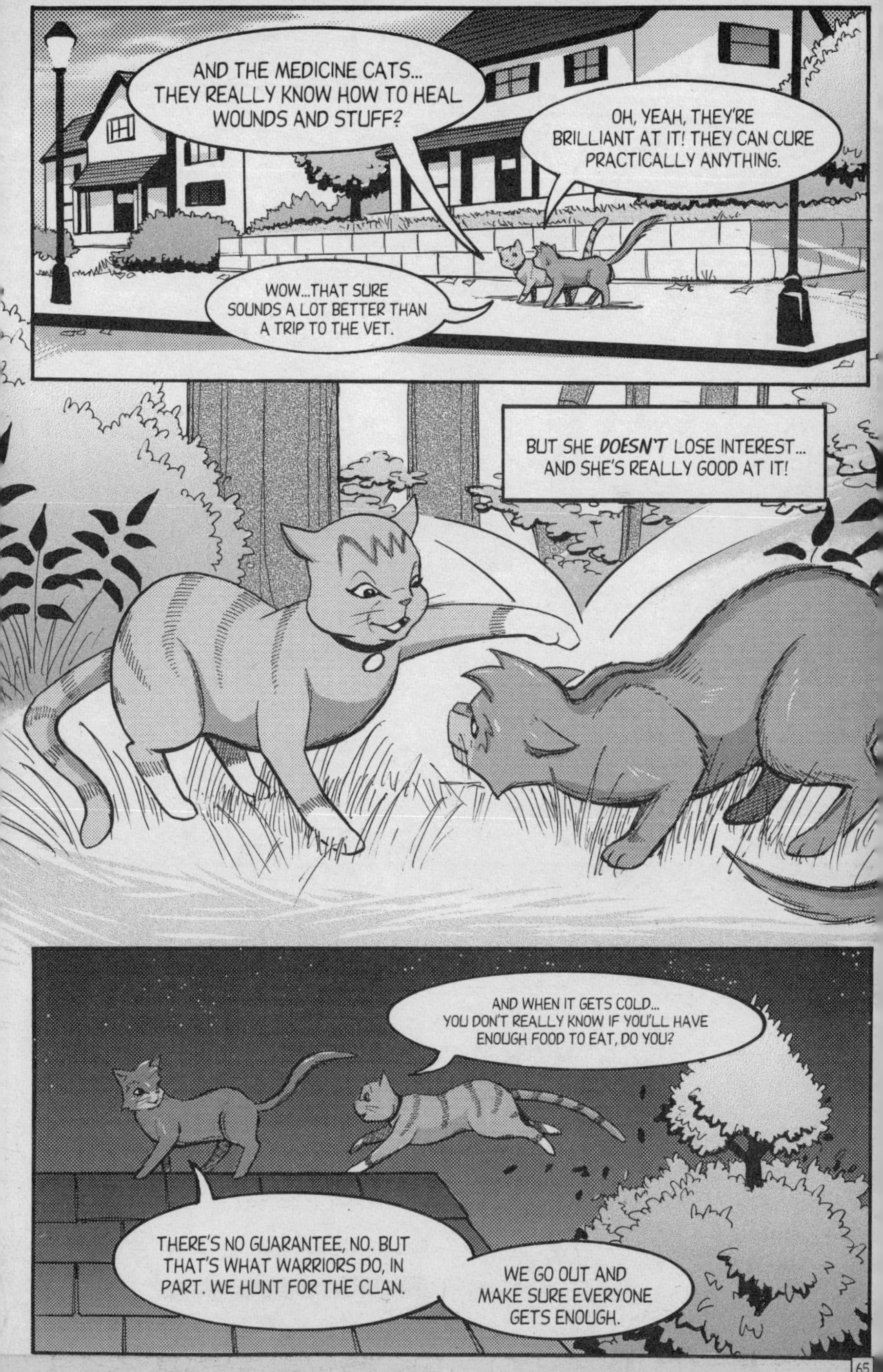
AND THE MEDICINE CATS... THEY REALLY KNOW HOW TO HEAL WOUNDS AND STUFF?
OH, YEAH, THEY'RE BRILLIANT AT IT! THEY CAN CURE PRACTICALLY ANYTHING.
WOW...THAT SURE SOUNDS A LOT BETTER THAN A TRIP TO THE VET.
BUT SHE *DOESN'T* LOSE INTEREST... AND SHE'S REALLY GOOD AT IT!
AND WHEN IT GETS COLD... YOU DON'T REALLY KNOW IF YOU'LL HAVE ENOUGH FOOD TO EAT, DO YOU?
THERE'S NO GUARANTEE, NO. BUT THAT'S WHAT WARRIORS DO, IN PART. WE HUNT FOR THE CLAN.
WE GO OUT AND MAKE SURE EVERYONE GETS ENOUGH.

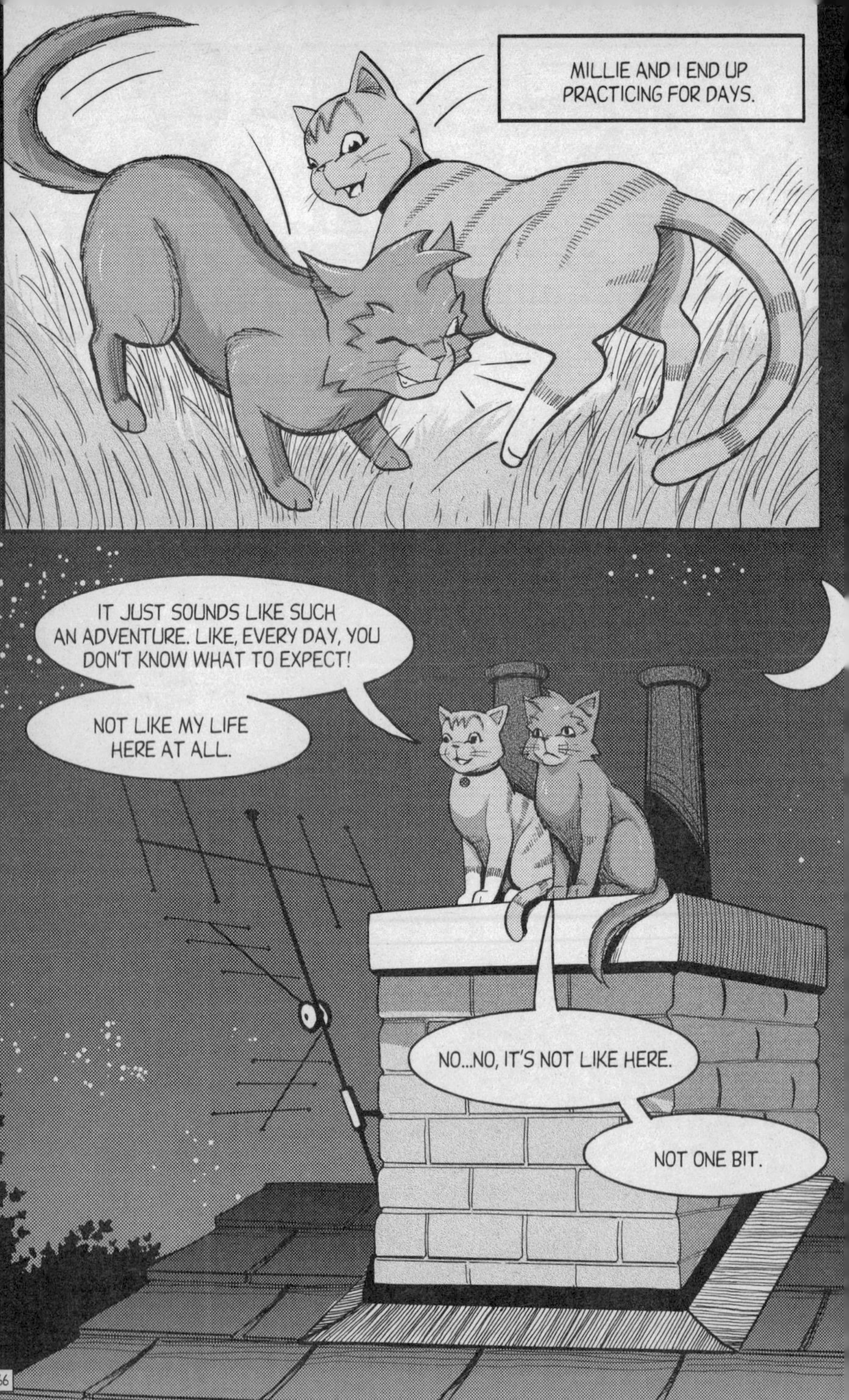

MILLIE AND I END UP PRACTICING FOR DAYS.
IT JUST SOUNDS LIKE SUCH AN ADVENTURE. LIKE, EVERY DAY, YOU DON'T KNOW WHAT TO EXPECT!
NOT LIKE MY LIFE HERE AT ALL.
NO...NO, IT'S NOT LIKE HERE.
NOT ONE BIT.

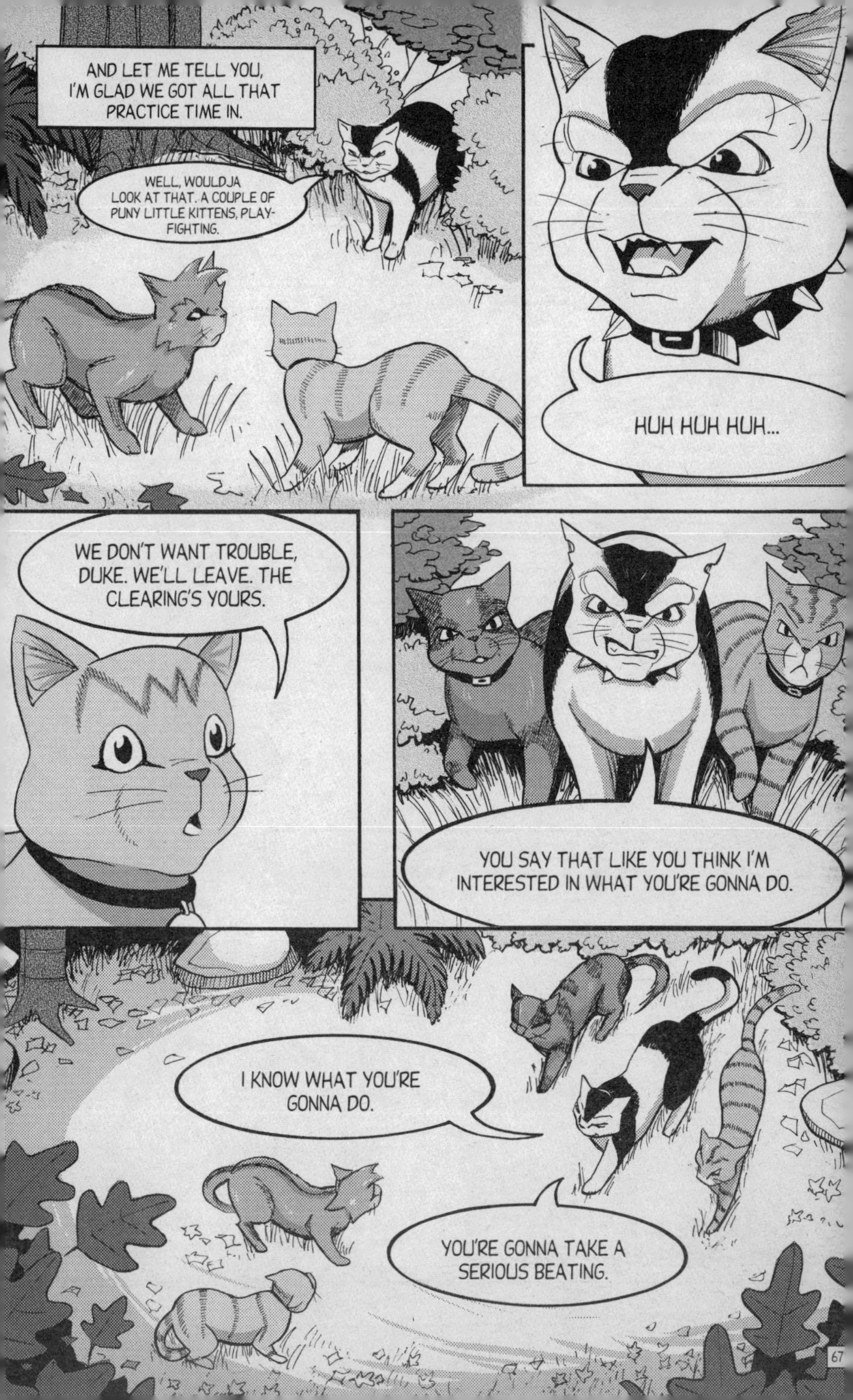
AND LET ME TELL YOU, I'M GLAD WE GOT ALL THAT PRACTICE TIME IN.
WELL, WOULDJA LOOK AT THAT. A COUPLE OF PUNY LITTLE KITTENS, PLAY-FIGHTING.
HUH HUH HUH...
WE DON'T WANT TROUBLE, DUKE. WE'LL LEAVE. THE CLEARING'S YOURS.
YOU SAY THAT LIKE YOU THINK I'M INTERESTED IN WHAT YOU'RE GONNA DO.
I KNOW WHAT YOU'RE GONNA DO.
YOU'RE GONNA TAKE A SERIOUS BEATING.

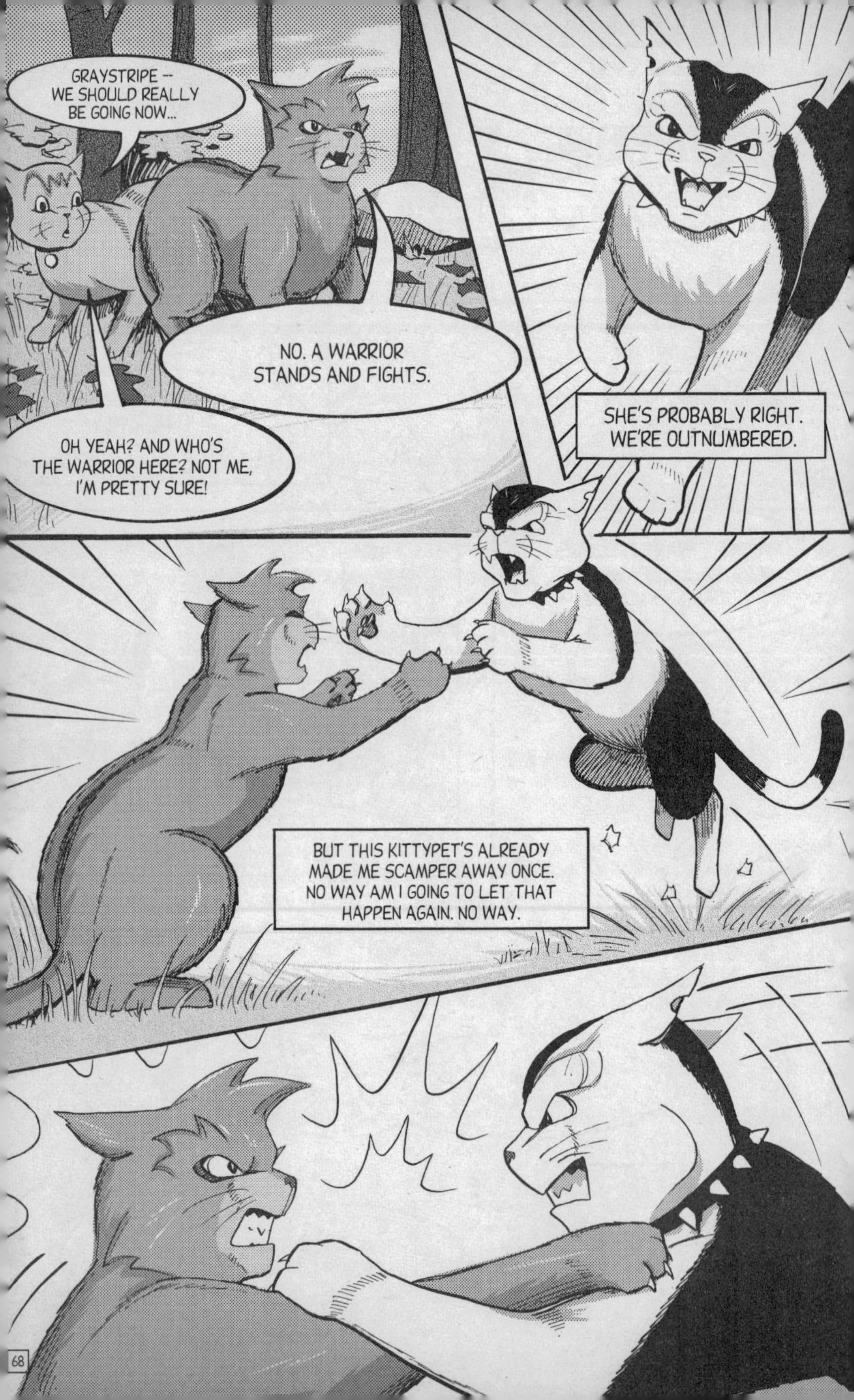
GRAYSTRIPE -- WE SHOULD REALLY BE GOING NOW...
NO. A WARRIOR STANDS AND FIGHTS.
OH YEAH? AND WHO'S THE WARRIOR HERE? NOT ME, I'M PRETTY SURE!
SHE'S PROBABLY RIGHT. WE'RE OUTNUMBERED.
BUT THIS KITTYPET'S ALREADY MADE ME SCAMPER AWAY ONCE. NO WAY AM I GOING TO LET THAT HAPPEN AGAIN. NO WAY.

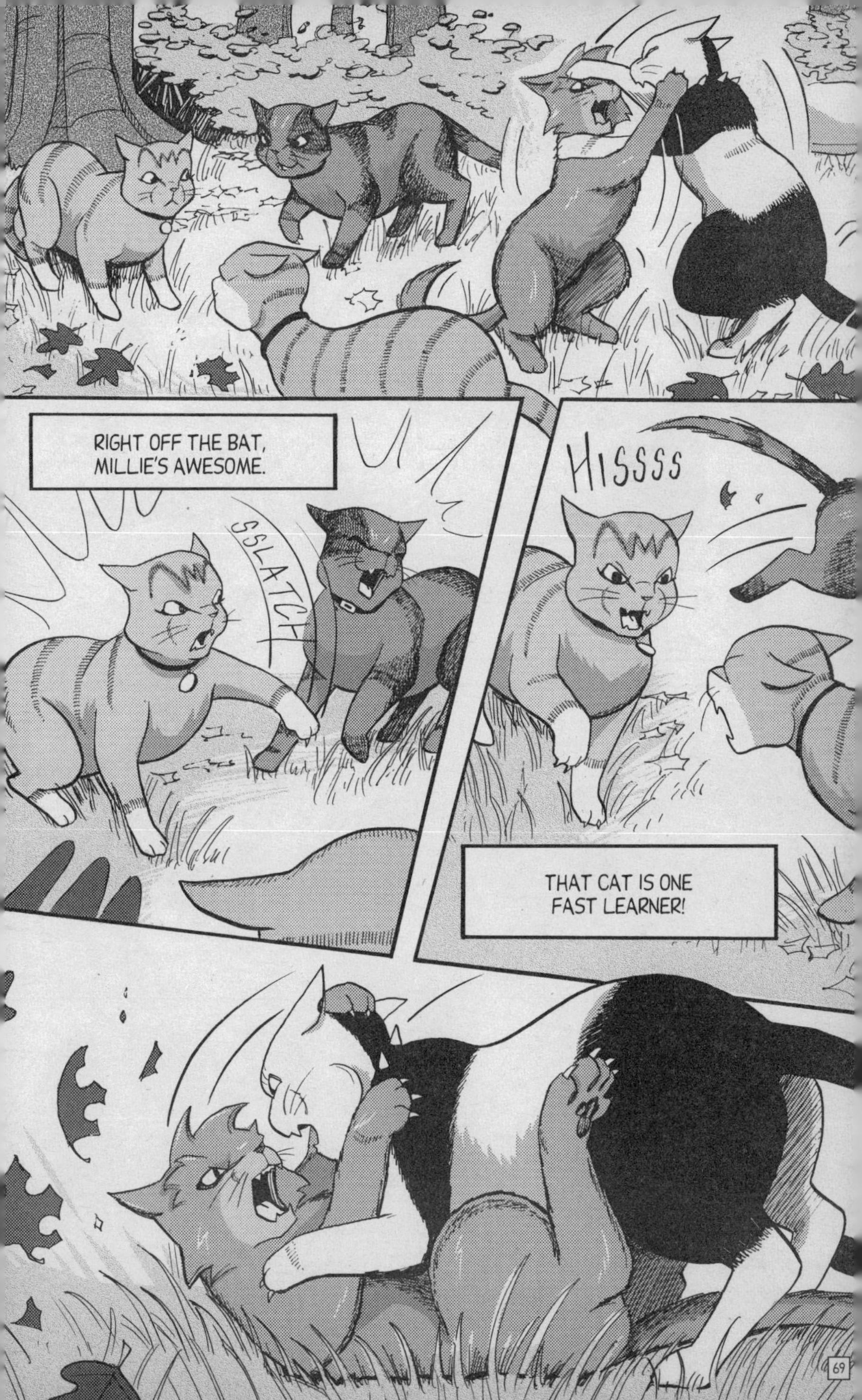
RIGHT OFF THE BAT, MILLIE'S AWESOME.
SSLATCH
HISSSSS
THAT CAT IS ONE FAST LEARNER!

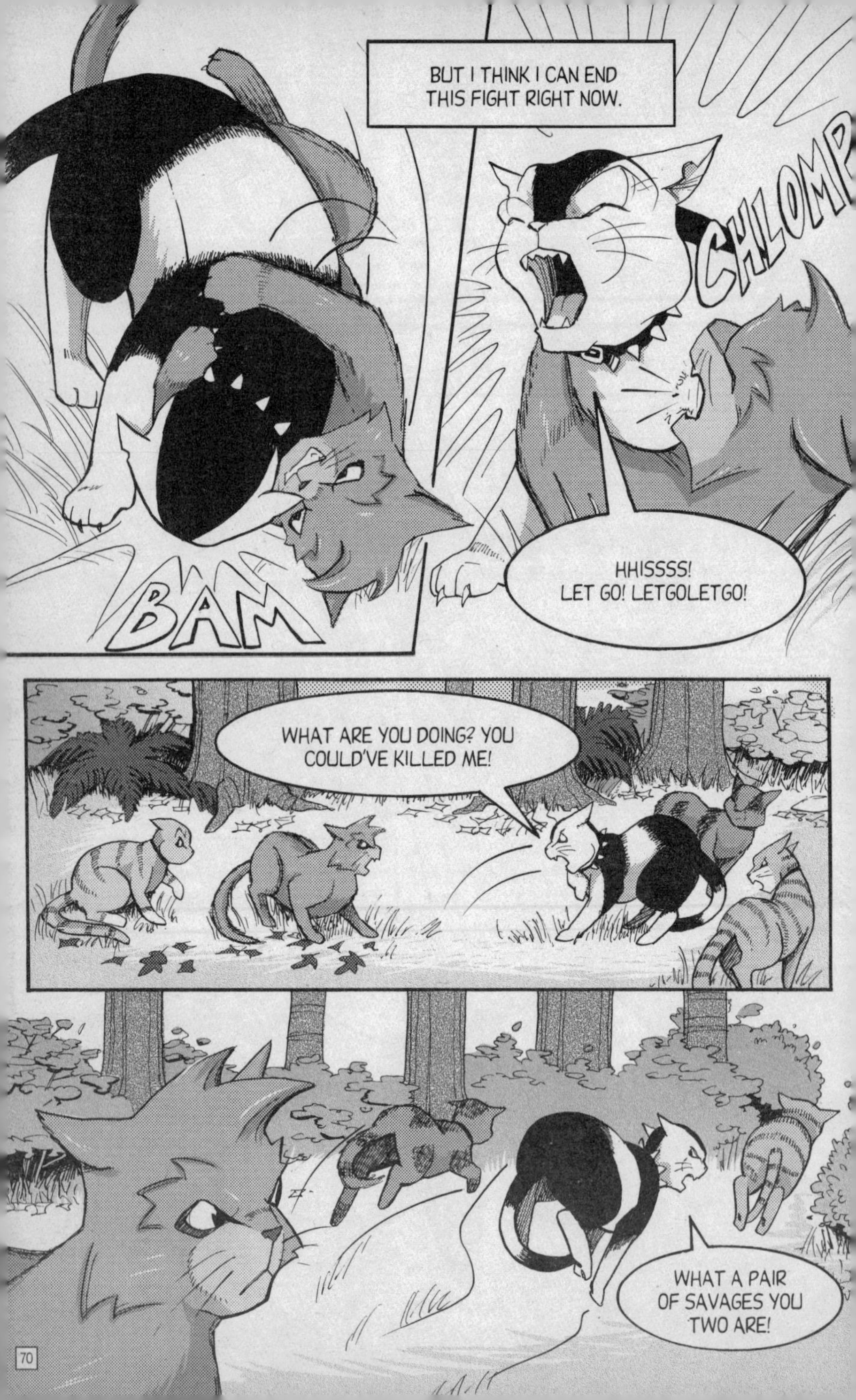
BUT I THINK I CAN END THIS FIGHT RIGHT NOW.
CHLOMP
BAM
HHISSSS! LET GO! LETGOLETGO!
WHAT ARE YOU DOING? YOU COULD'VE KILLED ME!
WHAT A PAIR OF SAVAGES YOU TWO ARE!

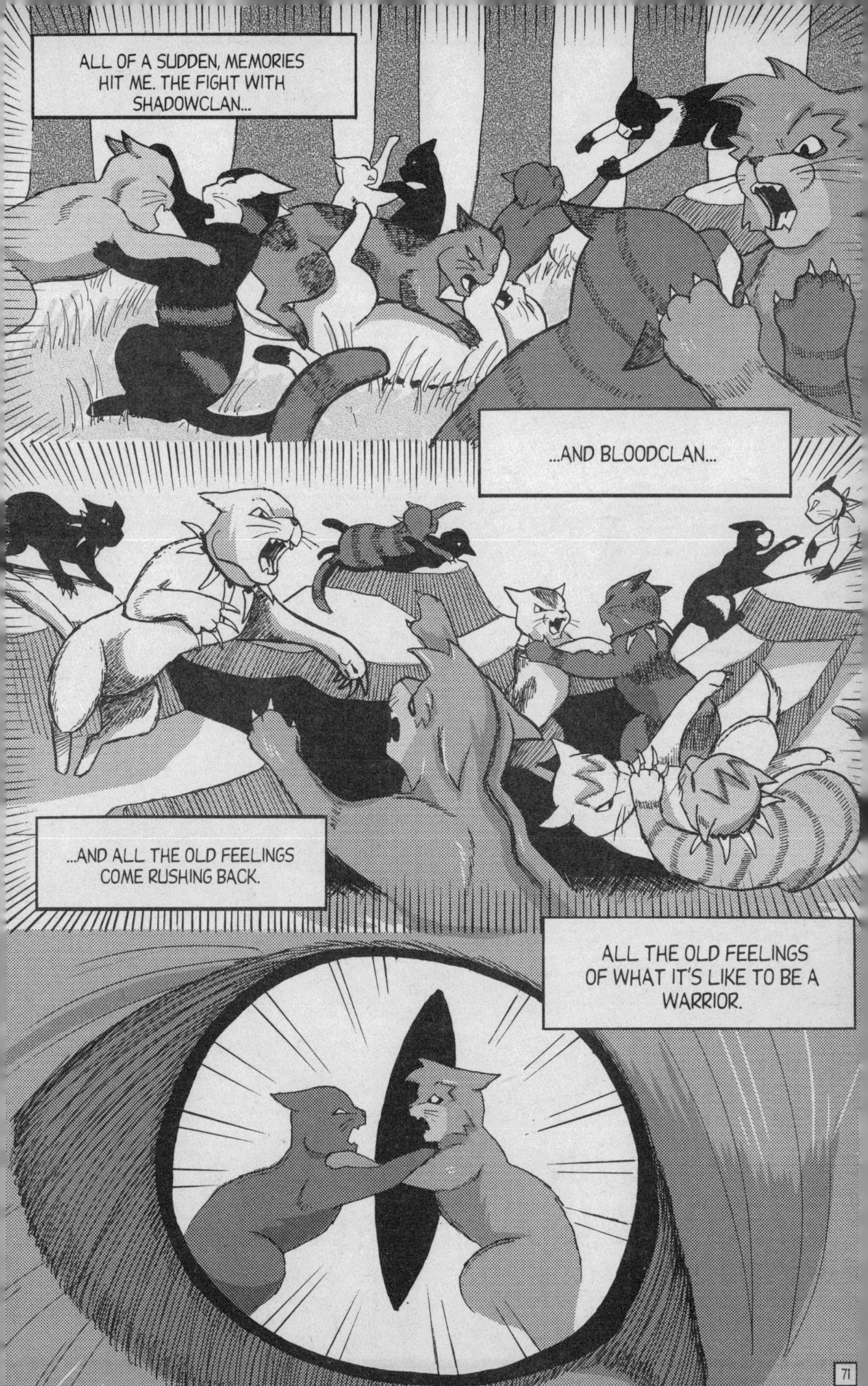
ALL OF A SUDDEN, MEMORIES HIT ME. THE FIGHT WITH SHADOWCLAN...
...AND BLOODCLAN...
...AND ALL THE OLD FEELINGS COME RUSHING BACK.
ALL THE OLD FEELINGS OF WHAT IT'S LIKE TO BE A WARRIOR.

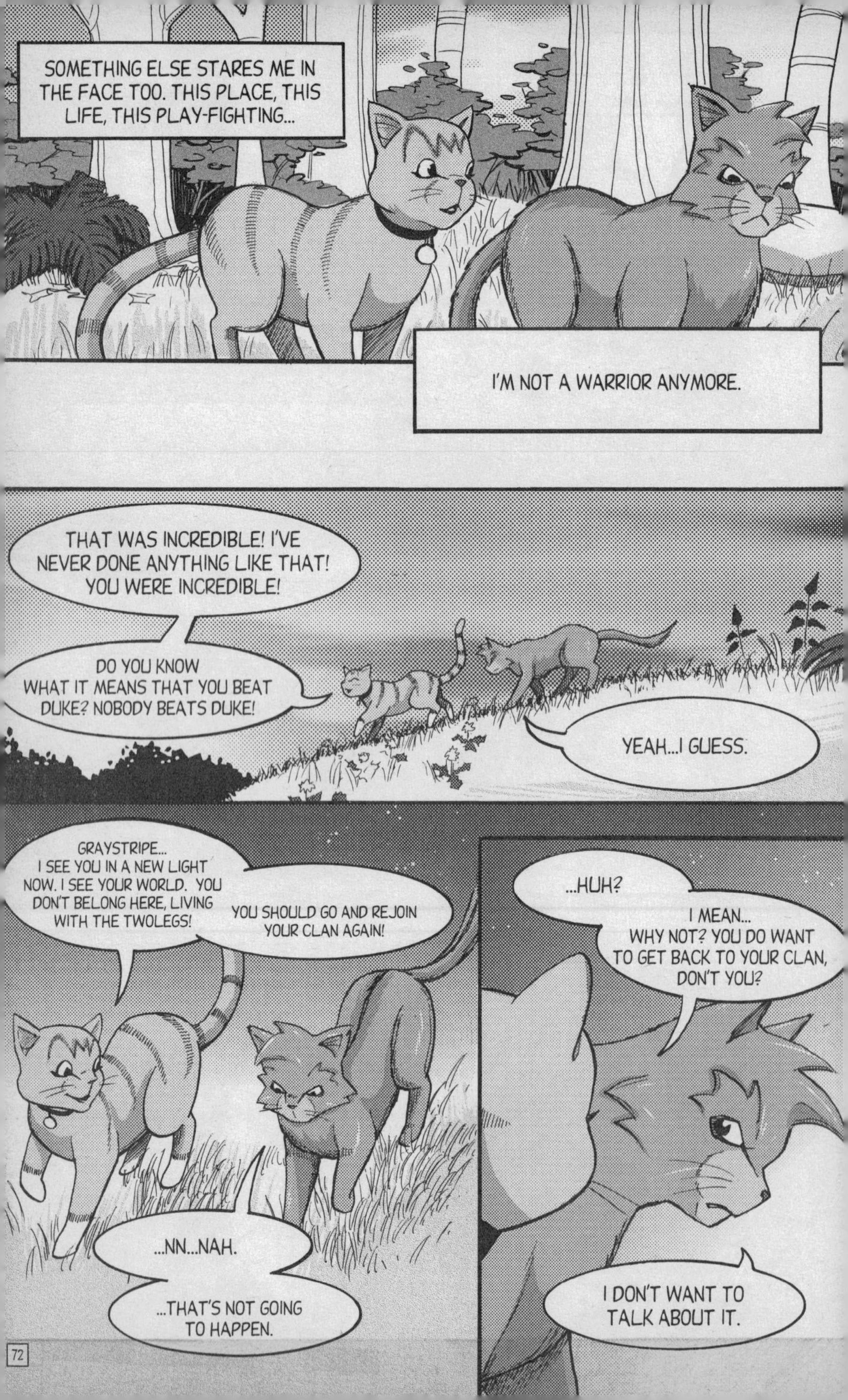
SOMETHING ELSE STARES ME IN THE FACE TOO. THIS PLACE, THIS LIFE, THIS PLAY-FIGHTING...
I'M NOT A WARRIOR ANYMORE.
THAT WAS INCREDIBLE! I'VE NEVER DONE ANYTHING LIKE THAT! YOU WERE INCREDIBLE!
DO YOU KNOW WHAT IT MEANS THAT YOU BEAT DUKE? NOBODY BEATS DUKE!
YEAH...I GUESS.
GRAYSTRIPE... I SEE YOU IN A NEW LIGHT NOW. I SEE YOUR WORLD. YOU DON'T BELONG HERE, LIVING WITH THE TWOLEGS!
YOU SHOULD GO AND REJOIN YOUR CLAN AGAIN!
...NN...NAH.
...THAT'S NOT GOING TO HAPPEN.
...HUH?
I MEAN... WHY NOT? YOU DO WANT TO GET BACK TO YOUR CLAN, DON'T YOU?
I DON'T WANT TO TALK ABOUT IT.

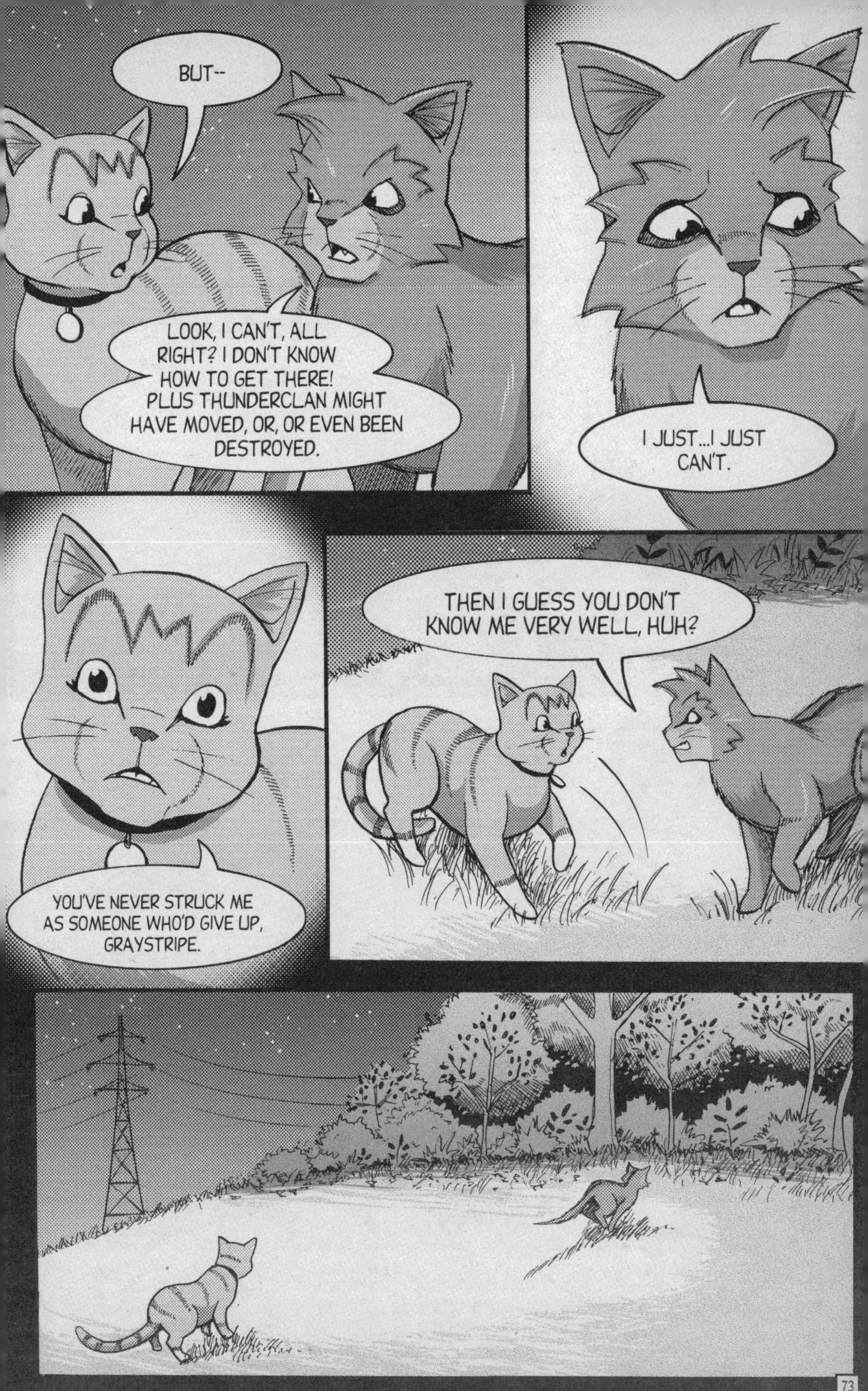
BUT--
LOOK, I CAN'T, ALL RIGHT? I DON'T KNOW HOW TO GET THERE! PLUS THUNDERCLAN MIGHT HAVE MOVED, OR, OR EVEN BEEN DESTROYED.
I JUST...I JUST CAN'T.
YOU'VE NEVER STRUCK ME AS SOMEONE WHO'D GIVE UP, GRAYSTRIPE.
THEN I GUESS YOU DON'T KNOW ME VERY WELL, HUH?

CHAPTER 4

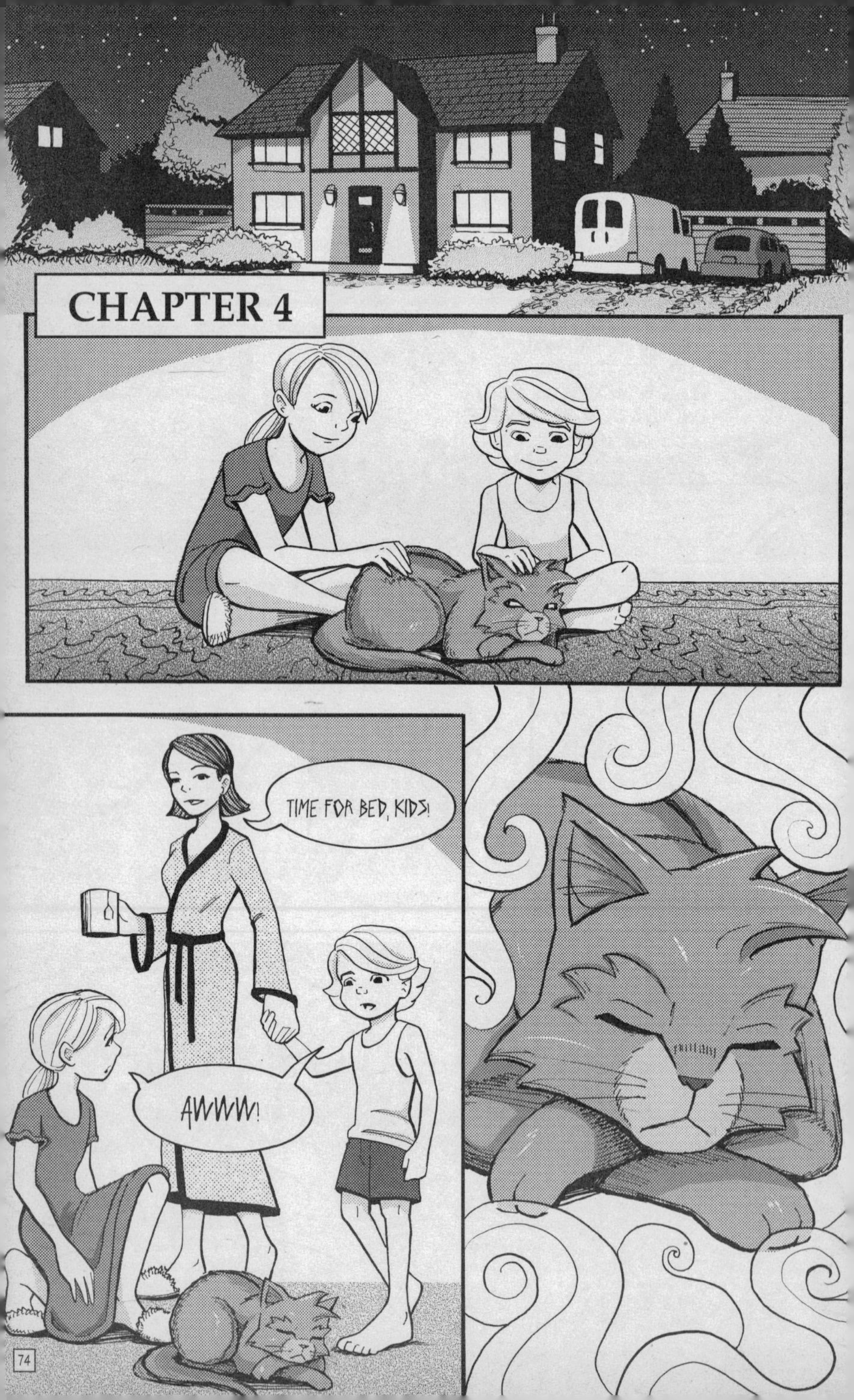

TIME FOR BED, KIDS!
AWWW!

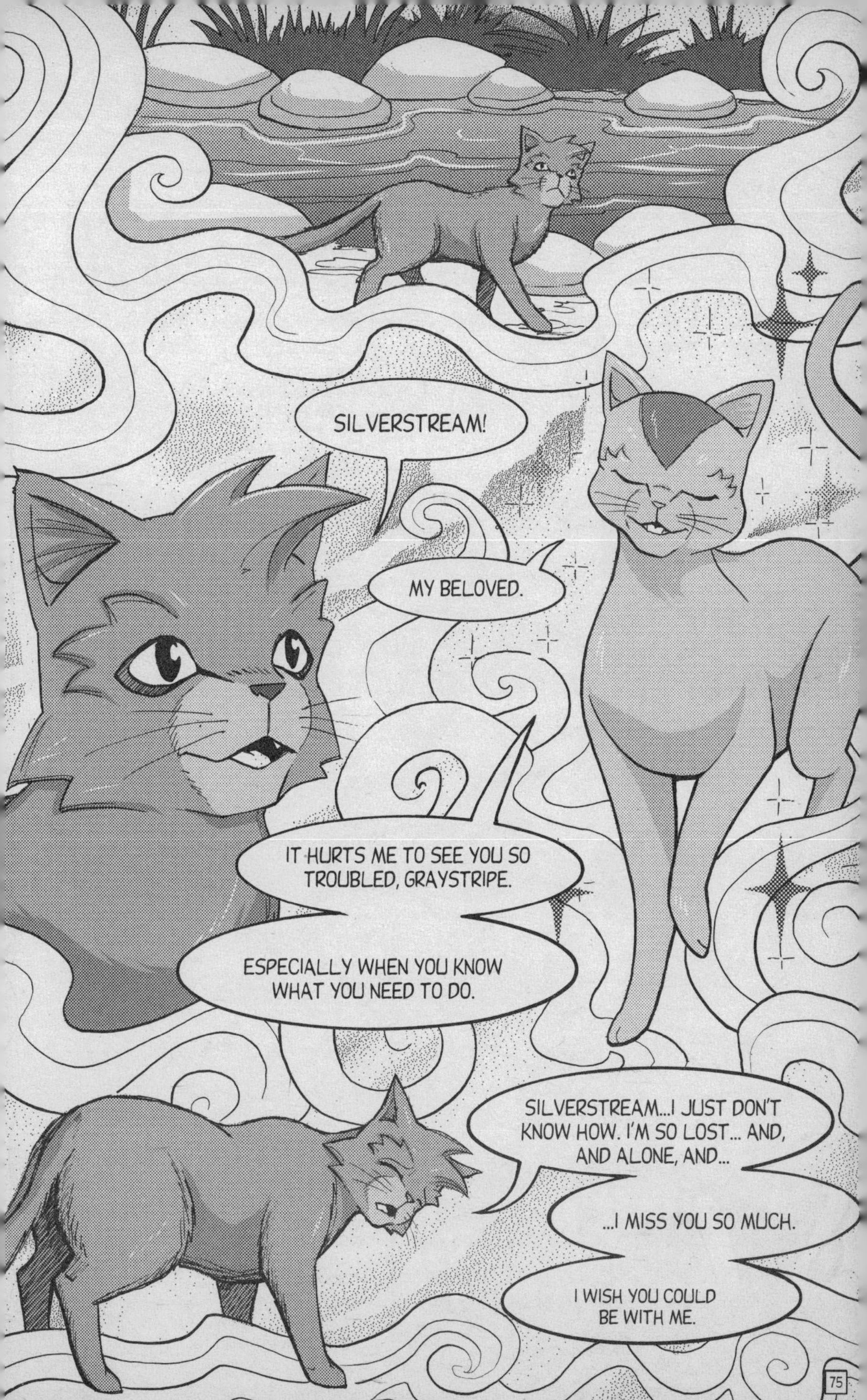
SILVERSTREAM!
MY BELOVED.
IT HURTS ME TO SEE YOU SO TROUBLED, GRAYSTRIPE.
ESPECIALLY WHEN YOU KNOW WHAT YOU NEED TO DO.
SILVERSTREAM...I JUST DON'T KNOW HOW. I'M SO LOST... AND, AND ALONE, AND...
...I MISS YOU SO MUCH.
I WISH YOU COULD BE WITH ME.

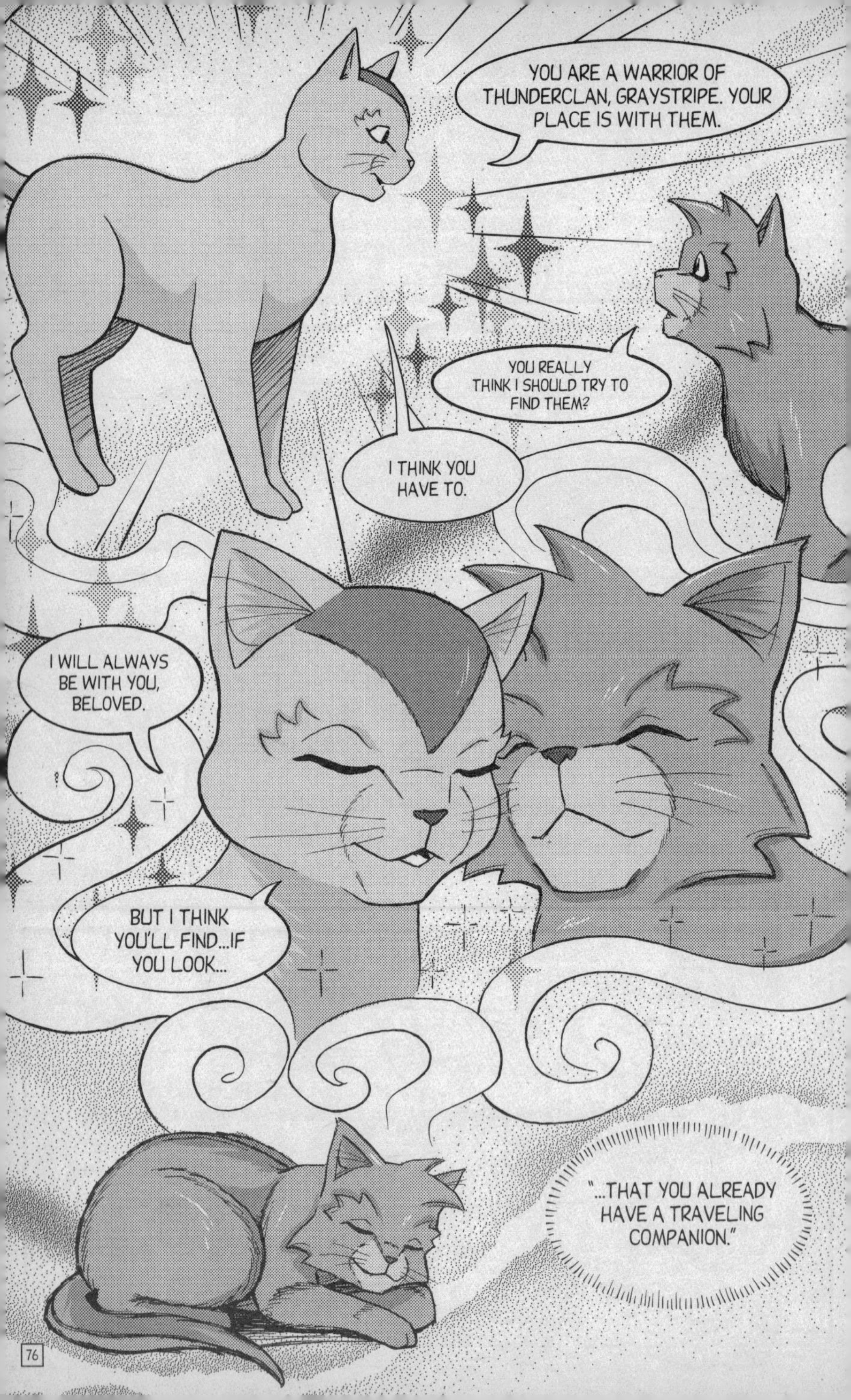
YOU ARE A WARRIOR OF THUNDERCLAN, GRAYSTRIPE. YOUR PLACE IS WITH THEM.
YOU REALLY THINK I SHOULD TRY TO FIND THEM?
I THINK YOU HAVE TO.
I WILL ALWAYS BE WITH YOU, BELOVED.
BUT I THINK YOU'LL FIND...IF YOU LOOK...
"...THAT YOU ALREADY HAVE A TRAVELING COMPANION."

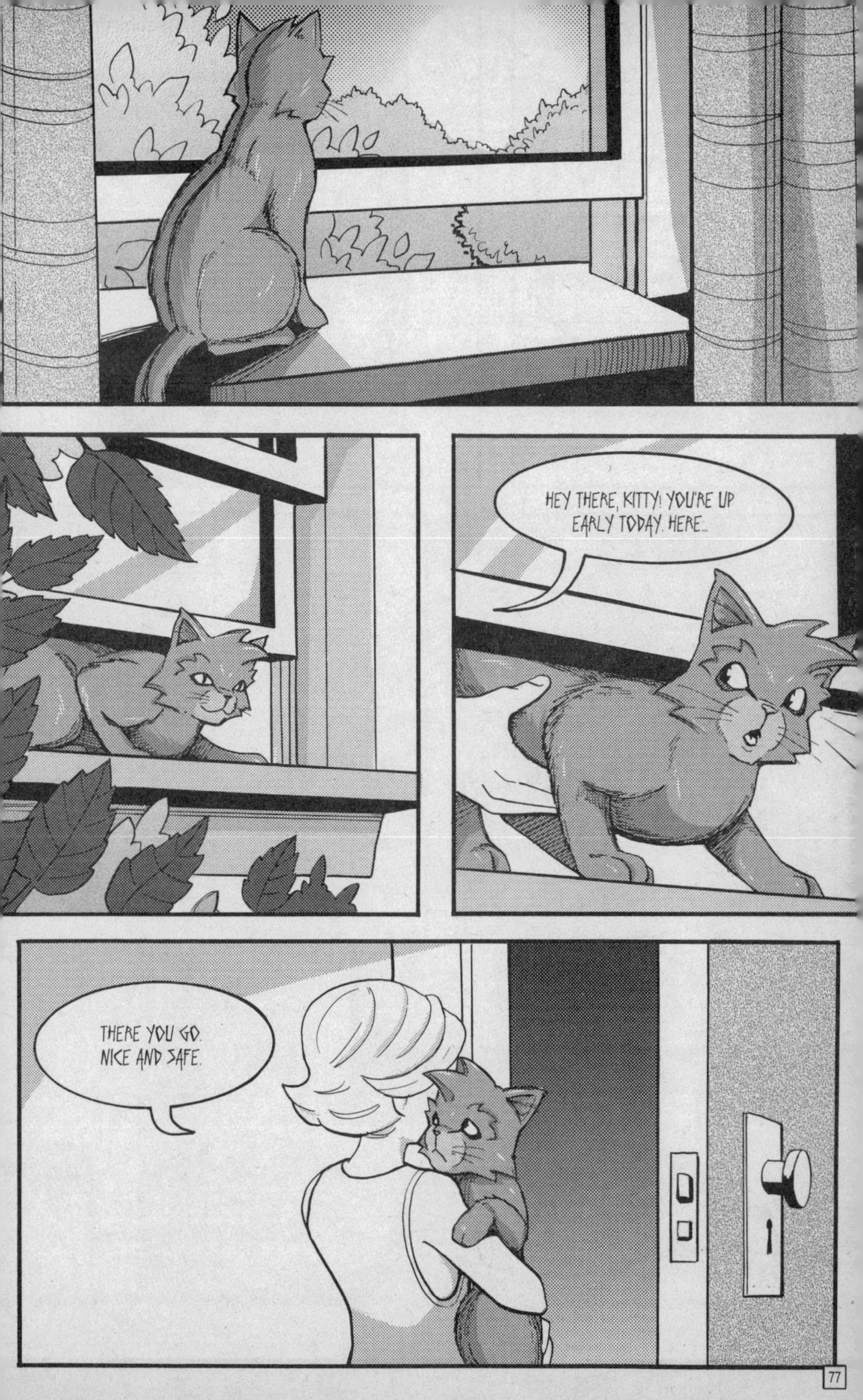
HEY THERE, KITTY! YOU'RE UP EARLY TODAY. HERE...
THERE YOU GO. NICE AND SAFE.

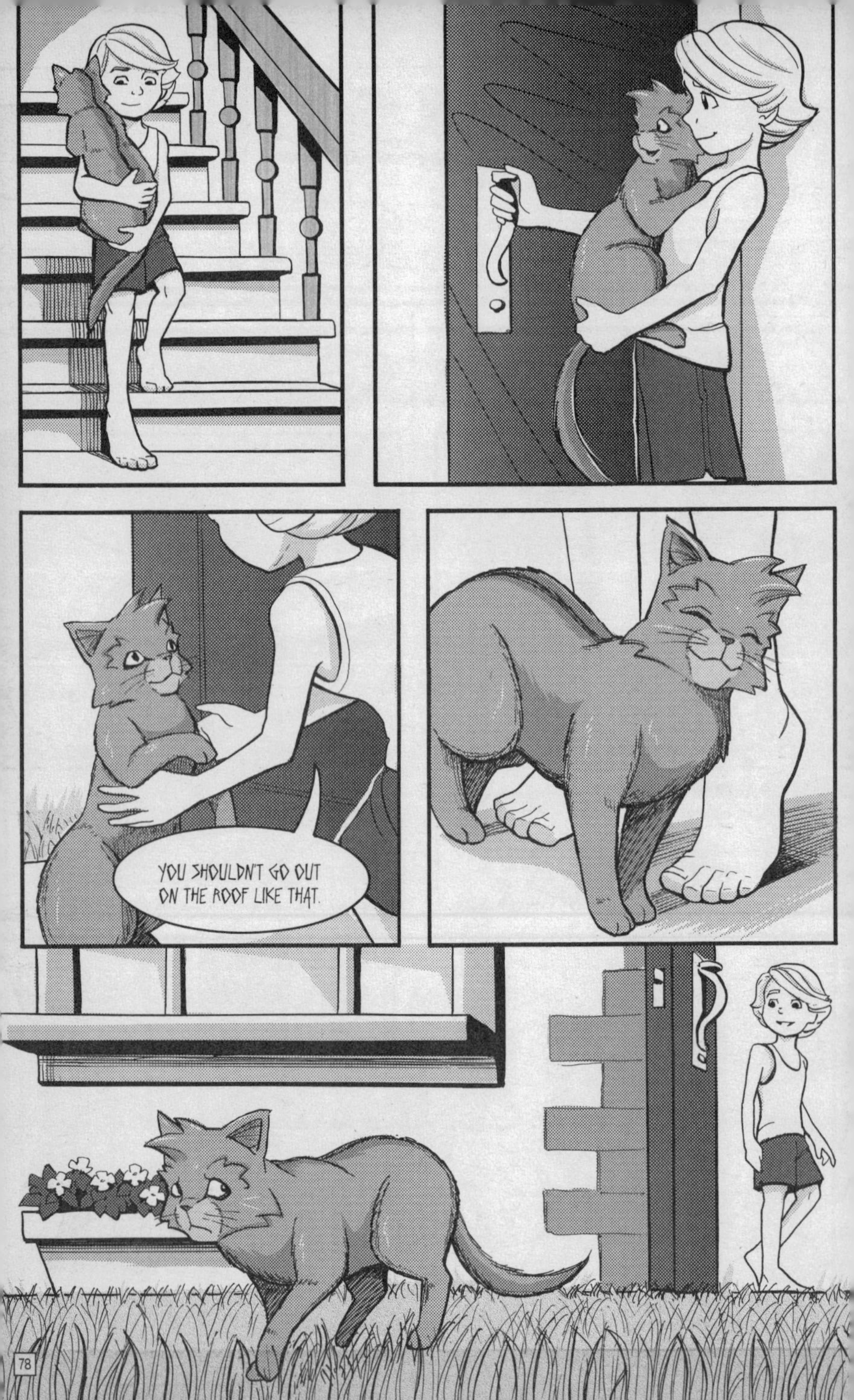
YOU SHOULDN'T GO OUT
ON THE ROOF LIKE THAT.

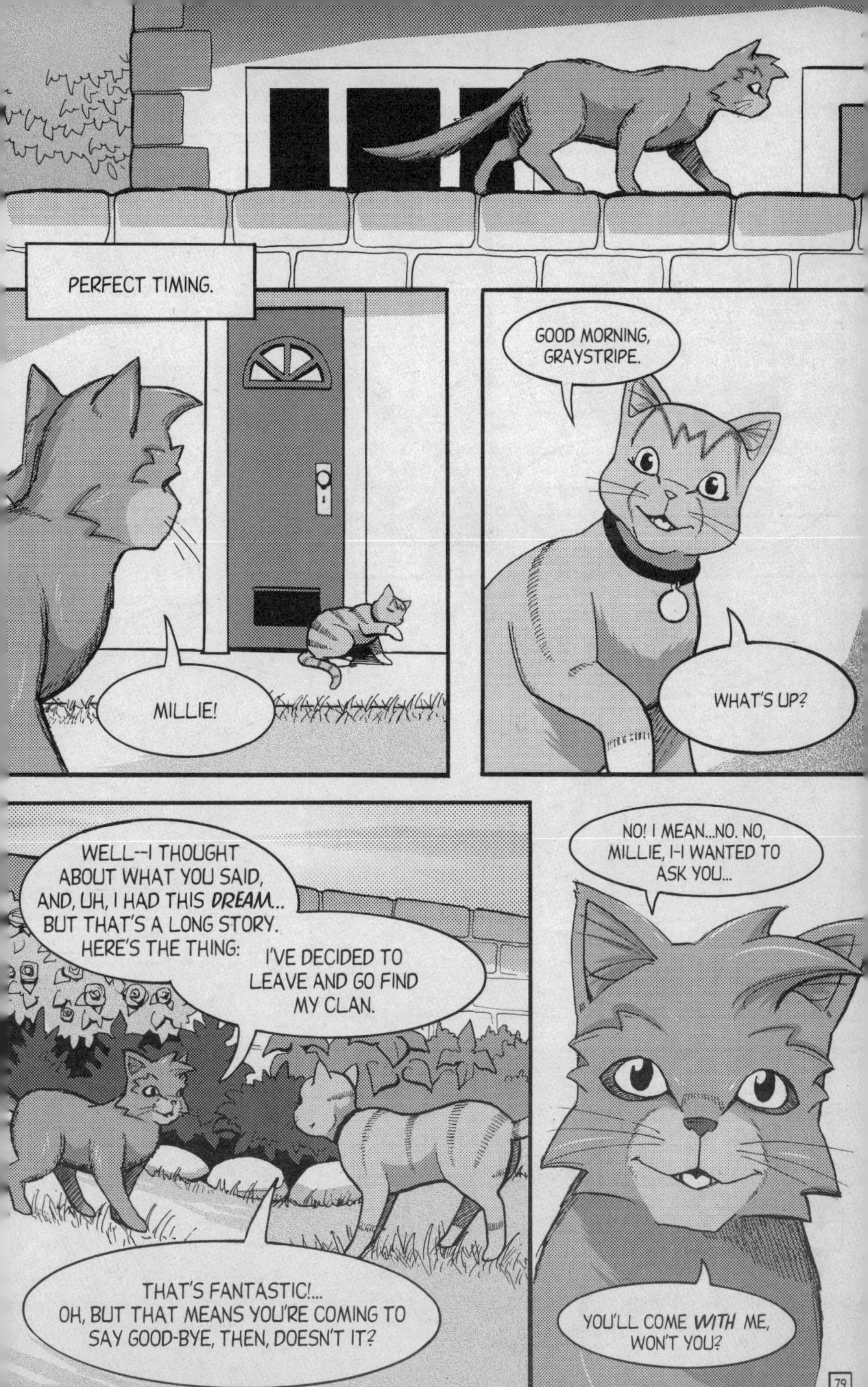
PERFECT TIMING.
MILLIE!
GOOD MORNING, GRAYSTRIPE.
WHAT'S UP?
WELL--I THOUGHT ABOUT WHAT YOU SAID, AND, UH, I HAD THIS *DREAM*... BUT THAT'S A LONG STORY. HERE'S THE THING:
I'VE DECIDED TO LEAVE AND GO FIND MY CLAN.
THAT'S FANTASTIC!... OH, BUT THAT MEANS YOU'RE COMING TO SAY GOOD-BYE, THEN, DOESN'T IT?
NO! I MEAN...NO. NO, MILLIE, I-I WANTED TO ASK YOU...
YOU'LL COME *WITH* ME, WON'T YOU?

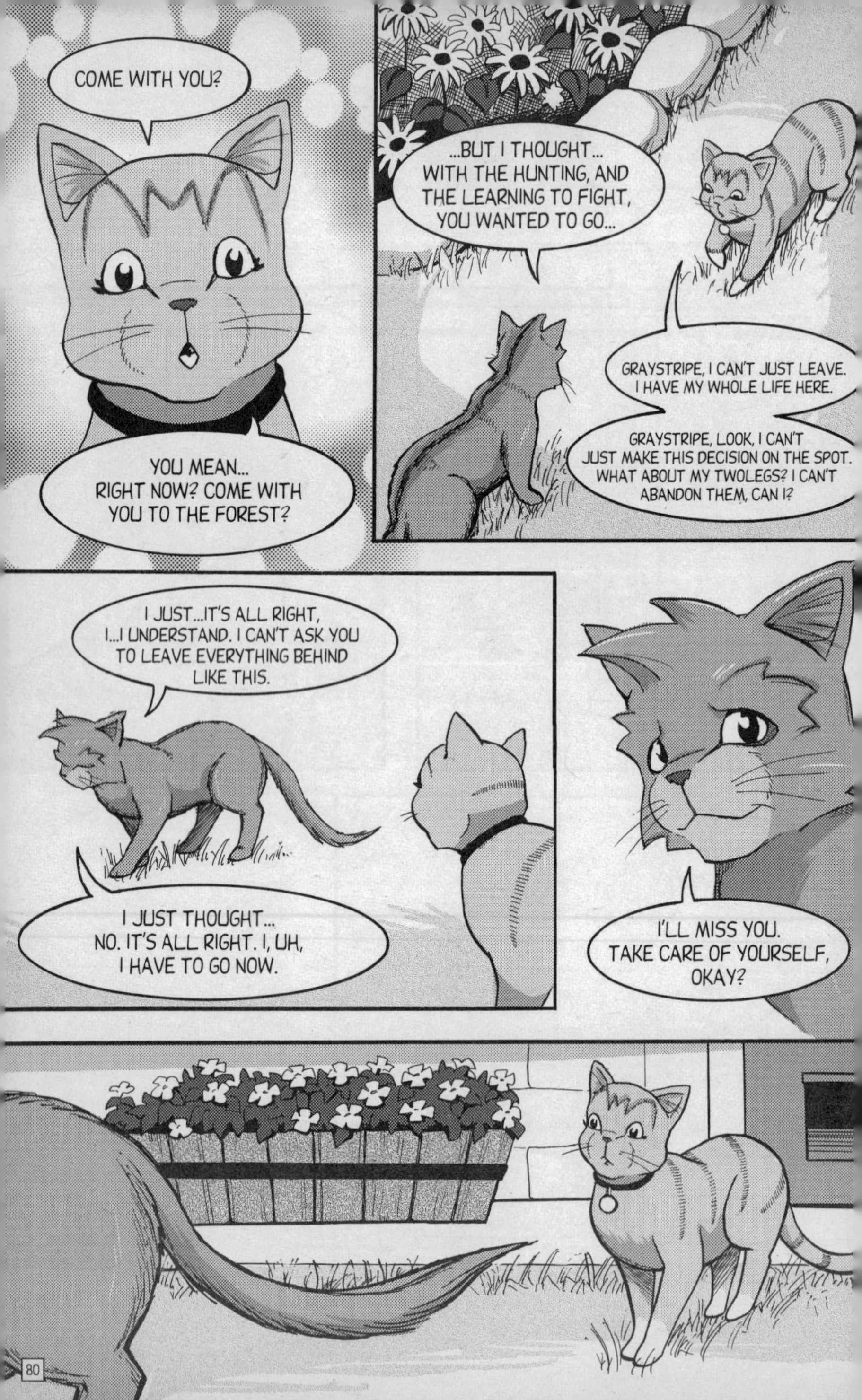
COME WITH YOU?
YOU MEAN... RIGHT NOW? COME WITH YOU TO THE FOREST?
...BUT I THOUGHT... WITH THE HUNTING, AND THE LEARNING TO FIGHT, YOU WANTED TO GO...
GRAYSTRIPE, I CAN'T JUST LEAVE. I HAVE MY WHOLE LIFE HERE.
GRAYSTRIPE, LOOK, I CAN'T JUST MAKE THIS DECISION ON THE SPOT. WHAT ABOUT MY TWOLEGS? I CAN'T ABANDON THEM, CAN I?
I JUST...IT'S ALL RIGHT, I...I UNDERSTAND. I CAN'T ASK YOU TO LEAVE EVERYTHING BEHIND LIKE THIS.
I JUST THOUGHT... NO. IT'S ALL RIGHT. I, UH, I HAVE TO GO NOW.
I'LL MISS YOU. TAKE CARE OF YOURSELF, OKAY?

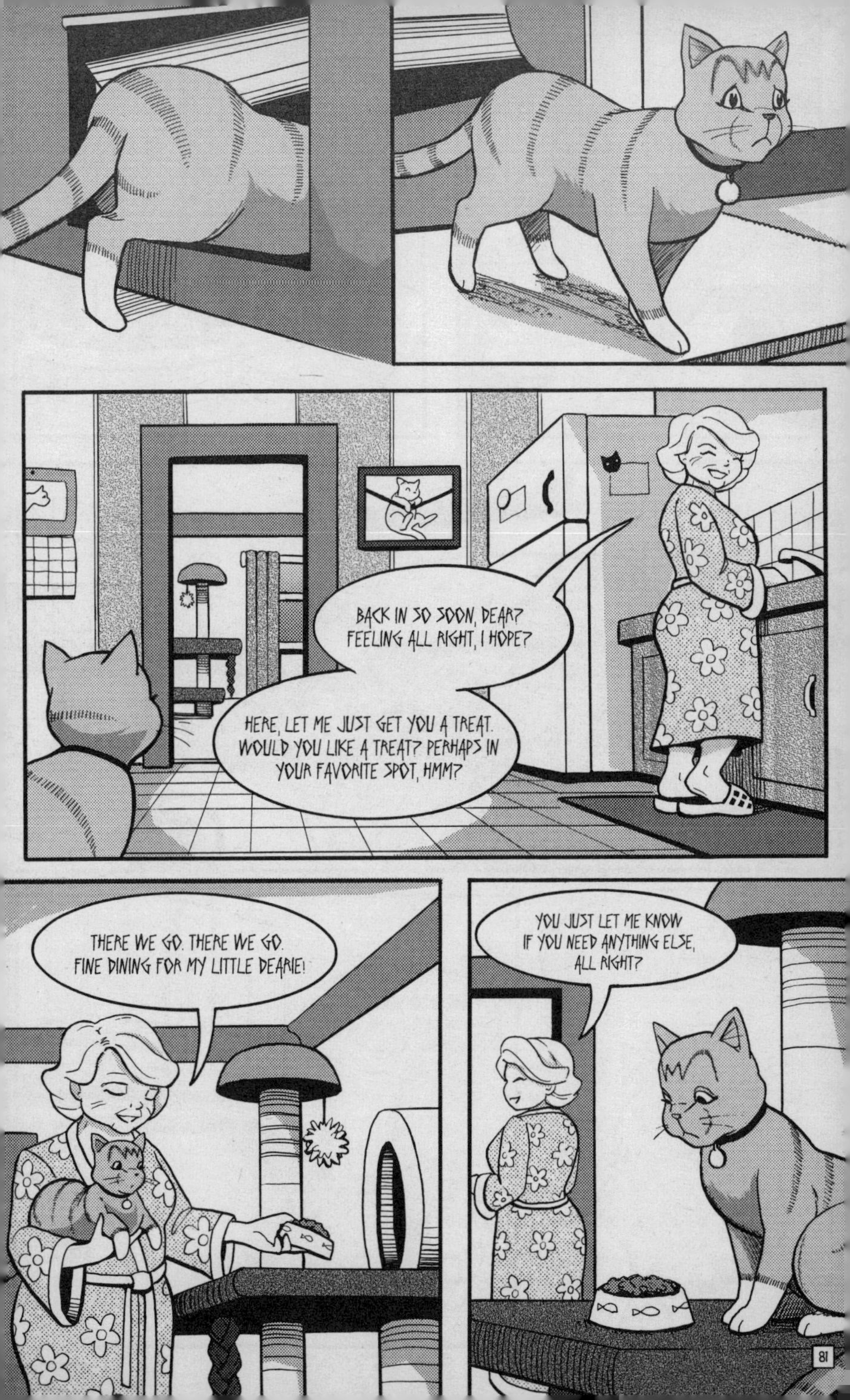
BACK IN SO SOON, DEAR? FEELING ALL RIGHT, I HOPE?
HERE, LET ME JUST GET YOU A TREAT. WOULD YOU LIKE A TREAT? PERHAPS IN YOUR FAVORITE SPOT, HMM?
THERE WE GO. THERE WE GO. FINE DINING FOR MY LITTLE DEARIE!
YOU JUST LET ME KNOW IF YOU NEED ANYTHING ELSE, ALL RIGHT?

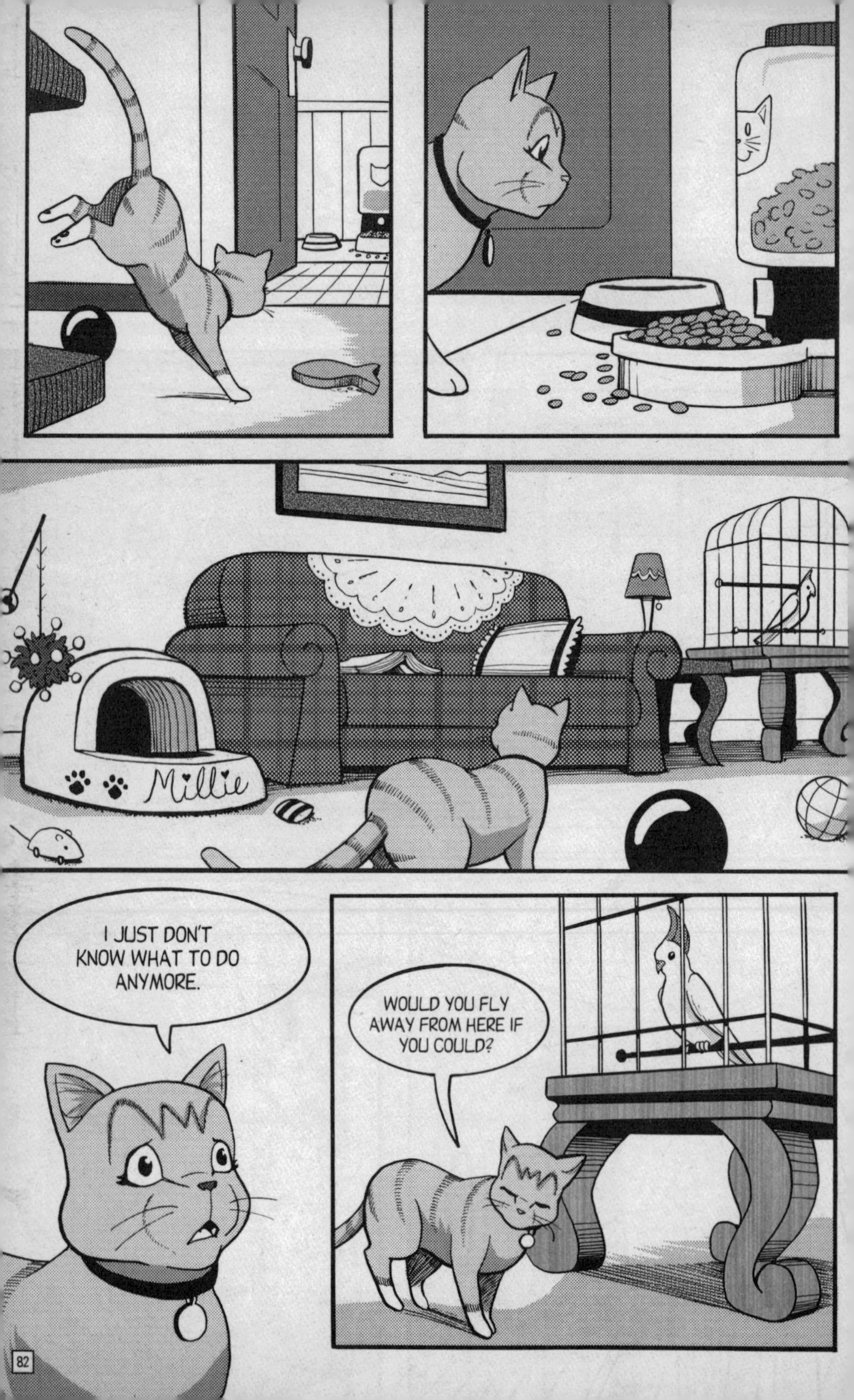
Millie
I JUST DON'T KNOW WHAT TO DO ANYMORE.
WOULD YOU FLY AWAY FROM HERE IF YOU COULD?

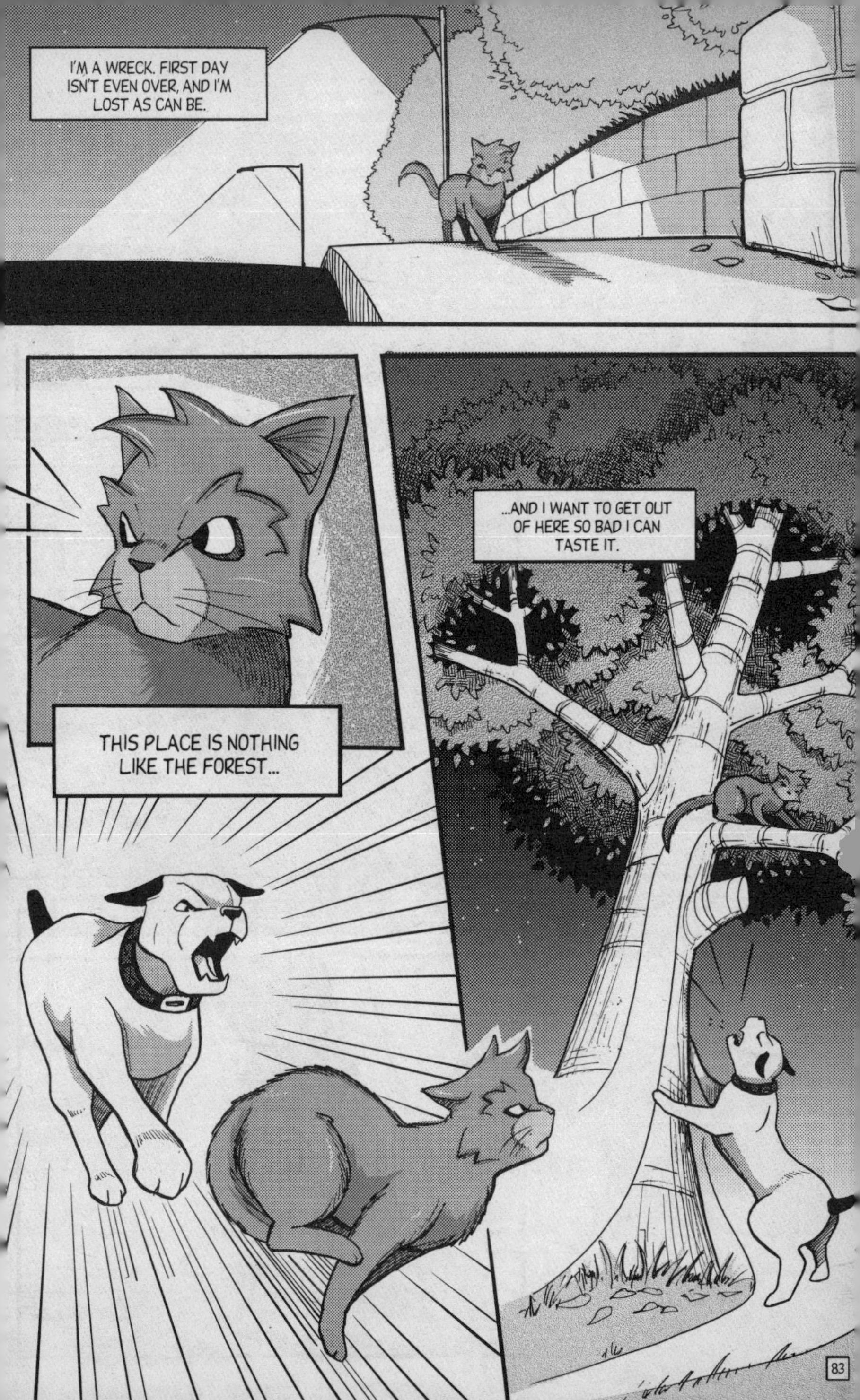
I'M A WRECK. FIRST DAY ISN'T EVEN OVER, AND I'M LOST AS CAN BE.
THIS PLACE IS NOTHING LIKE THE FOREST...
...AND I WANT TO GET OUT OF HERE SO BAD I CAN TASTE IT.

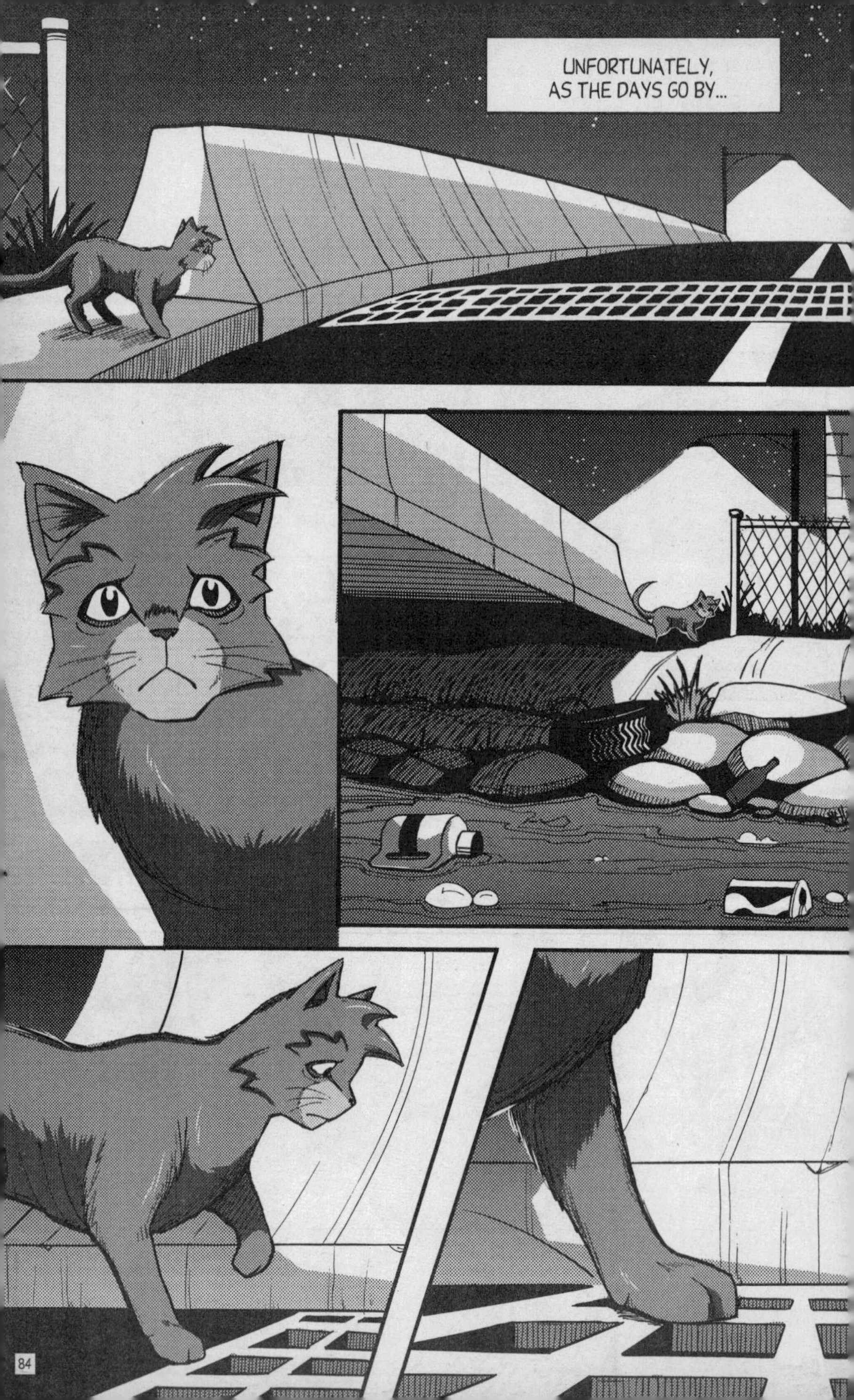
UNFORTUNATELY,
AS THE DAYS GO BY...

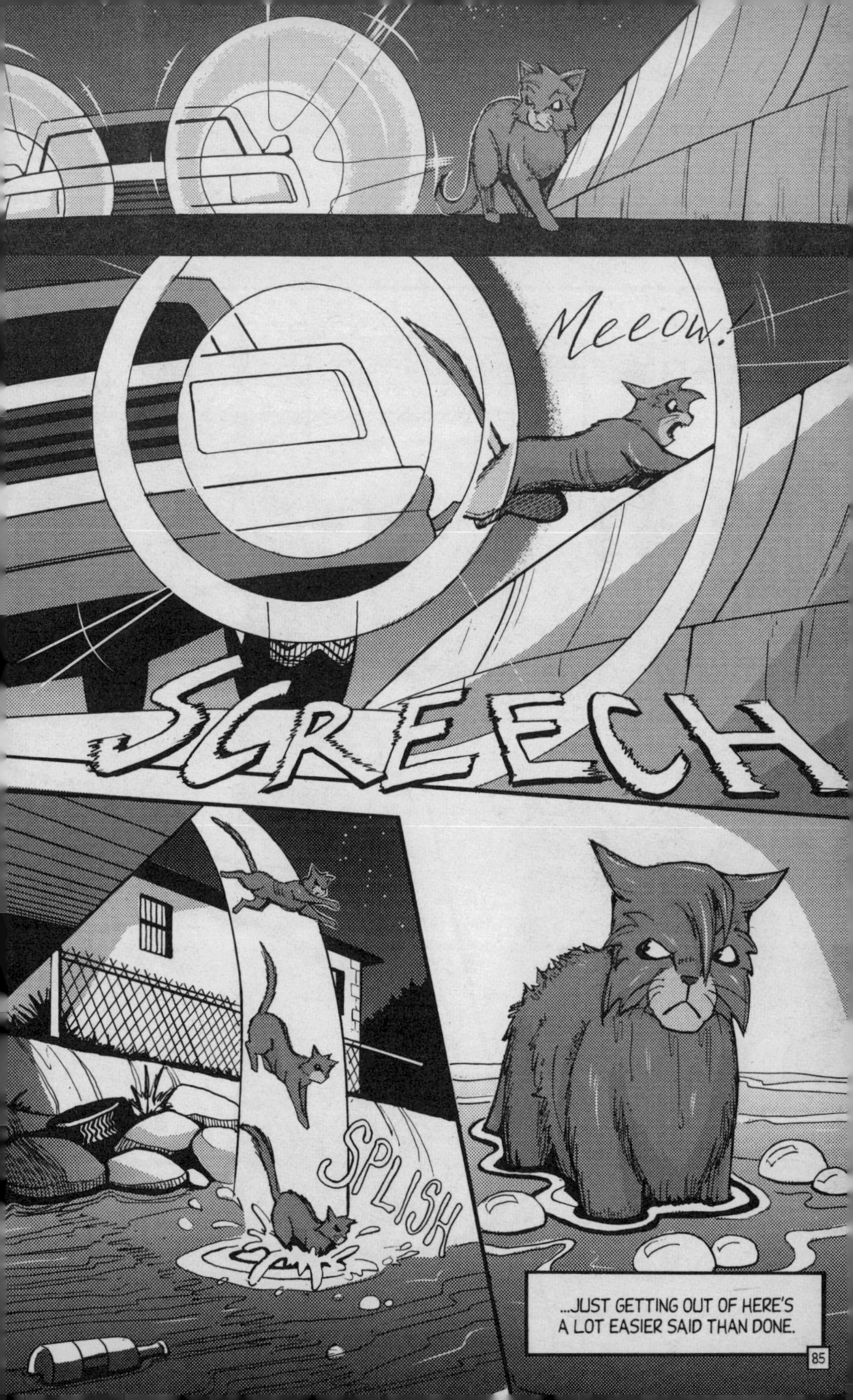
Meeow!
SCREECH
SPLISH
...JUST GETTING OUT OF HERE'S A LOT EASIER SAID THAN DONE.

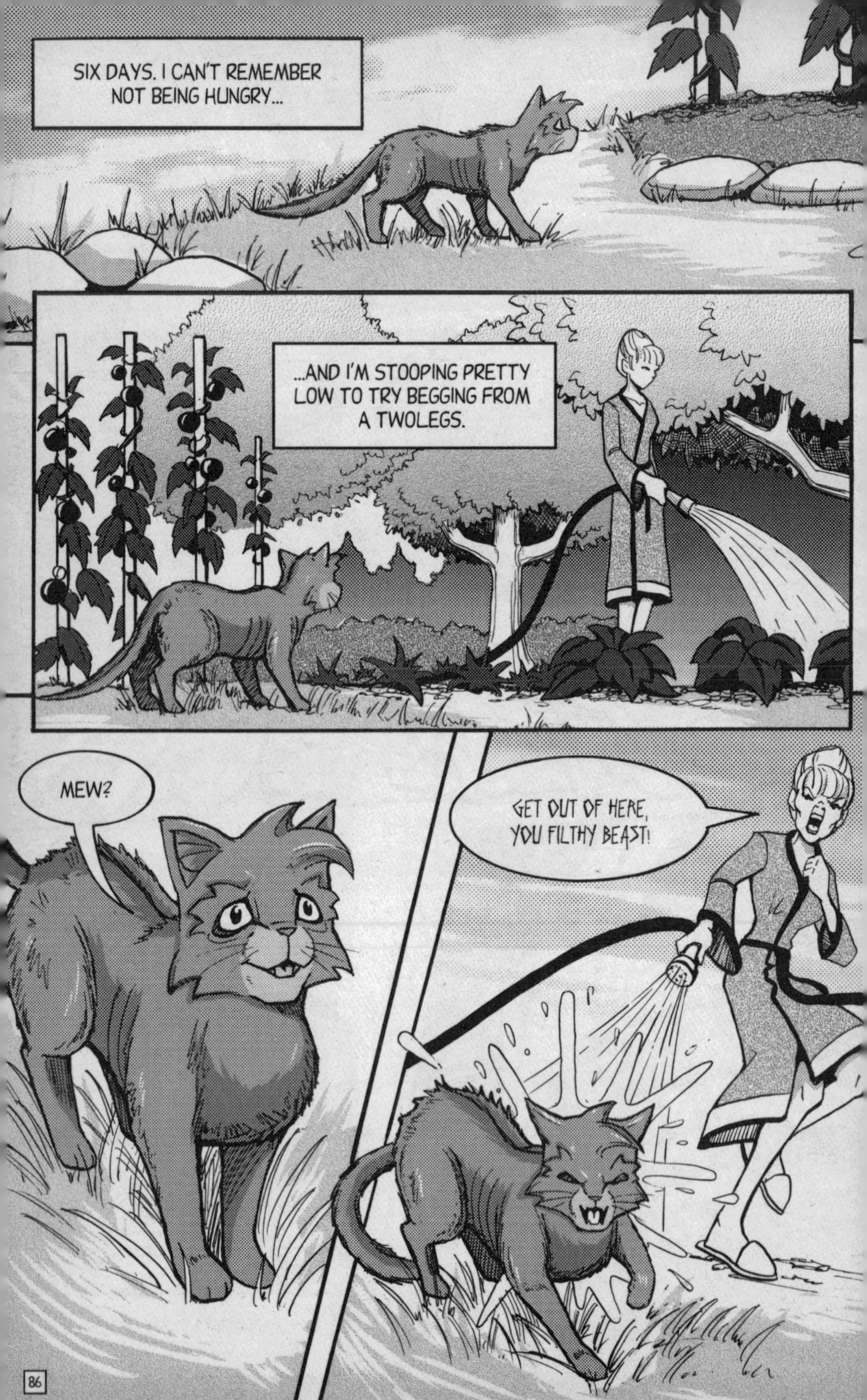
SIX DAYS. I CAN'T REMEMBER NOT BEING HUNGRY...
...AND I'M STOOPING PRETTY LOW TO TRY BEGGING FROM A TWOLEGS.
MEW?
GET OUT OF HERE, YOU FILTHY BEAST!

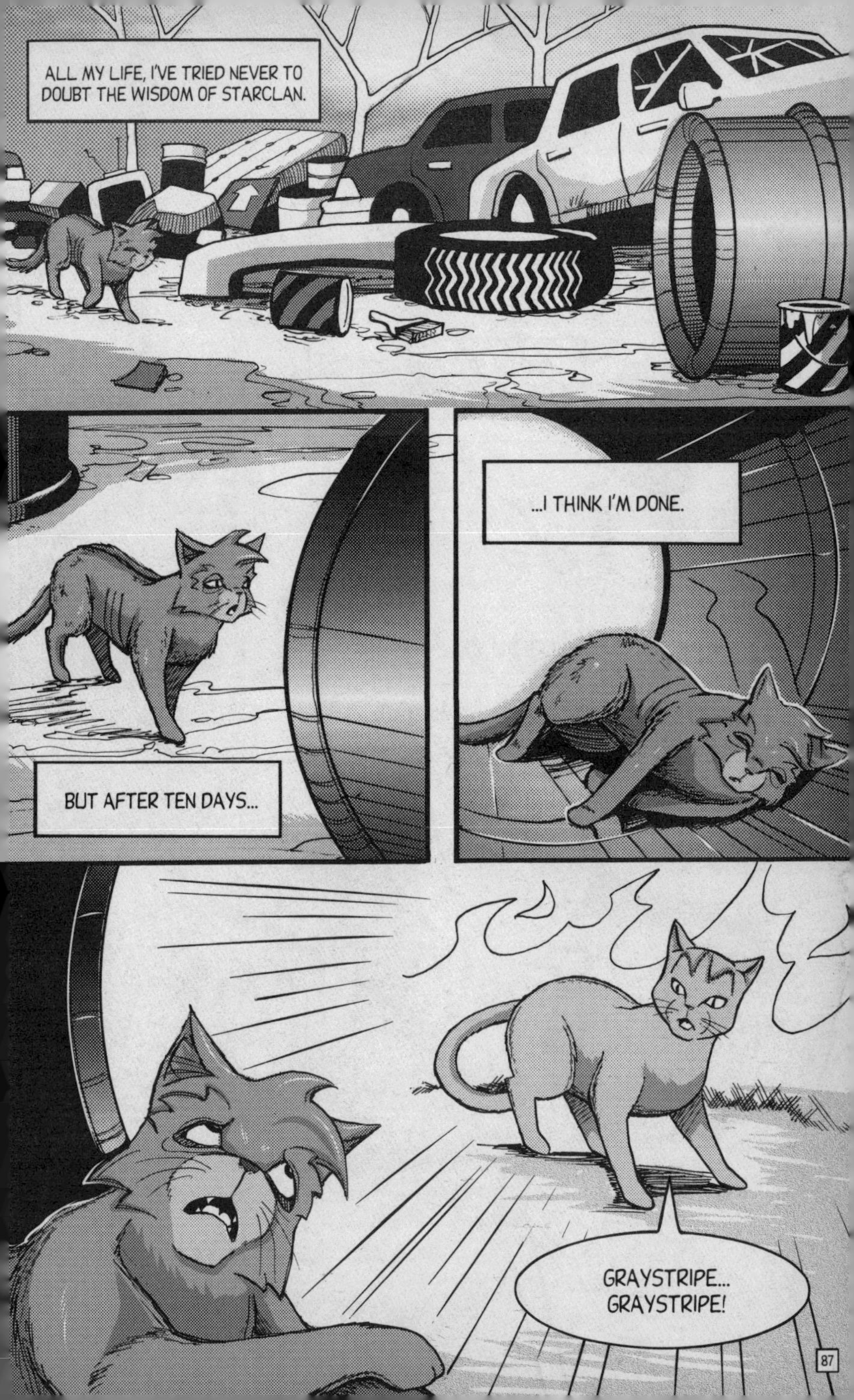
ALL MY LIFE, I'VE TRIED NEVER TO DOUBT THE WISDOM OF STARCLAN.
BUT AFTER TEN DAYS...
...I THINK I'M DONE.
GRAYSTRIPE... GRAYSTRIPE!

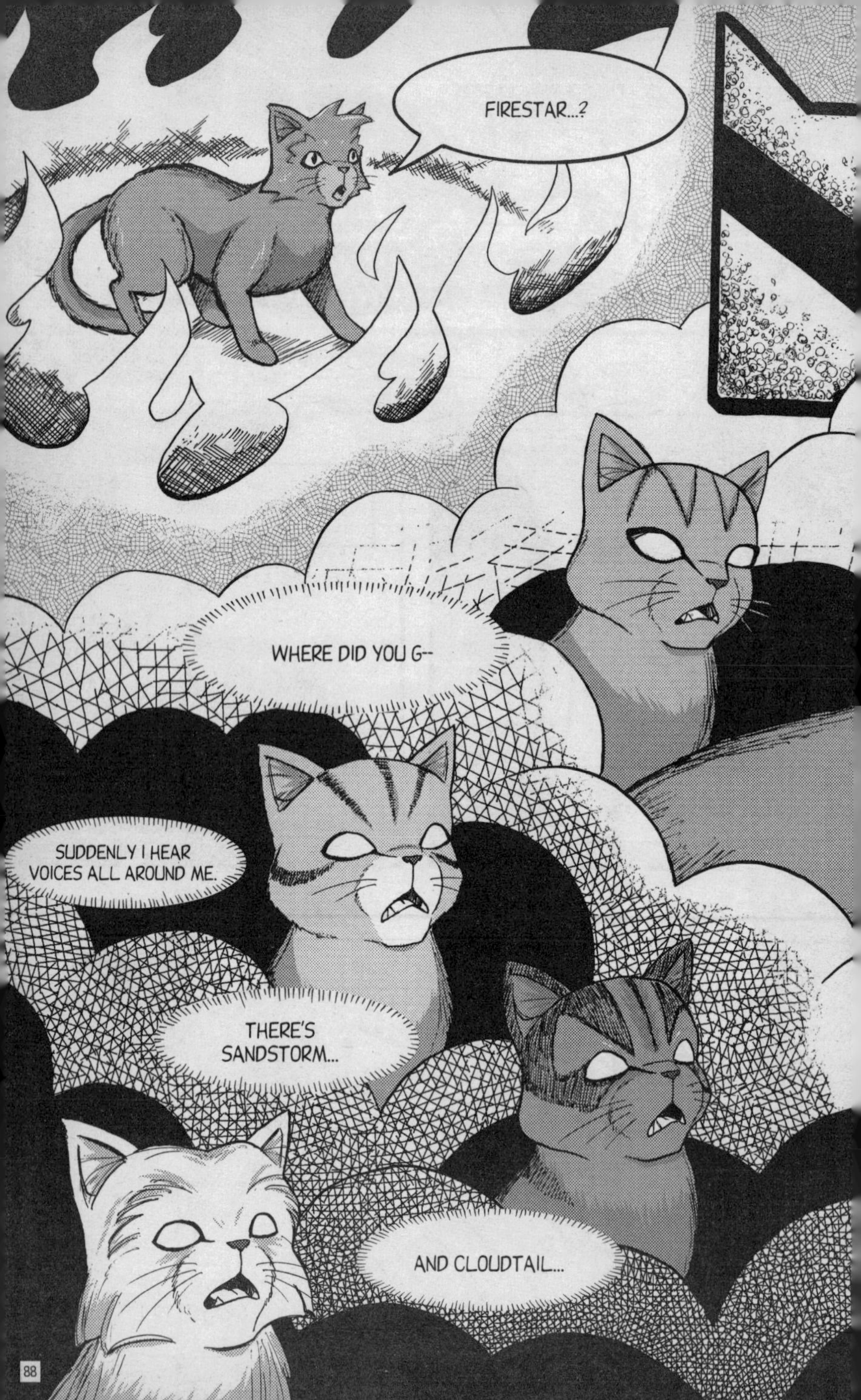
FIRESTAR...?
WHERE DID YOU G--
SUDDENLY I HEAR VOICES ALL AROUND ME.
THERE'S SANDSTORM...
AND CLOUDTAIL...

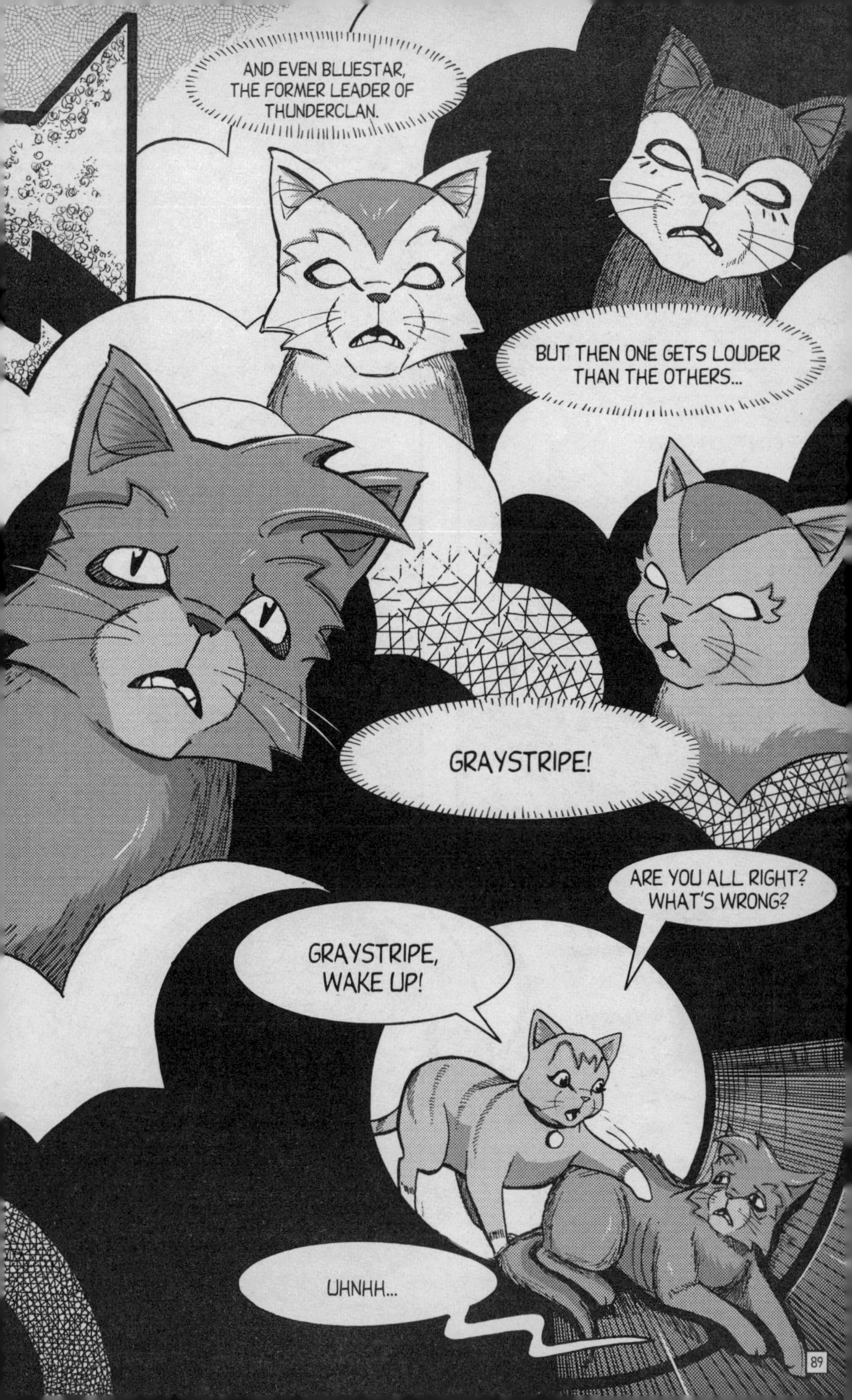
AND EVEN BLUESTAR, THE FORMER LEADER OF THUNDERCLAN.
BUT THEN ONE GETS LOUDER THAN THE OTHERS...
GRAYSTRIPE!
ARE YOU ALL RIGHT? WHAT'S WRONG?
GRAYSTRIPE, WAKE UP!
UHNHH...

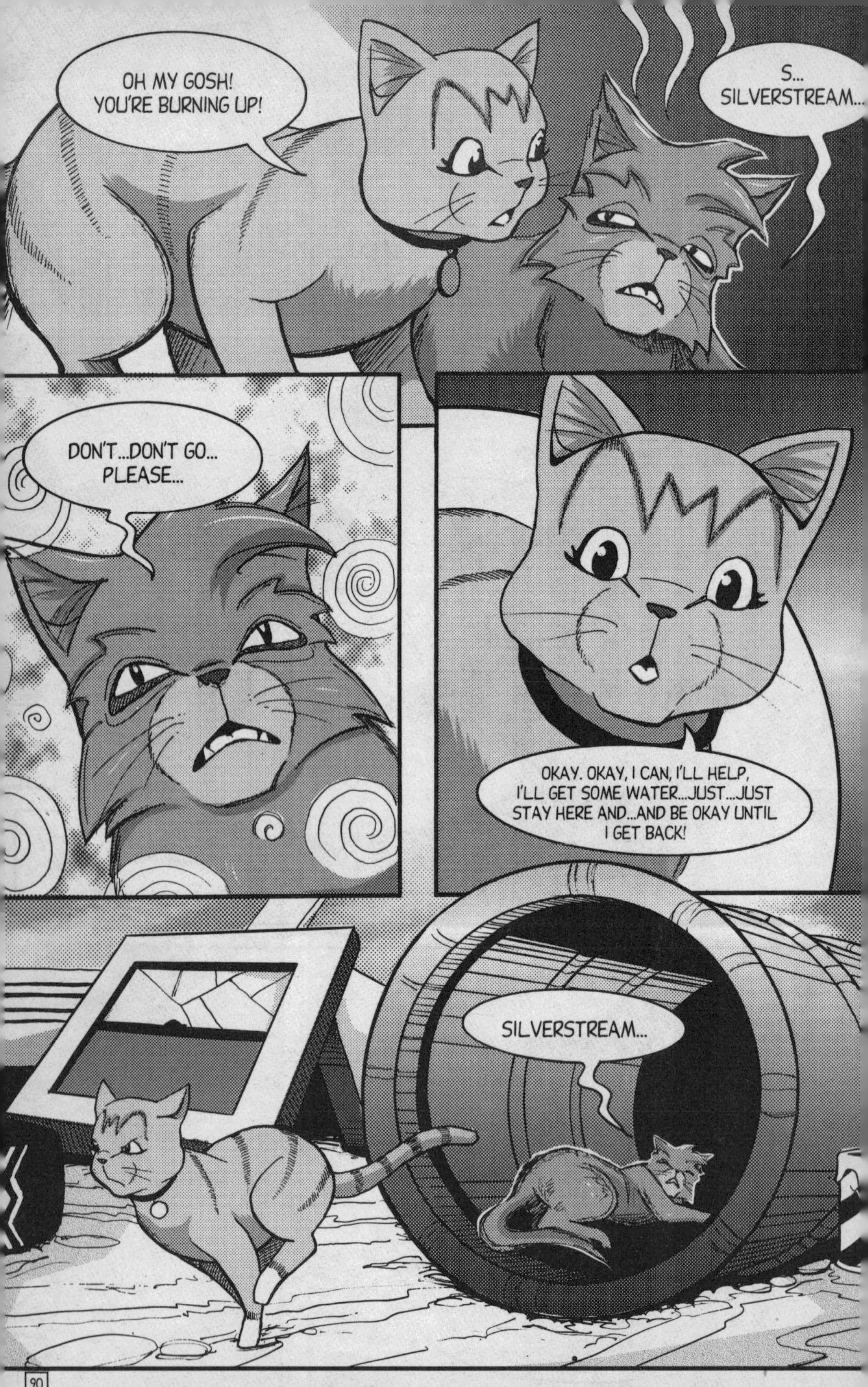
OH MY GOSH!
YOU'RE BURNING UP!
S...
SILVERSTREAM...
DON'T...DON'T GO...
PLEASE...
OKAY. OKAY, I CAN, I'LL HELP,
I'LL GET SOME WATER...JUST...JUST
STAY HERE AND...AND BE OKAY UNTIL
I GET BACK!
SILVERSTREAM...

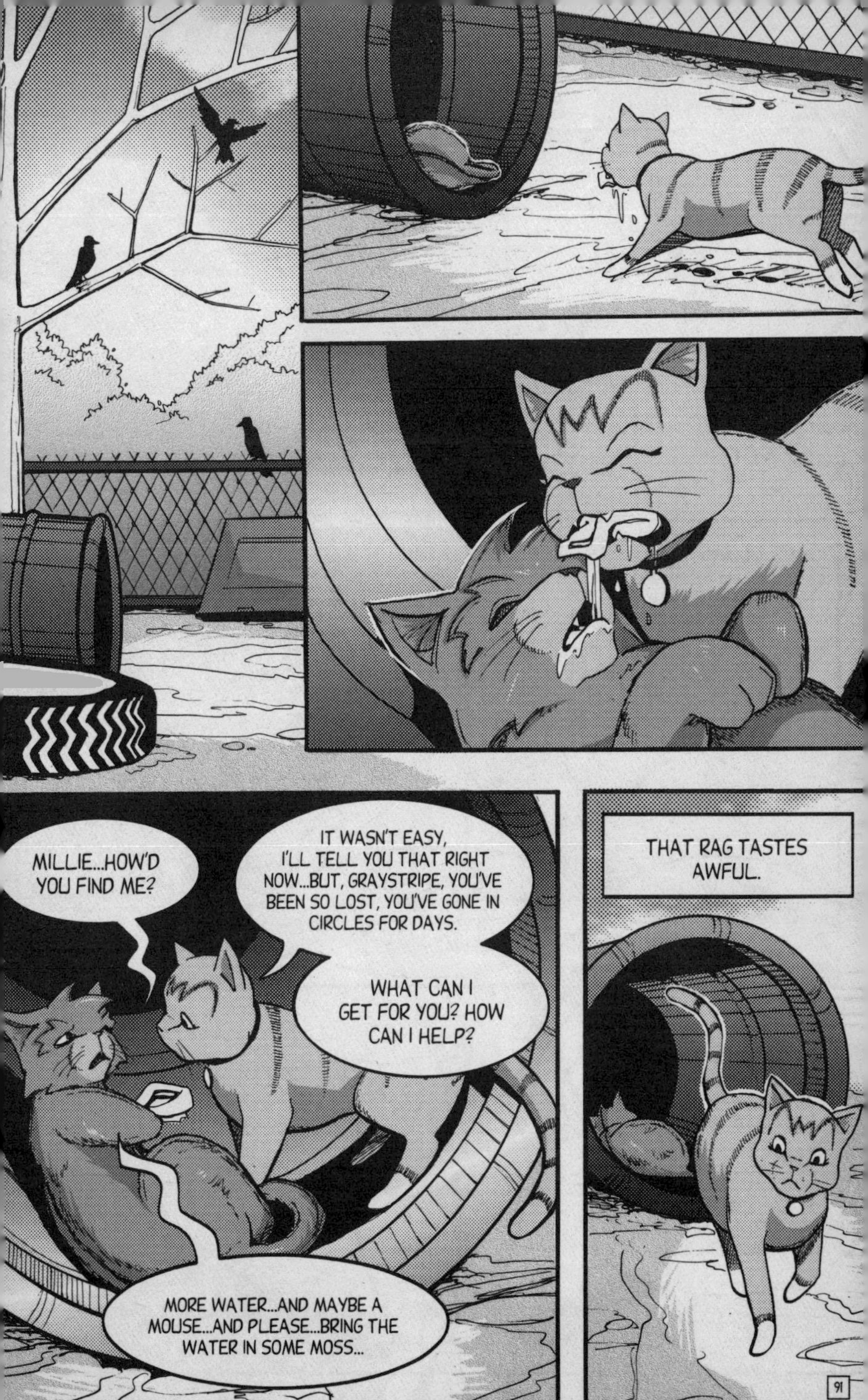
MILLIE...HOW'D YOU FIND ME?
IT WASN'T EASY, I'LL TELL YOU THAT RIGHT NOW...BUT, GRAYSTRIPE, YOU'VE BEEN SO LOST, YOU'VE GONE IN CIRCLES FOR DAYS.
WHAT CAN I GET FOR YOU? HOW CAN I HELP?
MORE WATER...AND MAYBE A MOUSE...AND PLEASE...BRING THE WATER IN SOME MOSS...
THAT RAG TASTES AWFUL.

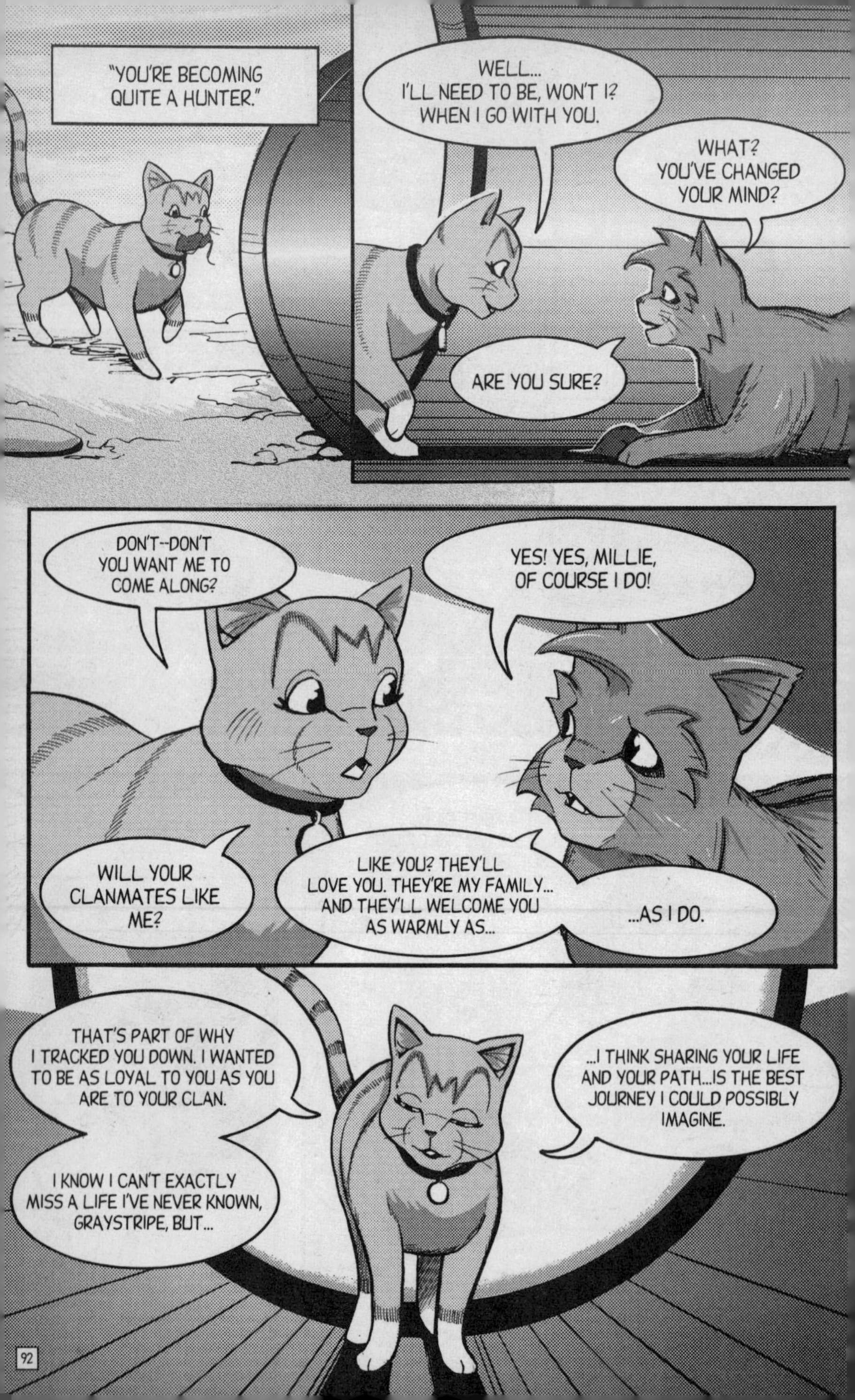
"YOU'RE BECOMING QUITE A HUNTER."
WELL... I'LL NEED TO BE, WON'T I? WHEN I GO WITH YOU.
WHAT? YOU'VE CHANGED YOUR MIND?
ARE YOU SURE?
DON'T--DON'T YOU WANT ME TO COME ALONG?
YES! YES, MILLIE, OF COURSE I DO!
WILL YOUR CLANMATES LIKE ME?
LIKE YOU? THEY'LL LOVE YOU. THEY'RE MY FAMILY... AND THEY'LL WELCOME YOU AS WARMLY AS...
...AS I DO.
THAT'S PART OF WHY I TRACKED YOU DOWN. I WANTED TO BE AS LOYAL TO YOU AS YOU ARE TO YOUR CLAN.
I KNOW I CAN'T EXACTLY MISS A LIFE I'VE NEVER KNOWN, GRAYSTRIPE, BUT...
...I THINK SHARING YOUR LIFE AND YOUR PATH...IS THE BEST JOURNEY I COULD POSSIBLY IMAGINE.

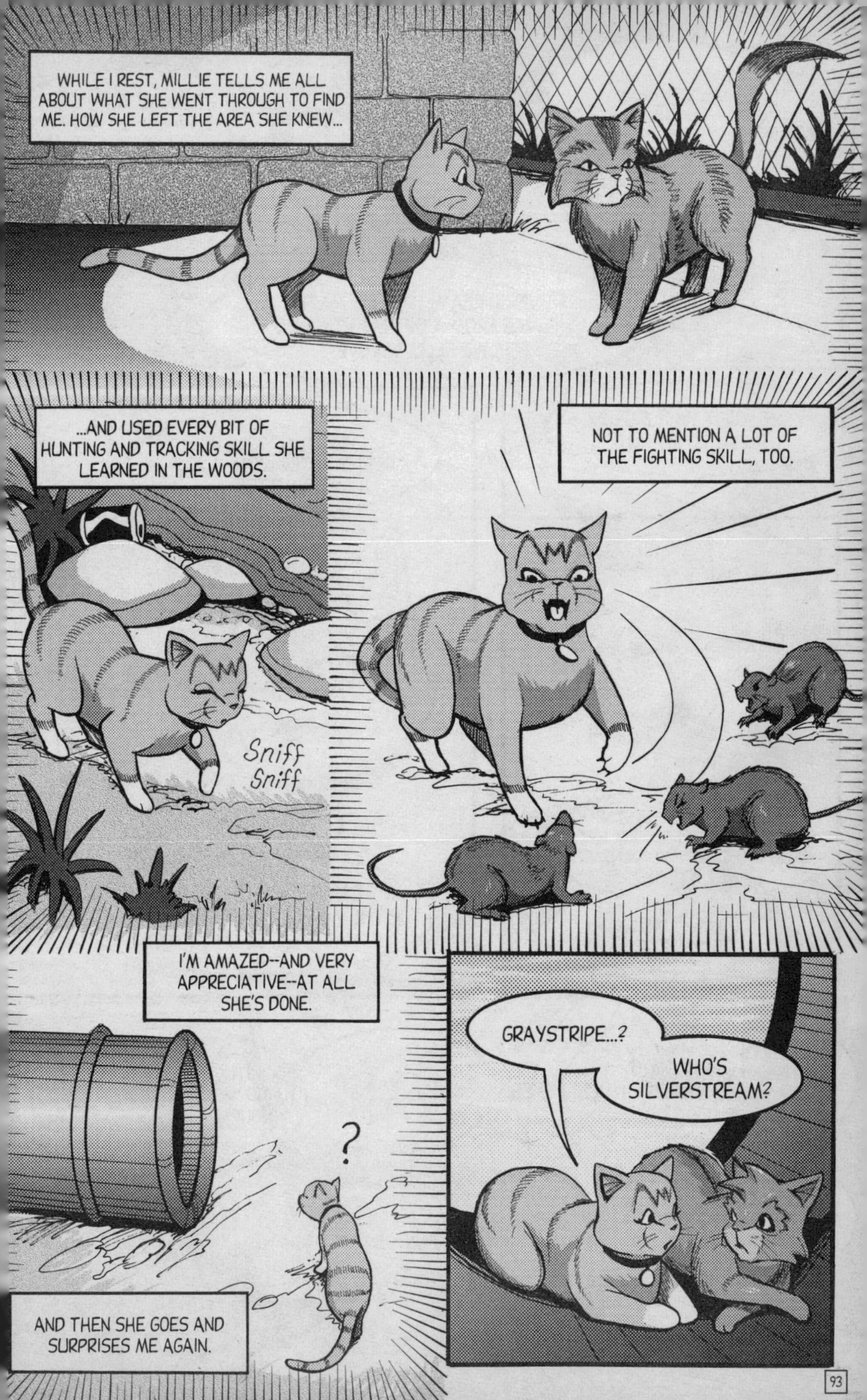
WHILE I REST, MILLIE TELLS ME ALL ABOUT WHAT SHE WENT THROUGH TO FIND ME. HOW SHE LEFT THE AREA SHE KNEW...
...AND USED EVERY BIT OF HUNTING AND TRACKING SKILL SHE LEARNED IN THE WOODS.
Sniff Sniff
NOT TO MENTION A LOT OF THE FIGHTING SKILL, TOO.
I'M AMAZED--AND VERY APPRECIATIVE--AT ALL SHE'S DONE.
?
AND THEN SHE GOES AND SURPRISES ME AGAIN.
GRAYSTRIPE...?
WHO'S SILVERSTREAM?

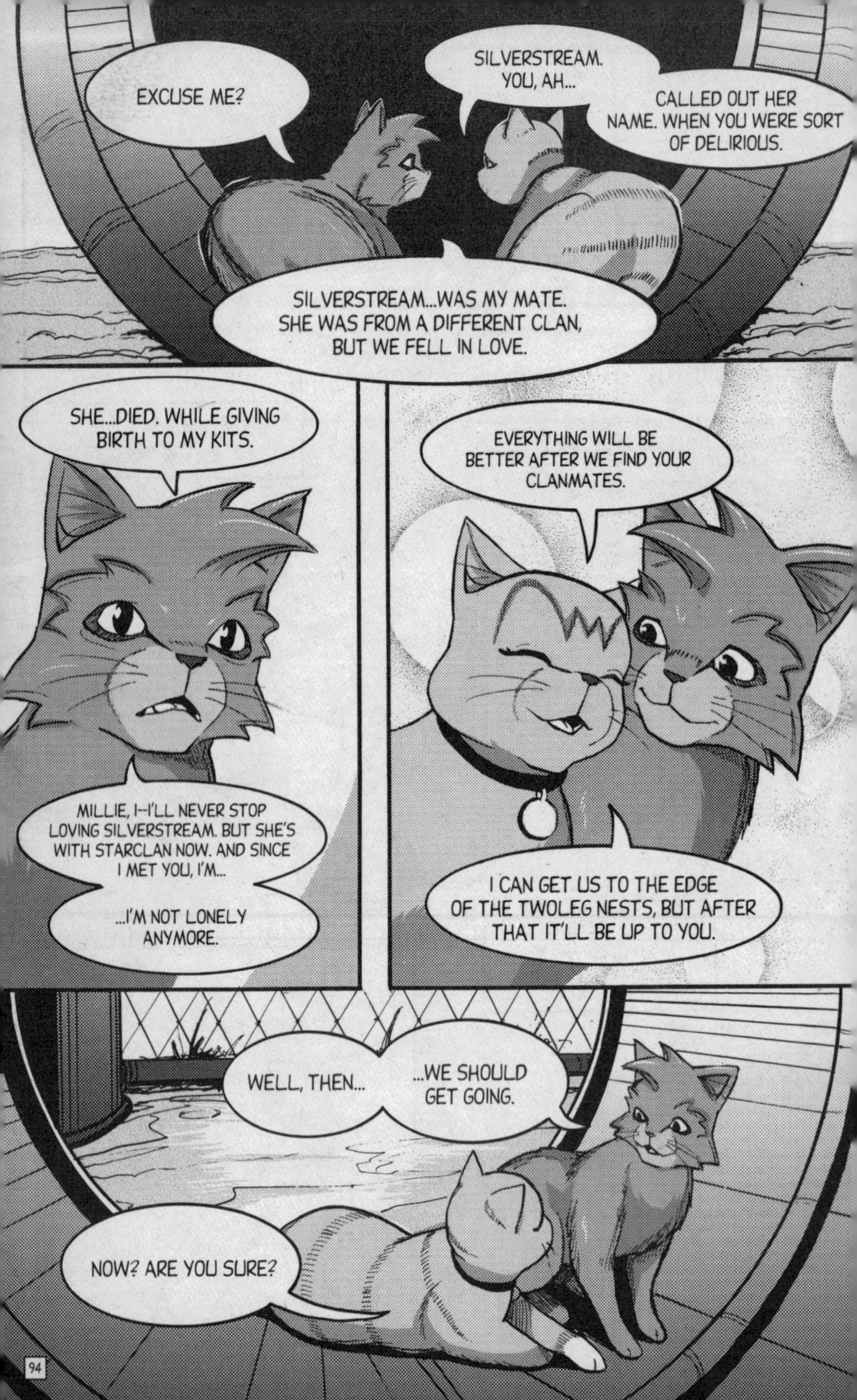
EXCUSE ME?
SILVERSTREAM. YOU, AH...
CALLED OUT HER NAME. WHEN YOU WERE SORT OF DELIRIOUS.
SILVERSTREAM...WAS MY MATE. SHE WAS FROM A DIFFERENT CLAN, BUT WE FELL IN LOVE.
SHE...DIED. WHILE GIVING BIRTH TO MY KITS.
MILLIE, I--I'LL NEVER STOP LOVING SILVERSTREAM. BUT SHE'S WITH STARCLAN NOW. AND SINCE I MET YOU, I'M...
...I'M NOT LONELY ANYMORE.
EVERYTHING WILL BE BETTER AFTER WE FIND YOUR CLANMATES.
I CAN GET US TO THE EDGE OF THE TWOLEG NESTS, BUT AFTER THAT IT'LL BE UP TO YOU.
WELL, THEN...
...WE SHOULD GET GOING.
NOW? ARE YOU SURE?

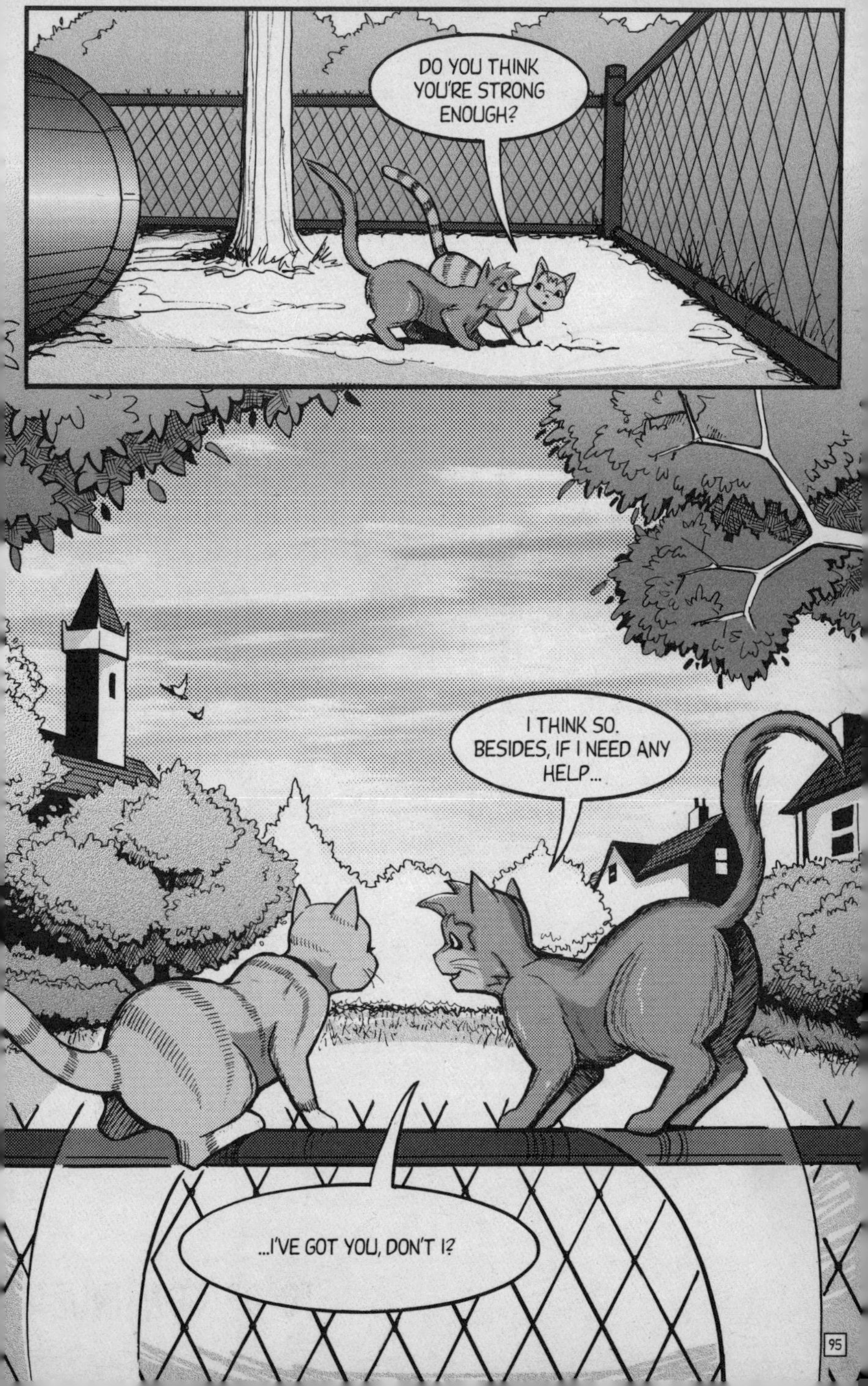
DO YOU THINK YOU'RE STRONG ENOUGH?
I THINK SO. BESIDES, IF I NEED ANY HELP...
...I'VE GOT YOU, DON'T I?

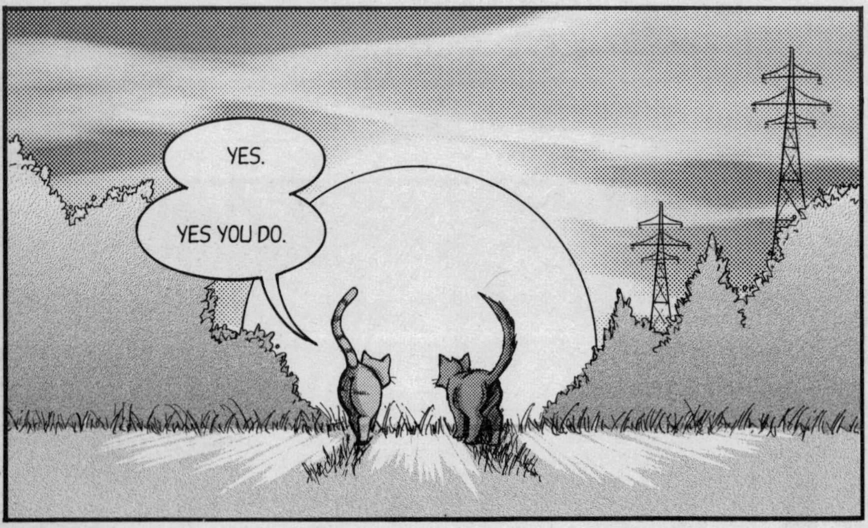
YES.
YES YOU DO.

TO BE CONTINUED

KEEP WATCH FOR

WARRIORS

VOLUME 2

WARRIOR'S REFUGE

Graystripe and Millie's journey to find ThunderClan has only just begun when the pair is faced with a series of obstacles that seem insurmountable. Getting out of Twolegplace alive isn't nearly as simple as expected, and Millie's unfamiliarity with life in the wild makes it a challenge for Graystripe to even keep them moving forward. But just when a temporary refuge is in sight, conflict with a tribe of barn cats threatens to break the travelers apart for good!

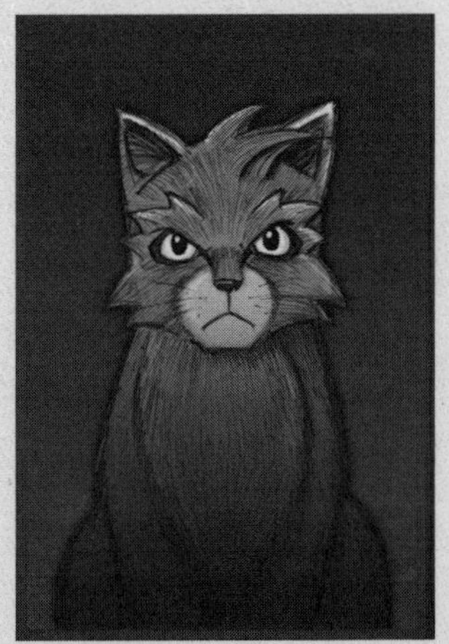

SEE WHERE THE ADVENTURE BEGAN!

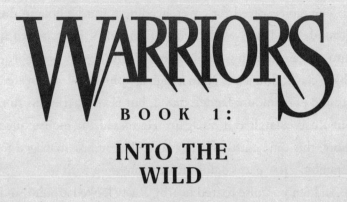

WARRIORS

BOOK 1:

INTO THE WILD

It was very dark. Rusty could sense something was near. The young tomcat's eyes opened wide as he scanned the dense undergrowth. This place was unfamiliar, but the strange scents drew him onward, deeper into the shadows. His stomach growled, reminding him of his hunger. He opened his jaws slightly to let the warm smells of the forest reach the scent glands on the roof of his mouth. Musty odors of leaf mold mingled with the tempting aroma of a small furry creature.

Suddenly a flash of gray raced past him. Rusty stopped still, listening. It was hiding in the leaves less than two taillengths away. Rusty knew it was a mouse—he could feel the rapid pulsing of a tiny heart deep within his ear fur. He swallowed, stifling his rumbling stomach. Soon his hunger would be satisfied.

Slowly he lowered his body into position, crouching for the attack. He was downwind of the mouse. He knew it was not aware of him. With one final check on his prey's position, Rusty pushed back hard on his haunches and sprang, kicking up leaves on the forest floor as he rose.

The mouse dived for cover, heading toward a hole in the ground. But Rusty was already on top of it. He scooped it into the air, hooking the helpless creature with his thorn-sharp claws, flinging it up in a high arc onto the leaf-covered ground. The mouse landed dazed, but alive. It tried to run, but Rusty snatched it up again. He tossed the mouse once more, this time a little farther away. The mouse managed to scramble a few paces before Rusty caught up with it.

Suddenly a noise roared nearby. Rusty looked around, and as he did so, the mouse was able to pull away from his claws. When Rusty turned back he saw it dart into the darkness among the tangled roots of a tree.

Angry, Rusty gave up the hunt. He spun around, his green eyes glaring, intent on searching out the noise that had cost him his kill. The sound rattled on, becoming more familiar. Rusty blinked open his eyes.

The forest had disappeared. He was inside a hot and airless kitchen, curled in his bed. Moonlight filtered through the window, casting shadows on the smooth, hard floor. The noise had been the rattle of hard, dried pellets of food as they were tipped into his dish. Rusty had been dreaming.

Lifting his head, he rested his chin on the side of his bed. His collar rubbed uncomfortably around his neck. In his dream he had felt fresh air ruffling the soft fur where the collar usually pinched. Rusty rolled onto his back, savoring the dream for a few more moments. He could still smell mouse. It was the third time since full moon that he'd had the dream, and every time the mouse had escaped his grasp.

He licked his lips. From his bed he could smell the bland odor of his food. His owners always refilled his dish before they went to bed. The dusty smell chased away the warm scents of his dream. But the hunger rumbled on in his stomach, so Rusty stretched the sleep out of his limbs and padded across the kitchen floor to his dinner. The food felt dry and tasteless on his tongue. Rusty reluctantly swallowed one more mouthful. Then he turned away from the food dish and pushed his way out through the cat flap, hoping that the smell of the garden would bring back the feelings from his dream.

Outside, the moon was bright. It was raining lightly. Rusty stalked down the tidy garden, following the starlit gravel path, feeling the stones cold and sharp beneath his paws. He made his dirt beneath a large bush with glossy green leaves and heavy purple flowers. Their sickly sweet scent cloyed the damp air around him, and he curled his lip to drive the smell out of his nostrils.

Afterward, Rusty settled down on top of one of the posts in the fence that marked the limits of his garden. It was a favorite spot of his, as he could see right into the neighboring gardens as well as into the dense green forest on the other side of the garden fence.

The rain had stopped. Behind him, the close-cropped lawn was bathed in moonlight, but beyond his fence the woods were full of shadows. Rusty stretched his head forward to take a sniff of the damp air. His skin was warm and dry under his thick coat, but he could feel the weight of the raindrops that sparkled on his ginger fur.

He heard his owners giving him one last call from the back door. If he went to them now, they would greet him with gentle words and caresses and welcome him onto their bed, where he would curl, purring, warm in the crook of a bent knee.

But this time Rusty ignored his owners' voices and turned his gaze back to the forest. The crisp smell of the woods had grown fresher after the rain.

Suddenly the fur on his spine prickled. Was something moving out there? Was something watching him? Rusty stared ahead, but it was impossible to see or smell anything in the dark, tree-scented air. He lifted his chin boldly, stood up, and stretched, one paw gripping each corner of the fencepost as he straightened his legs and arched his back. He closed his eyes and breathed in the smell of the woods once more. It seemed to promise him something, tempting him onward into the whispering shadows. Tensing his muscles, he crouched for a moment. Then he leaped lightly down into the rough grass on the other side of the garden fence. As he landed, the bell on his collar rang out through the still night air.

"Where are you off to, Rusty?" meowed a familiar voice behind him.

Rusty looked up. A young black-and-white cat was balancing ungracefully on the fence.

"Hello, Smudge," Rusty replied.

"You're not going to go into the woods, are you?" Smudge's amber eyes were huge.

"Just for a look," Rusty promised, shifting uncomfortably.

"You wouldn't get me in there. It's dangerous!" Smudge wrinkled his black nose with distaste. "Henry said he went into the woods once." The cat lifted his head and gestured with his nose over the rows of fences toward the garden where Henry lived.

"That fat old tabby never went into the woods!" Rusty scoffed. "He's hardly been beyond his own garden since his trip to the vet. All he wants to do is eat and sleep."

"No, really. He caught a robin there!" Smudge insisted.

"Well, if he did, then it was before the vet. Now he *complains* about birds because they disturb his dozing."

"Well, anyway," Smudge went on, ignoring the scorn in Rusty's mew, "Henry told me there are all sorts of dangerous animals out there. Huge wildcats who eat live rabbits for breakfast and sharpen their claws on old bones!"

"I'm only going for a look around," Rusty meowed. "I won't stay long."

"Well, don't say I didn't warn you!" purred Smudge. The black-and-white cat turned and plunged off the fence back down into his own garden.

Rusty sat down in the coarse grass beyond the garden fence. He gave his shoulder a nervous lick and wondered how much of Smudge's gossip was true.

Suddenly the movement of a tiny creature caught his eye. He watched it scuttle under some brambles.

Instinct made him drop into a low crouch. With one slow paw after another he drew his body forward through the undergrowth. Ears pricked, nostrils flared, eyes unblinking, he moved toward the animal. He could see it clearly now, sitting up among the barbed branches, nibbling on a large seed held between its paws. It was a mouse.

Rusty rocked his haunches from side to side, preparing to leap. He held his breath in case his bell rang again. Excitement coursed through him, making his heart pound. This was even better than his dreams! Then a sudden noise of cracking twigs and crunching leaves made him jump. His bell jangled treacherously, and the mouse darted away into the thickest tangle of the bramble bush.

Rusty stood very still and looked around. He could see the white tip of a red bushy tail trailing through a clump of tall ferns up ahead. He smelled a strong, strange scent, definitely a meat-eater, but neither cat nor dog. Distracted, Rusty forgot about the mouse and watched the red tail curiously. He wanted a better look.

All of Rusty's senses strained ahead as he prowled forward. Then he detected another noise. It came from behind, but sounded muted and distant. He swiveled his ears backward to hear it better. *Pawsteps?* he wondered, but he kept his eyes fixed on the strange red fur up ahead, and continued to creep onward. It was only when the faint rustling behind him became a loud and fast-approaching leaf-crackle that Rusty realized he was in danger.

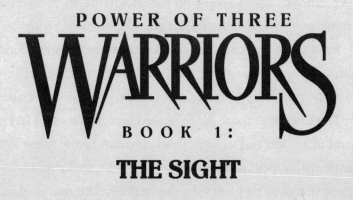

POWER OF THREE

WARRIORS

BOOK 1:

THE SIGHT

"They're looking in the wrong place," Jaykit mewed. He suddenly realized that despite the scents of the patrol and the dead fox, he could smell a far subtler and sweeter smell—milk. It was right here beneath the sycamore. "The fox came past this tree," he told the others. "I can smell her milk-scent."

"We've found her trail!" Hollykit mewed.

Lionkit scrabbled out from under the root. "Let's follow it! It'll lead us to her cubs!"

Jaykit turned away from where Thornclaw, Spiderleg, Poppypaw, and Mousepaw were plunging through the frost-blackened undergrowth. Heading out from the sycamore roots, he padded along the scent of the milk-trail.

"Watch out!" Lionkit warned. "There are brambles ahead."

His senses trained only on the milk-scent, Jaykit had not noticed the spiky bush.

"I'll find a way through!" Hollykit offered. She pushed into the lead and wriggled into the branches.

"But the trail leads around it," Jaykit objected.

"We can't afford to stay in the open," Lionkit told him. "We can pick up the scent on the other side, once there are brambles between us and Thornclaw's patrol."

Reluctantly, Jaykit followed Lionkit as their sister found a narrow tunnel through the tangle of branches. He was relieved when he picked up the fox's scent quickly on the other side.

The trees were more widely spaced here. Jaykit could feel the wind in his fur, and sunlight reached down to the forest floor, mottling his pelt with warmth. The fox's milky scent grew stronger and, as they neared a clump of bracken that shielded a small lump in the ground, Jaykit scented a new smell. The cubs?

"Wait here!" Hollykit ordered.

"Why?" Lionkit objected.

"Just wait while I take a look behind this bracken!"

"I'm coming too," Lionkit insisted.

"We don't want the cubs to know we're here," Hollykit mewed. "If all three of us go blundering in, they'll know something's up and we'll lose the element of surprise."

"My golden pelt will blend in better against the bracken than your black fur," Lionkit pointed out.

"What about me?" Jaykit mewed.

"We won't attack the den without you," Hollykit promised. "But first, you and I will wait here while Lionkit finds the way in."

Jaykit felt a twinge of frustration, but he knew Hollykit's plan was sensible. "Come back as soon as you find it," he called in a whisper as Lionkit disappeared into the bracken.

For the first time he wondered if taking on the fox cubs was a wise idea. But how else was he going to persuade the Clan that there was no need to treat him like a helpless kit?

He strained his ears for the sound of Lionkit returning. It seemed an age before his brother finally pushed his way out of the bracken.

"The main entrance to the den is right behind this clump," Lionkit whispered, shaking leaves from his pelt. "But there's a smaller entrance on the other side of the lump of earth —probably an escape route—which leads into the back."

"Are the cubs inside?" Jaykit asked.

"I didn't go in but I could hear them crying for food."

"They must still be young, then," Hollykit guessed. "Otherwise they'd have come out by now."

"It'll be easier to flush them out if we go down the escape passage," Lionkit proposed. "If we rush them, the surprise will be enough to get them out of the den and then we can chase them toward the border."

"Which way is the border?" Hollykit asked.

Lionkit snorted impatiently. "There'll be a border whichever way we drive them!" he snapped. "ThunderClan territory doesn't go on for ever. Let's get on with it before Thornclaw finds them and takes all the glory."

He surged away into the bracken before either Jaykit or Hollykit could reply. He led them up the slope, out of the bracken, and over the top of the leaf-strewn mound of earth.

"The escape route is here," he announced, skidding to a halt.

"It's no bigger than a rabbit hole!" Hollykit mewed in surprise.

"Perhaps that's what it used to be," Lionkit answered. "Who cares, so long as we can fit down it."

Thornclaw's meow sounded in the trees not far away. The warrior patrol must have given up searching the bracken near the dead fox and were heading toward the mound of earth.

"Hurry!" Lionkit hissed. "Or Thornclaw will find the cubs first!"

Taking a deep breath, Jaykit plunged into the hole. Its earthen sides pressed against his pelt as he scrabbled down it. He didn't mind that there would be no light down here; he trusted his nose to lead him to the den. He could feel Lionkit pressing behind him and pushed onward until he exploded into the foxes' den.

The air was warm and stank of fox—more than one. Jaykit let out a threatening hiss. Lionkit, at his side in an instant, spat ferociously and Hollykit gave a vicious yowl.

Jaykit could not see the foxes but as soon as he heard them scramble to their paws, he realized that they were far bigger than they had expected. Fear shot through him as the cubs let out a shrieking cry.